MERLIN'S WOOD

Robert Holdstock was born in Kent in 1948, and now lives in London. His first novel was published in 1976, and he has been a full-time writer ever since. Recent novels such as *Mythago Wood, Lavondyss, The Bone Forest* and *The Hollowing* have brought him widespread critical accalim and popular success.

SCIENCE
FICTION
FANTASY

ROBERT HOLDSTOCK

Merlin's Wood

or

The Vision of Magic

HarperCollins*Publishers*

HarperCollins*Publishers*
77–85 Fulham Palace Road,
Hammersmith, London W6 8JB

This paperback edition 1995
1 3 5 7 9 8 6 4 2

First published in Great Britain by
HarperCollins*Publishers* 1994

ISBN 0 00 648001 2

Set in Linotron Sabon

Printed in Great Britain by
HarperCollinsManufacturing Glasgow

To Etty — Happy Birthday
(late) March 1995)
31/3/95.
× × × × from

To *Scott* and *Suzi Baker*
Phantasmes de l'Opéra

Chris
+ Kerry.

Contents

Then in one moment, she put forth the charm
Of woven paces and of waving hands,
And in the hollow oak he lay as dead,
And lost to life and use and name and fame.

Then crying 'I have made his glory mine,'
And shrieking out 'O fool!' the harlot leapt
Adown the forest, and the thicket closed
Behind her, and the forest echo'd 'fool.'

From 'Merlin and Vivien'
part of *Idylls of the King*
by Alfred Lord Tennyson

PART ONE

Broceliande

A storm was coming, but the winds were still,
And in the wild woods of Broceliande,
Before an oak, so hollow, huge and old
It look'd a tower of ivied masonwork,
At Merlin's feet the wily Vivien lay . . .

From *Idylls of the King*

The People on the Path

(A time in childhood)

The boy's voice woke Martin from a spirit haunted sleep. It was pitch dark. A fragment of gravel cracked against the bedroom window, and again the voice: 'Martin! Martin! There are people on the path. *Martin!*'

People on the path.

Martin flung back the blankets and ran to the window. Below, in the faint moonlight, he could see his fair-haired brother Sebastian, pale-faced, and excited. He was pointing to the forest. 'Martin, there are three of them. Quickly.'

Martin pulled on his jeans and a grubby white jumper. He opened the window, dropping effortlessly to the ground. The old dog whined and yapped in its kennel, dreaming of the chase, too far away in other lands to be disturbed by this second escape from the farmhouse. Martin ran through the darkness. He vaulted the gate and chased after Sebastian.

'Wait for me!' he hissed, not wanting to raise his voice and perhaps disturb the people on the path, though he knew this had never happened.

Where was Sebastian? The moonlight waxed and waned as light cloud drifted over the forest, over the farm. Something ethereal flowed and glowed distantly. Faint birds seemed to be flying upwards, spiralling around the dark shape of a slowly spinning figure.

The boy who danced was Sebastian. Martin watched amazed as his brother, arms outstretched, danced among the people on the path, moving through the three milky forms, a man, a woman, a tall child with long hair. The child was looking back, nervously. Martin thought it was a girl, but the spectral features were hard to discern. All three moved in slow motion. Their ghostly shapes shed light like streams of plasma, where Sebastian passed through them, his voice a thrill of laughter.

'It feels cold. I can hear their hearts beating – it's weird. Their breathing too. The man smells of grease and smoke. Come inside, Martin. Quickly. It's the best yet! It feels like I'm flying and running and swimming all at once – I can fly like an eagle, Martin – come and feel what it's like.'

Martin followed his brother up the old path, but he felt apprehensive. There was a shifting, lurking movement in the wood and Martin thought at once of the old 'bosker', the murderous woodsman who lived among the pools and rocks of the deeper forest. Or perhaps it was Rebecca, spying, always spying on her brothers when they went out onto the path by moonlight.

The night air carried the strong sour smell of earth, emanating from the spectral figures that had emerged from the edge of Broceliande. The man, looking over his shoulder as he moved slowly along the path, seemed to be watching Martin. His mouth worked as if he was speaking, his face contorted as if in warning. Then he raised an arm and pointed, the pale finger freezing Martin in his tracks. The woman turned slowly. She too seemed to stare at the boy who followed them, unaware of the blonde lad who laughed and danced within her insubstantial form.

At length, Sebastian left the inside of the people on the path. He was shivering, almost ecstatic. 'It felt *strange*! The man's so frightened. They've had a *vision* of something. Like a long, thin bottle, with trees and earth inside. Like the one I drew last time. They're running away from something. How old, d'you reckon?'

Martin knew his brother was referring to the historical age of the figures. The people who walked the path sometimes looked quite modern, sometimes came in the uniforms of the cavalry from the time of Napoleon, or even earlier; Martin had once seen a Greek warrior on the path. The women occasionally wore dresses that swirled and sparkled with glass as they moved, but more usually were wrapped in heavy cloaks, or thick furs. But the people he watched tonight were wearing peasant's clothes and carrying rough sacks over their shoulders. Their hair was long and they had no weapons. They could have come from one of many times.

Martin shrugged and shivered, walking slowly behind the ghosts on the old track as they steadily ascended the hill to the ruins of the church. There, as they crossed the thorny hedge to the right of the lych gate, the figures began to fade.

Swinging on the wooden gate, aware of bright moonlight cutting an edge across the hollow tower and the broken walls of the chapel, Martin and Sebastian watched as the figures began to descend into the earth. The ghosts were outside the defining wall of the cemetery, beyond the hump of the prehistoric mound on which the church had been erected.

When they were waist high the boys waved and called 'goodbye'. Soon only the heads could be seen, bobbing through the thistles, and then they too were gone.

Where the people went from here, none of the children of this or any other time had ever discovered.

The path from Broceliande continued south into another realm.

The Stoneshifter's Tale

(Fifteen years later . . .)

A storm was coming, Martin noticed, as he followed the cart and the coffin along the path around the forest. And yet the winds were still, the air apprehensive, sharp with the first scents of autumn, seeping from the wild woods of Broceliande. As he drifted onwards to the graveyard and his mother's cold earth home, he watched the dark oaks in the green. Hollow, huge and old, their towering trunks veined and snaked with ivy, they might have been old men, their smooth and spreading roots the shapely limbs of women sprawled at their feet in careful, drowsy thought.

In those days, as in all days, Broceliande was a terrible place, a 'glooming' forest growing over boggy dells, forgotten stones, a place of hidden pools, falls of water and strangling thickets. Cut through by the village road from Gael to Guer, still the true heart of Broceliande could not be found, although the stink of that heart's corruption oozed from the edgewoods to lie, a sour miasma, over all the farms and hamlets to the west, the direction of the wild sea coast at Quiburon, of the stone-tattooed land at Carnac, the direction of the source of storms.

Yes, something lay rotting at the heart of the forest, a death that had been known for generations. It was a decaying place, shedding ghosts like autumn leaves. It held the farmsteads in a root-strong grip, the minds of the families too, though sometimes a youth escaped the shadow (to wait too long was to be lost) and Martin was one of these.

He had fled that shadow from the forest. He had been sixteen. He had promised that he would return only at his mother's death, a sad event which had now occurred, calling upon his conscience and his courage.

Again, then, he walked the slow path by Broceliande, a grieving son, a frightened man, confused by the flow of feeling from the wood.

Off the western shore the tide was turning, and with the ebbing flow the traveller was finally lowered to her cold earth home. The storm passed to the south as the priest spoke words over the grave, then walked through the two small fires to embrace and commiserate with Martin. The bell in the renovated tower tolled slowly.

'I'm sorry your sister couldn't be here. Eveline loved her very much. After little Sebastian died . . .'

Martin saw how the priest swallowed back the words, but he knew well what the man meant. Sebastian had been a special child to his parents, the deeply loved one; when he was gone, Rebecca had inherited the mantle of affection. Martin, too, would have liked to have seen his sister by the cold earth home, but she was lost, somewhere in the outback of Australia, following songlines, always following songlines.

Father Gualzator hesitated, shivering slightly as the chill wind blew, sending smoke swirling from the fires, the applewood sweet, the hazelwood smoke more acrid. Behind him, Martin's uncle Jacques and aunt Suzanne stood in respectful, watching, waiting silence, the old man's beret clasped at his groin, his long grey hair disturbed by the breeze. His watery eyes were filled with an odd longing; he was longing, certainly, for a cigarette, and to remove the too-tight shirt and tie. But there was something more disturbing him and Martin was aware of it. The priest was agitated, his rosy complexion now brighter with the embarrassment he was feeling. Martin asked him, 'What is it?'

'There are people on the path. I think they've followed us from the wood. Before I sing the hymn, I'd like to let them go.'

Martin looked back, to the place where the people used to sink below the hill. He could see nothing, sense nothing. The priest was blind to them too, but aware of them. He was a Basque, estranged from his strange land, and his language had given him a form of vision that was denied to the likes of Martin. *To speak old was to see old*, he had always said, and when Martin had been a boy he and Sebastian, watching the ethereal flow of people on the path, had tested the priest's 'old' eye, and found it unerring.

A few minutes of strained silence later the priest relaxed. 'They've gone,' he whispered, and turned back to the cold home. He tugged the rope that held the lid of the coffin and exposed the three linen-wrapped packs. He sang softly as he poured spring water along the length, then the breadth of each part of the traveller. Martin watched, remembering, as red berries and white were dropped carefully onto the wet linen. The flask of honey and the sack of meat were lowered, and then the small sun-wheel, resting on the traveller's chest. The lid was replaced, earth was scattered and more familiar words were uttered: 'Dust to dust, flesh to the fire . . .'

It was over. Jacques steered the ageing dray back to Eveline's farm, the cart riding smoothly on newly greased axles, the priest leaning forward on his knees, staring back at the rebuilt church. Martin was comforted by the over-attentive

Suzanne, whose black veil continually blew in his face as she held his arm, held the side of the cart, and talked non-stop about the traveller, Eveline, and the years of her trials and tribulations. Martin was not unaware that he was being gently criticised for having stayed away so long and he repeatedly tried to change the subject, talking about Amsterdam, the design business he ran – but Suzanne was quite single-minded.

Jacques had prepared a stew of rabbit and pheasant in red wine; the priest offered a whole *coeur de brie*, a succulent cheese which Martin had not tasted in years; and Suzanne had baked bread. There were several stone jars of still cider, and brandy wine.

They sat at the pine table, warmed by the smell of cooked wine and fragrant wood burning on the open fire; they raised their glasses to the traveller and spoke her full name aloud, 'Eveline Mathilde la-coeur-forte Laroche'.

Jacques was then allowed his single cigarette, which he smoked silently, curling the cigarette inside his fingers as he pinched the tip, inhaling deeply and staring at his empty plate.

When he announced that he wished to smoke another he was told sharply that he couldn't, but he glanced at Martin, defied Suzanne and rose from the table, lighting up as he moved and cocking his head meaningfully to the door. Suzanne poured herself more cider. Father Gualzator reached for the brandy, which he blessed (with a mischievous grin at the woman) before tipping the bottle to his glass.

Outside in the cold dusk, Jacques said, 'I don't know if you're intending to stay, but if you are you should come to the Quiburon peninsula with me. Maybe tomorrow, although I think it'll be a stormy day. What do you think? Will you stay?'

Puzzled by the man's words, Martin nodded, accepted a cigarette and lit it. Distantly a fox barked, and the wide scatter of hens moved suddenly towards the shelter of the shed. 'I have to stay. I have to sell the farm, clear up the paperwork, settle the taxes. I'll be here for a few days. Why Quiburon?'

'It's where your grandfather died, just after the war.'

'Oh yes. Of course. Eveline would never take me there . . .'

'Your mother was only twelve. My little sister. I was only a year older but I felt a lot of responsibility for her. How things changed!'

'Why go back now?'

'I want to tell you what happened to me. And to Eveline. I've never spoken about it, and nor did she, not as far as I know. But now I think I must. If only to encourage you to leave Broceliande, and not endanger your own life.'

'That's what Eveline said to me in her last letter.' Martin drew the envelope from his jacket pocket and removed the single sheet of blue writing paper. His mother's handwriting was neat and precise. He read aloud, '*You were always the sensible one. You avoided the path and I think you must have avoided the danger. I do hope so. If you come back to Broceliande, please don't stay. I have always enjoyed the trips to Amsterdam. You have always been a loving presence in my life. I don't need you at the farm when I finally travel on. It would be better to avoid danger and stay in the city where you have made such a good life for yourself. Please think carefully about these words and say the same to Rebecca, if you ever find her.*'

Jacques lit his third cigarette, glancing almost guiltily back at the house, but Suzanne's voice was raised with laughter and the glasses were clinking.

'For a reason I don't fully understand she was very

worried about you coming back. There are so many strange things about this place – the ghosts, the wood, the lost memories. We've all experienced them. They are part of life, *our* life, we take them for granted. But there's something not quite right. Something wrong. Something has changed in the last few years. I can't explain it. The priest has seen it. We probably all felt it when Eveline died, seven days ago. She seems to have been *acutely* aware of it. She was very concerned for you.'

'The evil in the heart of the wood . . .' Martin mused aloud, staring into the night.

'As I say – it's hard to know. But I would like you to come to Quiburon. Hear my own nightmare. It may help, it may not. It might help you understand your brother's death a little more. I don't know. But Eveline didn't want you to stay here. And the only way I have of persuading you to leave is to share my nightmare. It's up to you, then, to decide whether you should handle Eveline's affairs from here, or from your house in Amsterdam.'

The next day Jacques drove Martin to the sea-drenched cliffs of the western coast of Brittany, arriving in sleeting rain, below a grey sky that moved effortlessly over them from sea-horizon to misted hills behind.

As Jacques drove, he hunched forward in the seat of the old Citroen, peering through the running water on the windscreen, occasionally recognising a place name and exclaiming, 'There! It's OK. Now I know where I am!' or 'Hell and damnation. That last signpost must have been wrong. These damned coastal people.'

Through hamlets, closed against the rain, through country lanes, winding between grey fields and gleaming trees, they traced an erratic course southwards, driving near the cliffs, then looping inland, then back to the edge of the great sea. It was a journey in which they regularly passed the signs of habitation, yet saw not one single human being.

At last the road dropped towards a pebble beach. The restless sea curled and whitened as it heaved against the dark rock of the small bay. Stones, like a ring of black fingers, probed from that swell, out below the waves.

'There,' Jacques said, turning off the engine. 'There at last!' He took a moment to light a cigarette, then remembered to offer Martin one. The paper was damp, but the sharp smoke made Martin heady and relaxed. They peered through the rain for a while in silence. After a few minutes Jacques wound down the window and flicked the smouldering butt into the abyss. Martin did the same, then squirmed and twisted into his oilskin. He followed the older man, out onto a path that looked down on the drowned stone circle.

'There!' Jacques said again. 'You see?' He pointed through the rain beyond the circle. 'You see the stones of the second ring? Two rings together, side by side, stretching into the sea, one of them more drowned than the other. *Can* you see?'

Two dark fingers of smooth rock appeared then disappeared beneath the swell, a long way out across the ocean.

'Yes,' Martin said, adding, 'How old are they?'

'The rings?' Jacques shrugged. 'Six thousand years, some say. Or maybe only a few years.' He chuckled. 'It depends on how you think of them. When we built them, when we put them upright, they marked a land that was hallowed, but has now been swallowed. Maybe people around here are descended from the builders, eh? Who knows. The stones wear the sea like a skin. You can see how it gleams on them! At low tide, during the hot summers, you can walk among them. It's muddy, they're crusted –' he meant with barnacles, 'but you can touch them. I've heard stories that they sing, some that they dance, and some that they feed on the blood of young girls.' He laughed again, glancing at Martin curiously, green eyes narrowed against the wind and rain, but watching for a reaction. 'And of course, under certain circumstances, or maybe in certain minds, they do. They do. Everything is true. I've always believed in spirit,' he said. 'But it's something you just accept, not make into daft ritual. Do you have them in Amsterdam?'

'Girl-eating stones?'

'Ritualisers. The people who sing to the stones. The people who think that aliens made them. Crystal gazers.'

'We call them The New Age. The Age of Aquarius, in the sixties. People then used to long for it to come. I've worked with many of them. Most of their dream was hope, expectation. If their dreams *had* come true, they'd anyway have grown older, moved on . . .'

Jacques laughed throatily, then hawked and spat away from the wind. 'I agree with you,' he said. 'Dreams are for dreaming, not living. But that said, there's one dream I'd like to have come real, which is why I asked you here. I've lived my life with it. I stood here and hoped it. I longed for it. I dreamed of my father for years, for decades. If I could switch back the clock . . .'

Martin wasn't following his drift and said so. Jacques pointed out to sea again. 'There. Right there. Follow my finger . . .'

He was pointing to the outer ring of stones, perhaps to the tallest stone that could be glimpsed at the ebb of the swelling water.

'I was fourteen years old,' Jacques said. 'The storm had come in fast. The far horizon darkened, but Eveline and I

23

kept playing on the beach. My mother seemed alarmed, but we kept playing on the beach. The blackness spread like colour soaking through water. It swept towards us, although where we played was still in the sunlight. My father was on the small boat. Eveline and I had each had turns with him. Now he was alone, and enjoying a few minutes of peace away from us. The sail was full and he was turning to come back to the bay. The darkness was like a veil, like a net being flung towards us. The sea began to rise, and we were called from the beach and taken up this very path. Soon the sea began to heave into the rocks. The stone circles were awash. We watched the swirl of cloud, the blackness. It was flowing very fast. I had never seen a storm like it.'

Jacques was suddenly speaking strangely, almost dreamily. Martin felt that this story, this memory, had been rehearsed for years. He spoke as if reading from a book.

'My father got tangled in the rigging. The boat was very small. It seemed to skip for a moment in the sea-wind, nosing up then down and the man seemed to be sitting very precariously. He was drenched, his thick white hair draped about his face. The boat was awash. He saw his family, safely up on the path, and waved, then made signals with his hand.

'I remember my mother shouting something; I can't remember what. The boat was twisting on the sea, too far out for safety, the sail full one moment then flapping the next, and he hauled and tugged at the ropes as the ocean broke across the bows. Again my mother shouted to him, her words lost in the wind that was now beginning to scream from the west.

'Above us, the black swirled over, and the rain struck us, and our eyes became half blind so that all we could see was the white of the sail, the dark hull, and the black shape

24

of the man who struggled to guide the small vessel into the haven of the bay. When the boat tipped over it happened so fast I missed it, even though I was watching and shouting and crying for my father. One moment the white sail was a proud balloon, the next there was just the sea, and something splashing, a shape splashing.

'That was the moment when the sea became a monster, when the wind hit it, when the storm changed the cold water into a beast.'

Jacques was in a dream, his eyes almost closed, tears squeezing from the corners, his words oddly stilted, his description strange for this charcoal maker and handyman.

'It became a monster of many backs. The backs rose and heaved, green and scaly, flecked with white, shining as the monster rolled below the surface. You could see the muscles, the writhing limbs. On the beach, the monster's teeth exploded upwards, white enamel, sucked back into the tide just as the monster was trying to suck back the desperate man who was swimming for the shore. Around him, as he swam for his life, the limbs of the creature rose and fell, its huge back following him, trying to throw him, then suck him down as it subsided.

'He reached the stone. Do you see it? That stone there, yes, the dark one, the sharp one, you can see it now as the waves drop, the outermost stone of the second circle. It rises twelve feet from the sea bed. It was his only haven. And he reached it by sheer guts and reached around it, embraced it, and clung there. All the while the monster in the sea raged at him, sucked at him, tried to draw him back.

'I believe, or I have dreamed, that I saw him smile. He certainly waved. Believing himself to be safe, if cold, he clung to that great stone, to that great past, to the spirit of land, defying the sea. He clung like a limpet. Have you ever tried to prise a limpet from the rock it lives on? You need a chisel. When the creature sticks and grips, it cannot be dislodged, it cannot be sucked into the maw of the monster. And like a limpet embracing the old stone, my father resisted the tide that sucked at him, drew at him, tugged at him. It surged around him, it broke across him, it pulled and dragged at his legs, but he held on, he held on.

'So the ocean, seeing that it would not draw him back, now changed its tactics. It was the moment my mother knew we had lost him. It began to smash him against the friend who had found him. It lifted him and smashed him; it twisted him, drew at him, then flung him to the very stone to which he clung. His head became a bloody mess. It concentrated on his head, of course. It crushed his bones against the rock, stunned him, bruised him, broke him bit by bit, until soon his strength had gone and his whole body was lifted and broken on the circle.

'Three times, maybe four, the sea cracked my father against the rock to open him. And then the pulp was drawn away, down and gone from us, gone for ever.

'He never came back, not a single trace of him, not even the boat. Nothing.'

The rain beat down. It had found a way through Martin's oilskin and was freezing against his shoulder. Jacques had finished speaking and they scurried back to the car, squirming and twisting out of their waterproofs, flinging the wet garments onto the back seat before spending a few minutes smoking, listening to the drum of rain, to the odd silence that is invoked by that hollow sound.

'Why do you dream of him?' Martin asked at length. 'I don't understand. If you *could* turn the clock back, how could you help him?'

26

'I could have flown to him; or I could have moved the stone closer to the shore. I had the power to do it. For a year or more I'd known I was a stone-shifter, ever since I'd danced on the path. But I was too frightened . . . perhaps too young. I didn't trust myself to do it right.'

'I don't understand.'

'I could have *flown* to him. I stayed on the earth. I could have moved the stone. I didn't even try to grip it. My father died, but in my heart I know he *knew* that I could have saved him. That's why he waved. He trusted me. I had danced among the people on the path – the magic was in me. He knew this, he'd heard me talk. I failed him. That's all. And I think that's all I can say for the moment.'

Jacques opened the window and tossed his cigarette into the storm.

'I don't understand,' Martin said.

'I didn't expect the sea to change its game. I wasn't ready to take on the sea. I thought he could do it on his own.'

'And you thought you could move the standing stone?'

'It was a *gift*! I'd danced and played inside the ghosts. And sometimes you get a *gift* if you do that, and it lasts a while then goes. Like 'Old Provider's' Christmas presents, though, there's always a catch. Like nearly every child, I was too afraid to use the gift, and now it's gone, and your grandfather died when he might have lived.

'Eveline was there too and she too felt helpless, and yet she felt she *could* have helped. And whatever it was that happened to *her* during that terrible storm later made her frightened for you and Rebecca, which is why she encouraged you to go away and *stay* away.'

Jacques fumbled for the starter and the Citroen shuddered into life. Martin sat back, cold and confused and let the rain and the saturated land drift past as his uncle drove him home.

The Songliner's Tale

Four days after the interment, Martin dressed warmly against the chill weather and walked through the drizzle up the path to the cemetery. He'd had a restless night, waking at one point to the sound of movement downstairs. Half dreaming, half alert, he had imagined that someone was prowling about the house, at one point even entering the bedroom where he lay. Indeed, in the morning he found the back door swinging free, and the signs of sandwich-making. Not knowing his mother's routine, nor lifestyle, he was not unduly concerned by this intrusion.

He approached the old church, with its half-shroud of scaffolding, and as he reached for the gate, so he saw a crouching figure by the hump of green-cloth covered soil, the new grave. It was a woman, he thought, from the drop of auburn hair around the figure's shoulders, but he didn't recognise her. She wore a heavy lambskin coat, green cord trousers, and black leather boots that were scratched and muddied. She was hunkered down and singing softly, her arms folded across her chest, her head raised slightly, as if looking above the top of the gleaming marble headstone.

Her voice suddenly made contact!

'Rebecca?' Martin whispered. Her singing voice came clearer, sharper through the fine rain. 'Rebecca?' he called more loudly, and the woman turned to look at him. Martin stopped walking, shocked by the face that stared at him.

Slowly Rebecca rose to her feet, rubbed at the backs of her knees and came over to her brother. Her long hair was damp, framing a strong and handsome face, aged by sun and dust. She was as hard as stone, as carved as wood; when she smiled she revealed the absence of a canine tooth, something that the younger Rebecca would have never allowed to go unfilled. But the smile was a genuine gesture of pleasure, the wry turn of the lips, gladness conveyed in every movement of face and hands as she reached for Martin and hugged him.

'You look lean,' she said, stepping back to inspect him after the embrace. 'You've not been eating.'

'I try to keep fit. Genes for fatness run in the family; have to keep them at bay, like wild dogs. Not eating twenty-course Indonesian meals every day helps as well, excellent though they are.'

'*You'll* get fat,' she said with a smile. 'Just like daddy, it'll happen suddenly. But you look good now. Nice complexion.' She pinched his cheek. 'And no drugs, I think. No shadows. That's good.'

'I don't take drugs,' Martin agreed. 'You look rugged,' he went on. He touched the deeply etched lines about her eyes and mouth, his fingers gentle. She shrugged.

'I'm a rugged lass. The outback is a hard place. The land wants to take your water. Take my hand . . .'

They walked to the iron gate, then suddenly Rebecca ran, childlike, to leap and swing on the rusting hinges, looking out towards the village and the old forest – Broceliande, hazy in the rain, dark on the horizon. Martin stepped onto the gate as well.

Rebecca said, 'It's odd to be back. I can't tell whether I like it or hate it. I hate this bloody weather, of course. But the smells, the colours . . . I've been bleached yellow, burned red and charred umber at various times over the last few years. And I've heard the songs, such wonderful old songs, Martin ... But I've missed the colours, the greens. The *real* colours.'

'Can you hear songs now? Are there songs in *this* earth?'

She glanced at him, her expression one of deliberate if unfelt contempt. 'Don't be an idiot. Of course there are. The song is everywhere around us. It doesn't sing *from* us, Martin, it sings *through* us; which is why we forget so easily in this hemisphere.' She stepped from the gate and folded her arms, her characteristic gesture. She watched him through jet-lagged eyes, across the years of absence. 'I don't want to talk about the songpaths. I came here to watch my mother into her cold home and I missed it. I'm really sorry that I wasn't here. I missed dad down, ten years ago, and I promised myself not to repeat the negligence.'

Martin said, 'You must have got my letter ...'

'I did! It came fast. And I got the first flight available, but the bloody *engine* failed in Bombay. A day and a half in Bombay, confined to the airport, paying three kids a tip each every time I needed a piss, and all the cash I had was in Australian dollars! I tried to ring, but the lines just wouldn't connect.'

She laughed and clutched her brother's arm. 'That's funny, isn't it? Twelve years of my life I've spent connecting the lines, the lines between different shapes of spirit, but I can't connect with France Telecom from Bombay Airport. I like that. It's sort of ironic.'

'Pompous little bag of bones,' Martin murmured, echoing a childhood taunt, and Rebecca put him in a headlock, laughing as they struggled through the rain until Martin declared a truce.

'I *am* a bag of bones. But I'm five times stronger than *you*, my man.'

'Damn right. I said *pax*!'

'Can I stay with you?' she asked a while later, as they

30

straightened clothing and returned to the rough road back to the village.

'Of course. The house is as much yours –'

'Can I *stay* with you!' she repeated, and Martin felt the thump of his heart. It had been a long time and he flushed as he anticipated the renewed relationship. But there was no-one in his life in Amsterdam at the moment. 'I suppose so.'

'You suppose so. Great. You suppose so.'

'Yes. You can *stay* with me. It's been a long time, Beck. We've moved apart.'

'Of course we have! But the line is still there between us. Lines like that don't break. And I need to be close. That's all. That's it. I need to be close. To you. To them. I should have been here to watch them down.'

'I wasn't here when either of them crossed,' Martin said quietly. 'So they wouldn't have known you weren't here for the interment. They knew you'd be sent for. Eveline actually didn't *want* us here. Anyway, I watched them down. They were guarded. I swear it.'

Rebecca sighed as they walked, now linking arms, almost hanging on to Martin, jet-lag beginning to creep into her muscles. 'She'll be with little Seb. That's nice . . .'

'Not for thirty days yet,' Martin reminded her, and she glanced at her watch.

'Oh yes. I'd forgotten. Well . . . she soon *will* be with our little brat brother. It's so *odd* to be back,' the last statement made in a forceful tone of voice, the subject changed abruptly.

Martin felt the same shudder of realisation. He too was something of a stranger in a familiar land. His life had changed, he was out of place here; and yet he was needed.

'I know,' he said grimly. 'I think I have to stay. The farm

31

needs sorting out. I hardly know where to begin. It would be good to have some help, Beck.'

Martin was aware of her hesitation as they walked, the slight loosening of his sister's grip on his arm, the sudden tightening of her fingers again. Rebecca said, 'I'll stay as long as I can. I'll do what I can. But if the songs get too –' she broke off, then smiled and shrugged. 'I can't explain it, Martin. My line isn't here anymore. The sounds confuse me. If I get called back, I'll have to go.'

'Stay as long as you can. It'll be good to have you here.'

'I'll try. But when I go, I'll be gone before you know it. It's the way with me.'

'How very New Age,' he said with a smile.

'No. Just the way I am.'

He looked at her across years, across age, knew that the moments together would be short, that this sad reunion was an event in a life, hers, as rich and complex as any tapestry; he knew that Rebecca was here because her lines had brought her here, and that in her own world she would soon be so far from him that not even the sound-wires would be able to connect them, and again she would be gone.

His voice dropping, his voice resigned, he said simply, 'I know.'

Martin built and stoked the applewood fire until the small parlour was glowing with light and warmth. He spread a blanket on the hearthside, undressed and lay back. Rebecca finished her bath and ran naked into the room, clutching a bath sheet which she flung over the two of them, shivering beside him. Martin felt the steam and heat from her body, a cooling dampness. When the attack of shivering had passed she sat up, the towel around her shoulders, looking at the man, smiling and shaking her head. 'You *are* lean. You used to be so chubby! I don't think I've ever seen so flat a stomach.'

'Come on. Flynn is the most athletic man you've ever met. *Your* words, five years ago, last letter I ever had from you.'

Rebecca laughed, leaning her head towards the fire so that her coppery hair could start to dry. 'What are you talking about? I wrote every week. Didn't you get my letters? Obviously a bad postal service.'

'Obviously.'

'Besides, Flynn is nothing but bone and sinew. Athletic but not aesthetic, not that I give a damn. I don't want to talk about Flynn. I want to talk about us. So just get me warm. Please?'

'This reminds me of that first night. When I came here? Do you remember? I was a sad, bedraggled soul, and you and Sebastian hated me.'

Martin smiled as a vague memory of Rebecca's arrival in the family entertained him. 'They made such a fuss of you. They kept comparing you to me. I got really angry . . .'

'They were teasing you. I could see it so clearly. It was obvious. I thought it was funny –'

'What was funny?'

'– the way you *couldn't* see it. You were such a sheltered boy. Such a cautious boy . . . But I was hungry, and defensive, and new, and confused. I was missing my own home, my own parents. dad – *my* dad – was always teasing. I loved his teasing. It's what I missed most when he died. And then I found that my 'new' dad was just as bad – just as good! It was like coming home again. I missed it all so

33

much when I went to Australia. Flynn is so straight . . . "if it's irony it must be metal". "Say what you mean and mean what you say". It comes from having to dissect the literal from the symbolic in reconstructed languages, I suppose.'

'Do what?'

'It's his job. What he calls digging out the hard foundations below the crumbling ideas of walls and towers. And he's good at it. But he's: So! Serious! He's learned to cherish the clear signal of a clear statement. I'm not criticising him, you understand.'

'Of course you're not. Perish the thought.'

'Bastard! Anyway *you* were always easy to wind up.'

'Who's denying it? I didn't like you. Not at first. I didn't want you in the family. I didn't like the way you and Seb teamed up to dance through the people on the path. I felt excluded.'

'You *were* excluded. Which isn't to say that I didn't fancy you even then. You intrigued me. But you were a pain in the butt.' She looked at the fire. 'Poor little Seb. What the hell did he do, I wonder? What did he do that he had to die like that?'

Martin was surprised by her comment. 'You sound as if you think it had something to do with the path.'

'Do I? I'm not sure. But I am sure he went inside the people once too often. I bet every child around here still does it, of course. But most of us stopped seeing them after a while. As if we'd been . . . as if we'd been contacted. Or maybe completed. I don't know. Something like that. But Seb, he kept *on* seeing them. And he kept on drawing those funny bottles. Do you remember? Long, thin bottles, with little trees and little men inside them.'

'I do remember.'

Martin leaned towards the fire, puzzled. 'Contacted?

34

Completed? What does that mean, Beck? Do you feel completed in some way?'

Rebecca wriggled closer, her hand resting on his warm skin, just above the knee. She seemed to be shivering again. 'I think so. I don't know so. There's something in Broceliande that is seeping out. Merlin's spirit, of course. We've always known that, haven't we?' She smiled, then spoke the local lore, the belief based on forgotten legend. 'Merlin sleeps in the heart of the wood, trapped by the enchantress Vivien in a thorn tree, or an oak tree by some accounts, inside a column of air that hides him from all eyes but hers. His dreams, his nightmares, creep to the edge to provide for us, to divide us, to test us, to seek out the true hearts among us.'

'That's fairy-tale. The people on the path aren't dreams, or nightmares. And they don't interfere with us.'

'Don't they? But that's not the point. The point is, this *is* a haunted place, and it always has been. We take the ghosts for granted. Not everyone sees them, just a few, and all of us stop seeing them after a year or so and start to doubt our memory. But we never talk about them *outside*. Why is that? Why do we keep quiet? Is something *stopping* us? Have you ever spoken to anyone in Amsterdam about the people?'

'Never. They'd think I was mad.'

'But *why* do you say that? *You* know you're not. You're no more mad than everybody else. We share a common experience and we share a common fear of communicating that experience. It's as if we've become afraid of what happened to us as children, when we saw them, when we danced inside their skins. Except that you never did, of course –'

'In fact, I did. Just once. It was terrifying. It felt as if I

35

was gliding on a cold lake, and there was a woman singing, but it only lasted an instant.'

Rebecca frowned, staring at him for a moment. 'I didn't know that.' She turned away. 'Yes. I think I remember.'

'No, you don't. This is the first time I've mentioned it.'

'Well, my point is, most of us saw them for months. Some only got a glimpse. And for all of us there was a moment when we got frightened . . .'

'Christ. That's what Jacques told me . . .'

'Jacques? Is he still alive?'

'Very much so, still building sheds and making charcoal. He was at the cold-earthing, four days ago.'

'The funeral, Martin. We call them funerals in the outside world, these days.'

'I like the old terms. Anyway, he took me to Quiburon, out on the coast where the stones are. Told me about my grandfather . . . about how he'd felt that he could have saved him from drowning, even though he was a child at the time . . . And he said just what you've just said. He had suddenly got frightened, and known that it was time to stop the encounters.'

'With the path . . .'

'Yes.'

Rebecca sighed, stretching out across the rug, dry and warm, her hands behind her head as she stared at the black beams of the ceiling.

'To go away is to see more clearly, Eveline said, but she was trapped. She wrote to me – just once – she said she loved me but for my own sake, stay away. *We get blinded in this place*, she said. *We take too much for granted. We don't see how trapped we are, how used we are. All that protects us is that we are afraid to talk about it. But who's trying to stop us talking about it?'*

'You never talked about Broceliande to Flynn?'
'A little. I didn't find it easy.'

When I first arrived in your home, I didn't believe in the people on the path. I thought you were all crazy, dancing around at midnight, describing thin air as if there were human figures in it. I used to watch you from the garden. I was watching you the night Seb danced into the frightened people, the week before he died. You thought I was in bed asleep, but I never slept in the middle night; I was too frightened. There were too many prowlings and breathings, too many noises, and I was new to the house, and my new father still scared me a bit, even though I had no reason to be frightened.

I'd seen other children playing with the ghosts – do you remember Thierry? What a crazy boy. Always shouting, always calling to them: 'Tell me your story! Tell me your story!' And Suzi. Always nattering away, happy with all the people, always urging them to stay, having a *real* relationship with them. And all I could see were my new friends, and my new brothers, addressing the emptiness. But I'd also heard adults talking about their own childhoods, and the way they'd followed the people on the path, and some of the terrible and wonderful things that had happened to them shortly afterwards. So I was intrigued. I assumed it was just because I didn't know how to *look*. My eyes were wrong, which is why I started to rub them, and screw them up. It was so painful. I became so obsessed with seeing that I became crazy. When I finally cut the eyelids to let in more light – remember that? – I was finally taken in hand. I still have the scars, but they're lost in the skin-lines now, thank God.

I suppose Eveline knew that I was trying to see the things

which she herself had once seen, and long become blind to. She locked me in my room at night, although she always came back two or three times to cuddle me. The one night she didn't come and check on me was the night when you followed Seb dancing up the path inside *three* ghosts, although I didn't know this at the time. Eveline was ill, remember? And I managed to get out through the window when I heard Seb disturb you. He was always outside. I don't think he ever slept. It was as if he'd got some magical energy that kept him hunting, hunting the spirits.

I ran along behind you, hiding in the tree-line when the moon came out, and heard Sebastian shouting something like, 'This is the best ever. I can hear their hearts!'. You were hanging back; you always said you'd never go inside one of these ghosts. You were probably wise. I could only see you walking slowly and nervously, and little Seb twisting and laughing. The moon went in, everything was dark, and that's when I saw *my* person on the path.

He was right at the point where the track leaves Broceliande, where the tangle of rose-briar and hawthorn thins, that marshy area, with the aspens and broken oaks . . . He was standing there, holding a horse by the reins. Then he stepped forward, and I could see that the horse was heavily packed and that the man, who was young and lightly bearded, had some strange bagpipes over his shoulder. There was a stringed instrument on the side of the pack-horse, a piece of curved and decorated wood and a small soundbox. I didn't recognise it, and I never heard it played, but that this ghost, this shimmering man, was a musician was all that I could think of.

He drew back into the woods as you and Sebastian came running back to the farmhouse. He watched you carefully, and you didn't see him. That's odd, isn't it? Usually the ghosts are unaware of us.

When you'd gone, he led the horse forward up the path, hurrying slightly, although he was moving slowly, like a slowed film, but the haste was conveyed clearly. He knew I was behind him, following. I had never seen anything like it. I was enchanted. The glimmer, like fairy glamour, flowed from his edges. It filled the night air, and I tried to touch it, but felt nothing.

I caught up with him. I felt so alive, suddenly I forgot about my eyes, which were still hurting from the way I'd slashed the skin. I can recognise now that I was aroused, that my body was aroused by imagination, by the experience of seeing a troubadour, a ghostly one, but a sort of dream recreated on that autumn night. I was thrilled by the encounter, and desperately wanted to hear him sing. So I entered him, and copied Sebastian, turning and swirling inside the dewy ghost.

There was nothing but rage. It was terrifying. I was caught in a whirlpool of fear, of anger. The man was escaping. He was frightened of something, and secretive. The rage in him seemed to crush me. Every squirt of blood in his veins was the rushing of a waterfall; his heart was thundering. I was deafened by this man's retreat from some terrible encounter, or so it felt. I was strangling, gasping for breath, turning desperately to find fresh air as he carried me with him, up to the hill. It was like being buried alive.

Then, just at the last, just as I thought I was going to die, I heard the sound of pipes. He wasn't playing them, he was *remembering* them. He was singing to himself in his own language, remembering the skirling notes of the pipes he carried, and I shared that thought, that moment of internal music. I touched an ancient music. I was treated to such an old song, and a song filled with such despair . . .

I became haunted by that music, just as Sebastian had been haunted by his own encounter. I couldn't sing it. It made no sense. It made sense only in my head; I could jig to it, I could twirl to it, but it was inexpressible, except in dreams.

How old was I? I can't remember, now. Fifteen, maybe. I spent the holiday weeks of the next two years among the stones at Carnac, hating the tourists, the wretched families who came to picnic, to photograph, but not to listen. I was listening for the dreamsongs of that time, for the old tunes, for some clue to the magic that was now in me. But I realised that even that ancient earth wasn't old enough. To articulate the music that flowed inside me not so much like blood, more like . . . like a benign but omnipresent parasitic worm, invading my spaces, pulling back when it hurt me, growing inside me but as I say, *inexpressible*, because it was pure feeling, eroding me, fighting me, but carefully . . . to find out how to exorcise that music, to get rid of the ghost that something in Broceliande had driven into me, I had to go further back.

Which is why I went to Australia, to the place of songlines, and songtrails, and a way of singing that you would never understand, because it isn't singing at all, nor singing up the world of rocks and creatures as happened in the dreamtime, but being sung *through*. I can't describe it.

The other side is easier: I never had a good voice. I was always gravelly, you remember? The groaning background, Daddy used to say. But suddenly when I sang I seemed to have an effect on people. Whatever I sang, wherever I was, whatever the country.

I silenced the chief (and his family!) of the Memoragas people – the thunder people – out behind the Mann Ranges. They were singing to the sleeping rains and asked me to join in. I was already flowing with them, they seemed to be singing through me, and when I sang it was dizzying, it was like falling, then flying. Suddenly I was the only voice. They were entranced and puzzled, watching me in silence. I seemed to fly among them, and there were so many of them, and the land shifted and changed, the light, the colour, the warmth. I was travelling *through* the song, some silly ditty from childhood, 'Frère Jacques' maybe, I've now lost the words, I just remember how the world dropped away when I sang, and how my song went through those watching people.

In the morning I felt hungover, though I hadn't been drinking. There was so much excitement outside my private space that I got up, quite naked, and peered out.

Flynn was there, crouching with the chief and looking at water flowing from below their painted rock. There had never been a spring there, now there was new water, very cold, rich in calcium and magnesium – Flynn did the analysis – a new spring, which had come during the night.

My song, they said, had called the sleeping water to their hunt trail. They were amazed at the new spring. They made me bathe in it. They all wanted to wash me. I sat in the muddy stream for an hour, while I was anointed and sung to, and questioned, and played to with kazoo and bark drum. They put eucalyptus leaves on my head and insisted on daubing me with the image, in yellow ochre, of a gerbil, a creature that seems to find water everywhere. It was their totem creature.

The only truly embarrassing moment was needing to go to the toilet. Everything that I *didn't* want, they *valued*, collecting it and burying it below a small stone.

After that I got frightened. I was singing to people, singing anything, any rubbish, and it was affecting them profoundly. There was a touch of magic in my voice and I had no conception of it, only the knowledge that it worked. Flynn was both apprehensive and loving. He was never exploitative, although we did earn a few meals in the lean times by my singing in small town bars. I think he knew there was a spirit in me, he simply had no idea what it was and had no idea how to use it. We went into the desert for five years, built separate shacks, and entered our own Otherworlds. We'd meet on occasion to eat a ceremonial meal (of whatever we could find, or obtain), and spend a few hours on the mat, but most importantly we talked about our dreams. We'd end each visit by going to the small stream and bathing, then follow our separate lines again.

That was ten years ago. It was a hard time for me, a time in which I came close to death on several occasions. But with the song in me, this song, this magic, I always came back.

Then Flynn drowned – a terrible accident. I ran twelve miles to the billabong when I was told the news, and dragged his body from the muddy pool. He'd been dead when he was found, so they'd left him there. He was bloated with water, naked and fat, his skin fishbelly-white. He was quite dead. But I crouched on him and sang to him and the water started to ooze from him, came out of his mouth, his ears, his eyes, nose, out of his pores, his arse, even out of his cock. The water drained from him, a steady sweat, a steady flow in the cold dawn, and soon there was room in his body for the air again. He started to breathe and his body danced below me. The air went in, his eyes opened and stared at me, and I stopped the song.

If he was frightened of me before, he was terrified of me then!

It was the moment when my time with Flynn became fatally defined. I mean in terms of its intimacy, its . . . longevity? We were dying together from that moment on. But only because our time together was now defined by the *song*. He hadn't known he was dead. But when people

42

come up to you to congratulate you on being alive again you tend to get the idea that something weird has happened. Flynn was as muscular and lean as the desert where we lived; every part of his mind was trimmed to the bone. He had no time for doubt. He heard the story – that he'd had a stroke and fallen into the drowning pool – he heard the story of the songlady bringing him back to life, he knew that our friends in the wanderlands, the desert, weren't liars; and he accepted.

At that moment he was a dead man alive again; at that moment my song was magic. At that moment he was at a distance from me, because his own curiosity now extended not to the land which we loved, or to the past which we were trying to recreate in our minds, but to me, to a French woman, born near the forest of Paimpont, orphaned when fourteen years old, now a *possessor* of magic, not just an explorer of magic tradition.

The Lake-finder's Tale

The old 'bosker', Conrad, came to the farmhouse shortly
after dawn, a dark figure moving effortlessly along the
path, the early sun catching on his small, silver spectacles.
Martin had been unable to sleep, his mind full of Rebecca's
story and the idea that to dance inside the ghostly figures
from Broceliande was to become possessed by some
shadow of the past. Rebecca slept soundly in the bed
behind him. Martin peered down as Conrad rummaged in
the long grass by the hedges and found two eggs, which he
inspected and pocketed. He was wearing a wide-brimmed
leather hat – he had made it himself – and a long, grey
overcoat which flapped around him as he moved. He
carried two short wooden staffs, slung on his back like
rifles.

Seeing Martin at the bedroom window he waved, then
let himself in to the warm kitchen below. Martin came
downstairs. The old man stood, hat in his hands, white
hair combed back into a long pigtail, tied with grass-twine.
He was looking around sadly.

'I watched Eveline as she went to her cold home, the
other day,' he said. 'I was by the wood. I didn't want to
intrude by the fires.'

'I wish you had. You'd have been very welcome.'

'I'm going to miss her. She was just a girl when I came
here first, but she helped me build my houses in the forest.
She always let me have eggs – and bread, sometimes. I

traded foxes, after your father died. She couldn't bear to kill them, but they have to be controlled.'

'I understand,' Martin said quickly, feeling uncomfortable. 'But please stop controlling them from now. I'm more than happy to let you have eggs whenever you want.'

As Martin picked a dozen of the larger eggs from a wicker basket, placing them carefully in Conrad's sack, the old man said carefully, 'You're a fox lover, then?'

'Always have been.'

'So am I at heart. But trade is trade.'

Martin offered the remains of yesterday's heavy loaf and a farm cheese that was now over-ripe. The old bosker seemed delighted.

'Would you like some breakfast?' Martin asked him.

'I ate in the forest at first dew. Thanks all the same.'

Conrad seemed to relax. He pulled on his hat and lifted the pack to his shoulder. He was staring at Martin curiously, grey eyes bright in the weather-etched face. 'Are you still frightened of me, Martin?'

'Good God no.'

'You used to be –'

'Kids are always frightened of hermits. *And* you were once an enemy soldier, left behind by the war. We used to make up terrible stories about what you did in the woods.'

'A living demon, eh?' Conrad laughed. 'Yes, I remember. I used to listen – I could hear you all from a long distance. It's a talent I seem to have developed since coming here,' – he sounded wry – 'Sometimes your fantasies amused me, sometimes – not often – they made me sad. I was a long way from my first home, and harmless to everything inedible, which included children –'

'Ah yes, but we didn't think so.'

'All except Rebecca, your special friend Rebecca.' Conrad winked. '*She* wasn't afraid of me. Anyway, I would

45

watch you children chasing the ghosts from the forest as they walked the path. I couldn't see them, of course, no adult could. But I could hear them. It was an extraordinary experience. It still is. Which is chiefly why I came to see you. There's something I want to show you . . .'

'Shall I wake Rebecca?'

The old man glanced back. 'No. This is for you alone.'

Conrad might always have been a part of Broceliande. He was as eternal, as familiar, indeed as elusive, usually, as the strange ruins that could be found just inside the forest's skirts. But he had not been born here, nor come into existence here. In his own words, 'There comes a moment in every person's life, I now realise, when as they are marching forward they become aware that in fact they are running away. At that moment, home is where you are standing, and this place, this gloomy edgewood, became my second home.'

His army column had been marching past Broceliande. Conrad was sixteen, not particularly frightened, not particularly lonely. He was just a soldier in a column, moving forward towards the coast. There were not enough trucks to transport all the troops, in those early winter months of 1944, and so like Caesar's legions they tramped the rough roads to the west, sometimes aware that a watery sun was leading them on.

'But I had no faith, no real belief. My father had always talked of duty, and of family, but his words, sincere though they were, were of no comfort to me. I wonder sometimes if there can be any greater pain than realising that you are no longer part of a family that once was your whole life.

'As we marched past Broceliande my First Home broke into shattered memories. Everything simply fell apart. I hated where I had come from. I loathed that savage war. I despised the principles that drove it. I was not alone in this, of course, but the forest took me and me alone.

'I deserted quickly. I used a strip of oilskin to wrap my weapons and bury them; the rifle was a bolt-action Lee Enfield, more like twenty pounds in weight than nine, or so it seemed, and I was glad of the freedom from this burden.

'That first day, I walked a wide circle, walking to the limit of what I felt I needed. That circle, I discovered later, was more than two miles across.'

This disc of land had become Conrad's Second Home. He walked its circumference five times, first entering the dark forest, then emerging and skirting the villages, crossing the fields and the farmlands before entering the woods again. All of this was done at night because he was in fear of his life, now, and his uniform would certainly have been an invitation to murder.

In all the long years since then he had never once stepped outside the circle, as he had defined it during those February days. 'I belong here. I made it right that I belonged here. I became accepted, eventually welcomed. I don't belong across the circle, but I've lived long enough, and circled hard enough, to make this small land *my* land. My home.'

Now Conrad led the way into that small land and into the forest, following a wide, winding path that was tall with wet, webbed grass and purple thistle. He stopped occasionally to listen. The air was moist, almost stifling.

His first house was a shack constructed out of corrugated iron, wooden panels and old doors. It was covered with black oilskins. Around it, on a picket fence, hung thirty or so carcasses of grey squirrels, in various states of decomposition. Two foxes' heads on poles were a grim reminder of Conrad's main usefulness to the farms around the wood.

'Come in, come in,' the bosker said with a chuckle, glancing back at Martin. 'Into the place which terrified you once upon a time.'

Martin pulled aside the oilskin door, ducked through the small entrance space into Conrad's living quarters. The floor had been hollowed out and lined with sandbags and turves. His bed was at one end, in a stream of light from the only window, a gap below the metal eaves. His fire was at the other end of the small room, built out of bricks, with an iron chimney to the outside world. The walls were hung with skins and furs; hooks and leather ties dangled from the ceiling, ready for hanging game. He had a chair and a table, and a small chest on which stood two tiny, framed and faded photographs, one of a shy, fair-haired girl, holding a cat, the other of two people sitting on a garden chair, a couple who looked out of the frame with solemn expression.

As Conrad stored his new supplies, Martin noticed that above the bed were five crude paintings, all of the girl, all from different angles: one of each profile, her full face laughing, her face looking coy, a discreet nude that had been executed in crayon on smoothed and chalk-whitened wood.

Light spilled suddenly into the shack. Conrad had pulled back the doorflap, waiting quietly for Martin to finish his inspection.

'Just a ghost,' the old man said, and Martin felt embarrassed, stepping quickly away from the portraits.

'I'm sorry. That was an intrusion. I was too curious.'

'No intrusion at all. She's long gone, now. Long changed. But she keeps me in touch with my younger spirit.'

48

They continued inwards, the track narrowing and becoming more difficult, the oaks crowding from the sides.

'Be careful,' Conrad called, as he smacked at wet briar to clear the route. 'This is the way the ghosts come. If I say get off the path, do so immediately. They sometimes move very quietly.'

'What does it matter?' Martin called back. 'I can't see them or hear them any more. I'm too old. They can't harm me . . .'

Conrad's voice as he moved ahead was steely. 'They can harm you. Just do as I say. For Eveline's sake, for your mother's sake.'

The path spilled out into a clearing below the spreading branches of three massive beeches. The ground here was soft and golden brown, streaked through with the green of fern. Here, Conrad had his second home, a hemisphere of bent willow branches, covered with hides.

'Hunting lodge,' he said quickly, skirting the clearing. 'We've not far to go, now.'

Not far to go?

For an hour that seemed like ten, Conrad led them deeper into the wildwood, through half-lit dells and marshy, silent glades, down stone escarpments and over massive, mossy rocks which caught the shifting sun with a vibrant, emerald luminosity. Muddy watercourses wound through crushing woods of oak and holly; springs spilled from ragged ledges, misting in the thin light from the glistening canopy.

'We're lost. We must be lost.'

'Not lost at all. Look!'

And suddenly they had come through the wood to the rush-fringed shore of a wide lake, and the bosker's third home — a series of tarpaulins, slung between trees, open to the water.

'Fishing lodge,' Conrad announced, stooping to enter the shelter and beckoning Martin to follow him.

The lodge was full of dried and drying fish, crude rods and nets, a harpoon and a further pile of skins, rabbit and fox; the cured hides of two small deer were stretched on frames and could be pulled across the open front to block the wind.

They sat, squeezed together, and watched the gentle water. Mallards and moorhens wriggled through the rushes, dipping and pecking below the lake. The forest was solid on the other side.

'They come across in small boats, or sometimes on rafts,' Conrad said after a while. 'When I'm here at night, sometimes the water is covered with a low mist, and it swirls where the boat comes, the only visible sign of their passage from the heartwood. I hear the oars dipping, and the rustle of the sedges when it comes to the bank. I hear the murmur of voices, and on occasion the breathing of horses. The ghosts, which are invisible to me, follow the path by your farm, then up to the church and over the hill. The boat returns to the dark wood, after which there will often be nothing for months.

'Over the lake is the heart of Broceliande but it is an older forest than the forest behind us. It doesn't belong here.

'My circle of land ends as far out onto the lake as I need to go to spear pike, perhaps twenty yards. I would never dare go further.'

I had lived in the wood for ten years before I found the lake or perhaps I should say before the *lake* found *me*. There was no sign of it when I first came here. I had probably walked across its edge fifty times since I first circumscribed my land. It had hidden from me, or *been* hidden from me, but one bitter winter morning I heard the sound of moorhens and gently splashing water. I was curious, aware that there should have been a grove of trees there. I pushed through the dense holly to find the lake very much as you see it now. It was covered with ice, though, almost to the edge itself, where the rushes were white with frost.

This was the second event that convinced me of a source of magic at work, deeper in the forest. I'd already seen the strange behaviour of you children, at night on the path, your clear belief in ghosts and your parents' reluctance to contradict you. More than that, when hunting deep in the wood I had occasionally heard the sound of a man crying out. The wailing came from a great distance, and quite soon I realised that the distance was further than I'd thought, since I discovered I could also hear the whispered words of children from a mile away. That crying voice haunted me, though. It drifted through the glades, seemed to flow down the paths through the wood, and was usually followed by a woman's voice, laughing.

So when this lake miraculously appeared, one morning, I could no longer deny that I'd stumbled into a place which, to put it mildly, was quite out of the ordinary. The strange way of speaking among the farmers and villagers now became more important. The traditions, the rituals that I had watched from the edgewood, all had seemed eccentric, perhaps just local habit; now they seemed to echo an older thought: the fires you put at the head of each grave, the procession of the twelve trees, the drowning of grass images, with the hair-filled puppet of a child inside . . . They'd never been sinister, but now they became more meaningful, although I've never really understood that meaning.

I wasn't aware, when all this was happening, of the

association of Merlin with this forest. I hadn't read Tennyson or Chrétien de Troyes, knew nothing of Thomas Mallory, or the *Vitae Merlinis*, or the other sources. The priest talked to me about all of them. He lent me books. But before that education I only knew that there was a vision of magic, somewhere across the lake, and that it was seeping from the forest, shrouded in the ghostly forms of the people on the path, and in that terrible moaning.

You know how the seasons bring different scents, different feelings in the air? So it was with the wailing voice, as if there was a season for the agony, a certain day for the distress, an hour, just after dusk, when the moment of true desperation could be remembered and the air of the forest filled with the cry.

On one such evening, when the pain of that voice had gone, I crept from my hunting lodge again and heard the wildwood speak, an odd echo, like a girl's voice, but curiously slow. It seemed to breathe a word. I wasn't sure, but I thought the word was 'Fool', and moments later the word was repeated. 'Fool!'

I waited, fascinated, and soon a girl from the village came running and twirling along the path. I knew her by sight, though she had never entered the wood before. She was a slight thing, fourteen years old or so, her hair almost orange in the half light, her clothing a simple dress and a loose grey cardigan.

As she ran she seemed to dance, exactly as I have seen the children dance among the ghosts. She was murmuring as she moved. 'I have it. I have it now.'

She approached the clearing where I waited, unaware of me. Then she stopped and crouched, snarling and shaking her head so that her hair was wild. Laughing, she suddenly launched herself at a tree and scratched and bit at the hard bark, tearing with her fingers, stripping away whole lengths of wood. Embracing the torn trunk she flung back her head and howled and bayed, then laughed and again exclaimed, 'I have it!'.

I felt terrified of this feral child and inadvertently drew back, drawing attention to myself. She raced across to me, coming very close, then folded her arms about her body – her fingers were bloody – cocking her head as she peered at me. Then she leered forward, lips hideously drawn back from pearl-white teeth to expose the death in her head. 'I have it!' she hissed, and proceeded to dance a little jig, arms still folded. 'I have it,' she murmured, almost singing, delighted with herself.

At that moment a boy laughed from the darkness of the wood. The girl turned quickly, crouching slightly, then took off like a hare towards the source of the sound. The boy stepped into the half light and taunted her. 'No you don't! No you don't!'

'I *have* it,' screamed the girl.

'You have *nothing*. You took *nothing*!'

And at once his crowing ceased and his youthful face took on a look of great age, and great amusement, the amusement of an old man, listening to the pretensions of someone younger and still naive.

'Fool . . .' he added quietly.

It was the wrong thing to do, perhaps. The girl leapt at him and in a second had torn her nails across his grinning face. They struggled. He held her hair, but she was taller, stronger, and she hunched above him, bending him and crushing him, finally sinking her teeth into the back of his neck. She shook him, worried at him, like the wolf whose shape now seemed to envelop her. Girl-like, hair tossing, legs thrashing inside her simple skirt, the hunched form of a wolf was shadowed around her, an evil glamour.

The screaming boy was dragged away by this monstrous

creature. I ran towards her, but she turned and looked at me, the struggling boy still held in those perfect teeth. I felt as if I'd been struck by falling sickness. I couldn't move. I was on my knees. My arms fell heavily and I stayed there, watching the savage death, the boy dragged back towards the ponds, close to the village, close to the farm where the poor child lived.

Yes, Martin. I'm sorry. The child I saw murdered by the girl was your own brother. Sebastian.

I didn't regain the use of my limbs until after dawn of the following day. By the time I reached the edge of the forest I could hear the dogs, and the voices of searchers, and then the terrible cry of pain, your mother's voice, followed by the splashing of men in the shallow pond, dragging the body from its grave.

Later I came close to your farm and listened to the grieving voices. It was clear that a wolf was being blamed – as if a wolf would have treated its prey in such a way! Even if there had been any wolves *left* in Broceliande!

The children were more courageous in their suspicions, and I heard one of you say, 'The old woodsman. He's got one of us at last.' And someone answered, 'Let's get him. We'll burn him on the hill.'

But these were just the fears of you, your friends, still reconciling yourselves in your childlike ways to the loss of your littlest friend, Sebastian.

I approached the farm, very apprehensive, my mind a mist of uncertainty as to how to describe the events that I had seen. Eveline was on the garden seat, you on one side of her, comforting her even as you planned revenge on me, your sister Rebecca on the other, her face wet with tears as she held Eveline's arm.

Your father approached me quickly. He had two questions: had I seen or heard anything, and how should we organise a wolf hunt?

I was about to tell him what I'd seen the night before when Rebecca turned towards me. In an instant a *charm* fell away from my eyes, or perhaps away from her, it's impossible to tell. All I know is that she was revealed instantly as the girl in the woods, even wearing the same skirt and cardigan. I had simply not recognised her in the forest the night before.

I was speechless for a few seconds, then became terrified again as your tall sister ran towards me and hugged me, looking up through sorrowful eyes as she said, 'Don't listen to what the boys say. I'll always come and visit you. I promise. I promise. I'll not leave you alone for an instant!'

My head and heart had turned cold with fear. To this day I have no idea whether I was addressed by the true girl or by the wily sylvan monster. But I know she came and visited me often, before eventually she went away, to pursue new studies in Australia.

And I know that all thought of revealing my vision faded. How could I tell Eveline, mourning the death of her younger son, that it was her adored adopted daughter who had dragged him to the reed pond, and held him down?

The Shape-shifter's Dream

Martin was being shaken gently. He surfaced out of a dream in which he floated at night through drifting mist, the water of the lake lapping gently below his small boat. He woke with a shiver to find that he was still in Conrad's fishing lodge, the lake burnished with orange as the sun began to set. A swirling flight of dark birds crowded the sky above the heart of the wood.

'We should go back,' the old man said urgently. He looked very anxious. 'You've been asleep all day.'

'All day?'

'I couldn't wake you. We must get away from here.'

Martin was shocked by what he heard, and was still disturbed by Conrad's tale, and the revelation of the cause of Sebastian's death. He stood stiffly, groaning as he unlocked his knees. Conrad laughed sympathetically and held his arm, then offered one of his staves for support.

They returned to the iron-roofed shack and the bosker shed his overcoat and sheepskin jacket, stoked up the fire before uncorking a flagon of cider brandy. Martin sipped the potent drink with circumspection, not knowing who might have brewed it. Conrad was less careful, shuddering as the spirit burned its way to his cold bones.

'Will I make us supper?' he asked, but Martin shook his head.

'I should get back to Rebecca.' He hesitated, realising that suddenly the thought frightened him. 'Are you quite sure of what you've told me? About Rebecca?'

56

'Quite sure. Perhaps the possession was just a brief encounter. She grieved for Sebastian like all the rest of you. I felt no evil in her when she visited. I'm sure she had come from the lake, that deadly night, but she was completely unaware of it. Perhaps, as I say, the possession was brief. I do know that later she danced through another ghost and heard song, ancient song, and became obsessed with it . . .'

'Yes. That's why she went away.'

'And she must go away again. And you must too.' Conrad drank heavily from the flask again, then replaced the cork. 'Your mother sensed danger for you, just before she died.'

'That's what my Uncle Jacques said. But what danger?'

Conrad shrugged. 'She began to see the people on the path. She lay in bed, looking down, and saw their outlines again, just as she'd been able to see them as a child. Something she saw made her determined that even if you came for the funeral, you shouldn't stay.'

Martin rose from the floor by the crackling fire and turned to go. Then he asked, 'Why did you take me to the lake? Wasn't that a dangerous thing to do?'

'Yes. But if you take no heed of Eveline's wishes, then you may need to know it's there.'

Lights were on in the farmhouse, and the warm smell of garlic, herbs and red wine was on the air, suggesting a casserole under preparation.

Rebecca was at the wood stove, shaking an iron pan which sizzled loudly. The table was set, a candle in the middle, a bottle of claret opened, one glass half full. She glanced round and smiled as Martin entered staring at her in some shock. 'Won't be long,' she said.

There was a note from her, discarded on the sideboard.

It read, '*Hi early riser! 9 am. Gone to Vannes for clothes food hair a few special little things. No idea how long I'll be. Hope you're having fun.*'

'I'm sorry. I should have left a note for you before I went out . . .'

'Why?' she said, wiping her hands on her apron. 'If you'd wanted me to share in what you were doing you'd have woken me. I hope you're hungry. I bought far too much beef.'

'I'm starving. I appreciate it. I haven't eaten all day. Beck, you look . . . wonderful.'

She removed her apron and stood across the table, grinning, her arms outstretched. 'A transformation, eh?'

'Very sexy. Not that you need clothes to be sexy, of course. I didn't mean . . .'

She laughed as he contorted through the words, saying, 'Burble, squirm, burble. I know what you mean. Shut up and feast your eyes. It won't last.'

She'd dyed her hair jet black, cut the fringe in a straight line and made three thin ringlets on each temple, each strand decorated with golden amber beads. Her black silk blouse left her arms bare. It was cut low over her breasts. Her skirt flowed fully from below her tight waist, a green fabric patterned with lines of tiny red and purple squares. She'd rouged her lips and applied makeup to her face. The etching of her skin was hardly visible, now, and in this illusion she had shed ten years of age.

Amused by his scrutiny she laughed, 'One small nod to vanity, one huge dent in the purse. Don't worry, it's just for fun.'

'You look very . . . er . . . Romany?'

'Earlier than that. A lot earlier than those travellers. You'll see decorations like this on Bronze Age vases. But it's how my mother looked, it's how I remember her. A traditional look in the group of families. I wish you'd met her. I wanted to share a touch of her memory with you. May I please have a welcoming hug, now?'

She came round the table, oak-brown eyes flashing with pleasure, a hint of passion. Martin reacted apprehensively, his whole body stiffening slightly. She saw this and frowned, then put her arms round him and kissed him, holding the kiss for a few seconds then pulling away, turning away.

'Some wine? I opened it an hour ago. It should have caught its breath by now.'

'Mm.'

She passed him a glass, then raised her own. 'To health.'

'Health,' he echoed and sipped the wine appreciatively. He raised the glass again. 'To the traveller.'

'Bright path, Eveline.' She drained her glass and set it down, then leaned back on the table and folded her arms, looking at him curiously. 'The question, then, is this: do you tell me now, or after we've eaten?'

'Tell you what?'

Rebecca laughed, but there was little humour there. She shook her head, saying, 'Anxiety is a song that sings from eyes.'

'French proverb?'

'Thunder people *spiritlook*. It's part of a long chant teaching how to read the inner songs when the words are unclear. In other words, body language and heightened sensory perception. What's made you apprehensive all of a sudden? You seem almost frightened of me. You're not regretting last night, are you?'

'Of course not.'

She came over to him quickly and put her arms round him, fixing him with her level gaze, dark eyes searching. 'Where did you go today?'

59

'Into the forest. With the old bosker. Conrad.'

Rebecca smiled, 'I'm glad he's still around. I want to see him. How is he?'

'An old man, living rough. People round here look after him, clothes, barter, disgusting cider brandy. It's hard to remember the ogre in him. In fifteen years I don't think he's changed a bit.'

After a moment Rebecca said, 'Let's eat. I've bought haslet. Your favourite, if I remember.'

Sitting across the table they ate the thick slices of brawn in silence. Rebecca was about to fetch the casserole when Martin said, 'Where were you the night Seb died? Can you remember?'

She sat down, quizzical, then ran a finger and thumb down an amber-beaded ringlet. 'I was with you and your friend Peter, chasing the woman and child on the path, the ones who were running . . .'

Martin felt his face go cold. Rebecca hadn't been with him that night. He'd been with Peter, but the people on the path had been two men with staffs and unstrung longbows, one of them a heavy set man with bushy beard, the other aristocratic looking, dressed in half armour. Martin had watched Peter dancing inside them, but as usual simply ran in circles round the figures, studying them in great detail.

He told as much to Rebecca, who said angrily, 'Nonsense. I was there. We went back home together, climbed through the window together, and the next morning woke up to the shouting. What the hell is this, Martin? What's going on? You're white as a sheet. What's frightened you? What's going on?'

His heart thumping, unexpectedly anxious, he said, 'The bosker said he'd seen you by the lake in the forest the night Seb drowned.'

Rebecca frowned for a moment. 'What lake? Do you mean the pond?'

'No, the lake at the heart, the big lake.'

'There's no big lake in Broceliande. Not that I know of.'

'He says he saw you there. The night Seb died. You were dancing in the forest, behaving like a wolf.'

'Like a wolf?'

'That's what he said.'

'Why didn't he speak to me, then? Why didn't he contact me? I wasn't afraid of him, I was the only one of you who wasn't.'

'I don't know,' Martin said. 'I don't know why he didn't speak to you about it.' He regretted the lie as he spoke it and so transmitted the lie instantly.

Rebecca looked disgusted. She picked up a napkin and wiped the make-up from her face, an angry, pointed act. The years, the sunburn, the hard side of her came back. She was upset, clearly confused, aware that Martin was keeping something back from her but frightened by something deeper.

'Have you seen this lake?' she asked.

'I saw it today for the first time.'

'He took you there?'

'For the first time. Yes. It's a long way in, and it's a difficult route, but I'm damned sure it wasn't there when we were kids.'

Rebecca stared across the table, thinking carefully. 'Everyone knows there are ghosts on the path. So why not a lake that magically appears? Maybe it's an adult vision. Maybe as we age we can start to see things inside the wood. It's just that we never look.'

'That's more or less what Conrad said. He thinks he's a lake-finder.'

'Nice talent. But I still don't understand why thinking I

might have been in the forest when Seb died should make you upset.'

She grasped the point suddenly, leaning forward on the table, beads rattling in her hair. Her eyes gleamed with a terrible, controlled fury. She spoke in a whisper. 'Or maybe I do. You say Conrad saw a girl. He must have thought it was me – and he thinks I might have seen him . . . that's right. Not a wolf at all, then . . . Not a wolf that killed Seb. The old bosker's been guilty all these years, and he's made you suspicious of me. He's trying to implicate me.'

Her voice rose in pitch. 'And you believe him. You believe him. You unbelievable shit!'

Martin said quietly, 'Beck – I'm telling you plainly: you were not with Peter and me that night.'

'Liar! You know I was.'

'We were alone, Beck. The encounter you're talking about was a week or more before. You weren't with us that night. And your fingers were all torn at the ends, as if you'd been scratching at rough bark, which is what Conrad claims he saw.'

She was silent for a long time, looking at Martin, yet somehow through him, fiddling with her hair, then shaking her head. 'I scraped them sliding down a trunk after watching the two of you on the path.' She too was speaking quietly, almost sadly. And suddenly her eyes closed and her face grimaced with pain.

'My God. Oh my God.' She looked at him again. 'You do think I killed Seb. You think it was me. Don't you? Why don't you speak? Don't just stare at me. Oh Christ, I feel sick. I'm going to be sick. How could you? How could you think such a thing? I loved Seb. I loved him. I wouldn't have hurt him.'

She stood slowly and left the kitchen, closing the door slowly behind her.

Later, Martin heard her moving around upstairs. He thought she might be packing her things to leave, but eventually he heard the bed-springs, and then silence.

'I've lost her,' Martin said to the silence after she'd gone, experiencing an aching despair as this fear became a reality. But later he woke suddenly, cramped up on the small sofa, a blanket over his clothed body. Moonlight streamed into the sitting room, illuminating Rebecca, who sat on the sofa's edge, her eyes sparkling as she watched the waking man.

'Beck?'

'After Seb died,' she said softly, 'I had a recurring dream. It was very strange, quite frightening, and I never told it to anybody. After what you said this evening, I can't get it out of my mind; I think it came back again, I probably woke in the middle of it.'

Martin sat up and made more room for her, reaching out to touch her arm. She sat motionless, unresponsive. He said, 'Beck – forgive me. I'm confused. It's this place, the old fears. And the old man confused me . . .'

'Be quiet – please – be quiet. Let me tell you the dream.' She turned away from him, arms across her chest.

'I'm in a clearing, a glade in an old forest. I'm running round the glade with a torch, and everything is burning, the flames sweeping high, the smoke billowing, and cloth and skins and parchment are being consumed by the fire, burning brightly, shedding charred fragments into the air. There's the tall, thick shaft of an old thorn lying on the ground. I've hacked its branches down to stubs, then decorated it with bracelets in bronze, and torques and brooches, and there are bones around it, and clay pots filled with stinking liquid and coloured powders. All of them are

63

melting in the heat. And I'm dancing around a swirling column of earth that rises above me. A man is screaming. The more I dance the faster the rising tower of earth spins, the louder the cries, and the more I laugh!

'Then I'm dancing with a man, spinning round among the flames, only it isn't a man it's a stone statue, a horrible effigy, the ears cut off, the eyes gouged out, the nose slit, the mouth gaping tongueless, no fingers on the hands, no toes on the feet, the sex has been broken from the groin. I twirl this gruesome statue across the glade, and around the rising earth, singing all the time, even kissing the cold stone lips. There is a feeling of terror. A cairn of stones holds the centre of the glade and I fling the dancing stone across it.

'I run from the burning grove, swim hard through dragging, sucking waters, shaking myself dry on the shore, then running through the forest, swerving and ducking, but dancing all the time. Only I'm not a woman, now . . . I'm on all fours, my tongue lolling. I howl and scream at the sky as I run, I bay at the moon, I bark at shadows, I scratch at bark. It is a run of great triumph, and great delight.

'But suddenly a man is there, naked and blind, blocking my path. He is the man of the statue, stripped of senses, sex and touch; but his presence ahead of me – laughing! – fills me with fear and I plunge off the path and into the bushes. The land gives way into a pit and I fall, screaming, spinning in the air, endlessly falling, reaching for the branches and the stone outcrops that will save me, reaching for safety but always missing, falling and falling until I wake up terrified!'

She turned back to Martin.

'I felt a moment of that wild dance and the wild wolf run tonight. It woke me up. It brought the dream back to me.'

She was trembling. Martin sat next to her and enfolded her, feeling her tears as a cool moist touch on his neck.

'Perhaps it *was* me,' she whispered. 'Perhaps I *was* possessed.'

Suddenly she sat up, strong again. 'I'm frightened, lover. I think we should get the hell out of here. First thing in the morning. What do you say?'

'The paperwork will take two days. Don't go near the path. Avoid the bosker. We'll be safe for two days. Come on, I'll take you back to bed. We'll talk more about it in the morning.'

PART TWO

The Unquiet Grave

My breast, my love, is cold as clay,
My breath smells earthly strong;
But if you kiss my cold clay lips,
Our days they will be long.

From *The Unquiet Grave*
(folksong, variant ca. 1750)

The Unquiet Grave

1

A child was laughing, outside in the night, running along the path towards the church. Martin got out of bed and watched the small boy, visible by moonlight. It was Adrien LeConte. He whirled and slipped in the darkness, his eyes alive with the vision of enchantment, his head filled with the sounds of ghostly hearts and voices.

'It goes on,' he whispered, and turned to look at Rebecca, realising at once that she had gone. Her clothes were no longer over the chair.

With an apprehensive glance back through the window, over the field to Broceliande, Martin murmured, 'Don't go to the forest, Beck. For Christ's sake, don't go to the forest . . .'

He couldn't eat breakfast. He fed the chickens and the ailing retriever, walking the dog for a few hundred yards, but the creature was long past her prime and preferred the warmth by the wood stove. Jacques called by, his Citroën belching exhaust fumes, his breath even stronger with tobacco smoke. He had brought a pile of boxes for packing, and a suitcase for the clothes that he would be taking for his and Suzanne's own use. He stayed for coffee, then went back to his house. Martin took the opportunity to enter the forest's edge and look for the bosker, but Conrad was off hunting, or fishing, perhaps exploring.

Bess's barking brought him running back to the farm. The bitch was up on her hind legs, forepaws on the gate, barking towards the path. She was not normally disturbed by the phantoms from Broceliande, so perhaps she was aware of something in the woods themselves. Martin scratched the animal's head and patted her, calming her, and the barking changed to a nervous wheezing. 'What did you see, old girl, eh? What did you see?'

There was someone in the house, the door was open. 'Rebecca?'

She called back, and Martin found her inside drinking coffee and reading a magazine.

'Where did you go?'

'Up to Seb's cold home.'

'Don't you mean his grave?' Martin was trying to be light, but Rebecca stared at him, unsmiling.

'It feels cold up there, Martin. It's a cold home. I wanted to make my peace, in case I *did* have something to do with the death.'

She was very matter of fact, and Martin nodded, irritated with himself for not having thought of something so obvious.

'*Is* he at peace?'

She sipped at her cup and nodded, eyes skimming the text of the magazine. 'I think so. I know *I* am. But it still feels cold where he lies.'

'I thought you might have wanted to talk to Conrad.'

She closed the journal and looked up thoughtfully. 'I do. I think I'll wait for a while, though. But I do want to talk to him. Last night I was afraid, very afraid. That dream, your story, your hostility . . .'

'It wasn't hostility, Beck. I was frightened too.'

'Yeah. Well . . . it was all suddenly overwhelming. But the fact is, *I* didn't kill Sebastian, even if my fingers did. There's the ghost of that moment inside me, and that's why I felt so frightened, but I don't see why we should run from here because of the past. It feels good to be here, I feel I belong again. I thought the songpaths would be too weak to keep me, but now I'm not so sure.'

What was she saying, that she wasn't going to return to the outback?

'And Flynn?'

'Flynn is dead,' she said, looking at Martin sharply. 'I don't mean physically. I mean, he and I are dead. The songpaths are a closed part of my life. Eveline's death was the final marker of that experience, the defining moment. I had to come back when she died, and now I have to stay. I feel quite calm about this, Martin. If you want to leave, you go ahead. But I'm staying.'

There was a certainty about Rebecca that was so intense it was almost stunning. A few moments before, Martin had been clear that he would sort out the affairs of the small estate and then leave for Amsterdam, or perhaps for a long vacation by the southern shore. Now he was confused. Eveline's urgent demand, through her letters and the mouths of friends, that neither he nor Rebecca should risk their lives in Broceliande was still a powerful consideration, yet he felt himself weakening, his resolve to depart going.

This was his home. This was the only place, in all the world, where he truly belonged. Rebecca belonged here less than he did, and yet she, too, was finding that old spirit again, the attachment to a place of ghosts, farms, rural existence and peace.

'Why don't we stay for a week,' he said, 'then review the situation. Eveline was quite adamant that we're not safe here. There must have been a reason for it.'

'Have some coffee,' Rebecca said, filling a wide cup for him. She was smiling as she spoke. 'Eveline was afraid for us, Martin. But she's gone, now. It's up to us to be aware, to be cautious. Whatever she was afraid of, maybe it had only to do with little Seb's death, all those years ago. Maybe she knew that I had something to do with it – but what she couldn't know was that whatever the possession at that time, whatever was in me, it's gone. My new possession is song, ancient song, the songs of the earth, call it what you like, you know what I mean: song was always used in magic, and a little of that song-magic came into me from the people on the path. You couldn't know it because you never went inside one of them. Well, only for an instant. And perhaps that was wise. I can't in my heart feel any danger here.'

'But we should be cautious,' Martin said, and Rebecca smiled at him.

'Of course. What else?'

Martin worked on the details of the estate with Uncle Jacques, and a solicitor from Rennes, a jocular man, with bushy side-whiskers and a florid complexion, ill-at-ease with the pin-stripe of his suit.

Eveline had left an estate valued at two million, two hundred thousand francs, of which a quarter was in investments, insurances and savings. The farm stock accounted for very little of the remaining value, which was substantially contained within the building and outhouses, and in the land, twenty five acres, including woodland, that was divided between grazing and broccoli. There was a good water source, a spring that had been enclosed and channelled in the Middle Ages, and only two tumuli cut into the useable cultivation space.

The farm was, of course, heavily untended. In her later years, Eveline had concentrated on pigs and chickens, with Uncle Jacques and another farmer, raising broccoli and maize in rotation on five acres. For the first time, reviewing the estate, Martin became aware that his father had had a not unreasonable business sense, since the investments he had made out of the very meagre profits from the farming business had performed excellently on the Paris stock exchange. His mother had lived comfortably in her last years, and there were sufficient disposable assets almost to cover the taxes due upon the transfer of her estate.

Martin and Rebecca were the main beneficiaries under her will, and the stipulation that they receive their due inheritance only when they had left Broceliande was discreetly, at Rebecca's persuasive insistence, deleted from the document, witnessed and approved, albeit against his better judgement, by Uncle Jacques.

Martin quickly organised the selling of land to cover the balance of the death duties, negotiated rental deals for the remainder of the farm space, and within two weeks the paperwork was more or less completed.

The old retriever, Bess, was ailing and had taken to uncontrollable, pointless barking, and though it broke their hearts to do so they put her down, Rebecca taking care of the difficult arrangements.

It was mid-October by now, and the weather was generally bad, a series of rainstorms, grey days, the occasional crisp, frosty morning. When the sun shone, one Saturday, and the air was sharp and scented, the woodlands alive, the fields flowing with bright shadow, Rebecca went quickly around the houses in the neighbourhood inviting everyone to the farm. Martin dug a fire-pit, Jacques rigged up a spit to take a whole piglet, a vat of cider was wheeled from the LeContes, bread was made, salads fabricated, or bought ready-made from the nearest hypermarket, and Martin and Rebecca hosted their first garden party as a couple.

In the late afternoon Father Gualzator blessed the succulent and roasted creature and reminded everyone of the old custom by which the priest received the first cut from the best meat, the neck fillet, a tradition that was rapidly challenged, and which proved to be invention. Amidst the hilarity, as the priest staked his claim with wilder and wilder stories across the fire-pit, each outmatched by Johann deClude, a storyteller of wild exaggeration, the snout and tail of the pig were prepared on a bed of lettuce and presented, with ill-restrained giggles, to Father Gualzator.

'I *will* eat this!' he declared solemnly, holding the plate before him. 'But only if I can have the squeak as well.'

'Long gone,' someone said.

'Not at all! I believe I saw it earlier. There it is – hiding in the *fillet*!'

The roasting, the feasting and the hours of horseplay helped to create a special warmth on this cold, hard day. Then the fire was stoked and fed to make a warm place where there could be dancing until darkfall. Martin was very drunk. Rebecca danced alone, wide skirts swirling, hair flowing as the accordion wheezed out its jig, and feet stamped on the stone flags at the edge of the field, where the pit had been dug.

'We haven't had a party like this since 1946,' said Father Gualzator, as he bobbed to the accordion and nibbled at a finger of cheese. 'By the way, Conrad is over there, in the gloaming. Do you see? By the well. He's watching us. But he won't come into the fire-glow. I've asked him, but he's staying out.'

Martin couldn't see the shadow that the priest had seen. 'Have you taken him something to eat?'

'No. I didn't like to.'

Martin cut four thick slices of meat from the pig, and two of bread from the heavy cob. The salads had all been consumed. He found a small china flagon and filled it with the raw cider from LeConte's vat. As he began to walk across the field to the copse, Rebecca stopped him.

'It's for the bosker. He's up in the trees.'

'I'll take it. You're very drunk,' she laughed.

'And you aren't?'

'Out of my skull. But I want to say hello. Where is he exactly?'

'The copse, by the stone well.'

With the words, 'Don't expect me back too quickly,' she took the plate and flagon and strode off across the night field, to become a shadow among shadows.

It was after midnight before Rebecca crept into bed. She was naked and bitterly cold. She pressed her feet against the complaining man, warming her hands on his stomach, laughing as Martin struggled. They soon relaxed below the covers and eventually turned to face each other, kissing gently, savouring the fumes of garlic and cider.

'You were a long time. I would have been worried, but I passed out. Must have had a lot to talk about to Conrad.'

'He didn't stay long. I think he was still a little frightened of me. He ate what I took him, and we shared the cider and remembered old times. He didn't want to talk about Sebastian and the wolf-thing that had killed him. I told him you'd told me and all he said was, "Then everything, now, is in its cold home. It's done with, and with Eveline gone, and the lake so quiet, perhaps the storm has passed." Then he went back to the forest, asking me to thank you. I stayed by the well. It's a nice place, there. You can smell the water rising through the hill. Everything by that well is vibrant, very pure, very clear. I spent a long time thinking.'

'Thinking about what?'

Her touch was suddenly intimate. He felt aroused and reached around her to draw her body very close.

'Thinking about what?' he repeated.

As they kissed, Rebecca whispered, 'About staying in Broceliande, learning how to run a small farm. About you, how much I love you, now that I allow the feeling to surface. About us, how natural it feels to *be* us. About a child . . .'

Martin was stunned. His lips found Rebecca's, his hands found hers, fingers entwining as she wrestled him underneath her, to lie on him, her hands, then, holding his face, her mouth a moist presence on his eyes and cheeks as she took him into her, holding him close, holding him tightly until first light, first dew, and the first call, an urgent one, for the bathroom.

The first green had been on the woods for a week, now, and the last of winter had been seen off.

Martin waited by the gate as the eight horsemen cantered towards him, doffing his beret as they swept past leading a riderless mare. One blew a short, brass horn, the others waved flowered staves and screamed at the tops of their voices as they passed. Laughing, they wheeled around and trotted back, resplendent in their short white jackets and black trousers. Bells on the spurs of their black boots made a constant jangling as they waited for the groom.

Martin climbed into the saddle of the ninth horse, feeling the strength of the animal below him, holding her head back as she tried to stretch. Further away down the path, towards the village, the bride's canter was approaching noisily, the five horns sounding their high-pitched, sweeter notes. Rebecca, in the centre of the gallop, was a tall shape, robed in green and white. The women in her entourage were trousered in black, with white jackets and wide-brimmed, rose-decked hats. The arc of flowers-and-ivy, held between them, wobbled as they approached, and the groom's party kicked-off for the church, mud spraying, laughter punctuating the high-pitched challenge of the party.

Father Gualzator opened the main gate to the church grounds as the groom's riders cantered through and reined-in. The horses were led aside, and Martin and Jacques (who was battered, bruised and stiff from the ride) walked into the church, which had been cleared of the pews and chairs, a wide hall, the thorn and the cross in the centre.

When Rebecca rode through the open doors, cantering noisily around the edge of the stone-flagged floor, she streamed confetti behind her as was the custom, but watched Martin all the time with eyes that were radiant and longing. The child inside her was almost unnoticeable below the green dress, although she held her belly carefully as she swung from the saddle by the door, and was escorted to the thorn and the cross.

In the light from the high windows they were married. The child kicked as they kissed and took the two blessings. They went outside into bright, cool sunshine and paid respects at the cold-earth homes of Eveline and Albert, and then of Sebastian. The horses were straining at the tethers. Martin led Rebecca to the carriage. The riders mounted and led the way through the gate and along the path to the first village, and for two hours, with the sounds of car-horns, hunting-horns, klaxons, timbrels and the ululating voices of the younger women, they paraded the countryside and villages near Broceliande, collecting the presents and offerings of flowers, money and charms that were flung to them.

*   *   *

77

Daniel Tristan Laroche was First Named at the moment of his birth; ultrasound scans had confirmed the child's sex some months before, but Rebecca was superstitious and no items relating to the child, not clothes nor crib, nor bath were allowed in the house until the safe delivery.

Daniel was an enormous infant, over nine pounds in weight at birth, eyes bright in the red, wrinkled skin. He was completely silent, no cry, no breath of complaint as he was confronted with the world. He took to the breast with fervour, and remained calm and compliant during his Welcoming as cold water was splashed on him at the stone well, among the hazels. The name given to him was *fort de vie*. Since he was fit, and grew normally for the first few weeks, feeding avidly and lying contentedly below the spinning objects on the playframe, it was easy for a while to feel no real concern at his silence, or his seeming unawareness of what was happening around him. Indeed, it was a boon, since Martin had anticipated disturbed nights and short tempers.

But quickly the mood changed. Rebecca became frustrated by the silence, and Martin's concern grew as well. Daniel slept solidly for hours at a time. He woke on being touched, and fed normally. He lay quiescent on being placed down and stared into space. Sudden sounds didn't alarm him. Sudden movement had no effect.

Four weeks after his birth the health visitor was able to say with certainty that something was wrong.

Daniel was taken to a paediatrician in Vannes and Rebecca's worst fears were rapidly and thoroughly confirmed. Daniel was without sight, without hearing . . . and therefore it was necessary to entertain realistically the possibility that he would be without speech. Genetic tests taken by amniocentesis had shown no irregularities, and in every other respect Daniel was a perfectly healthy child.

Rebecca was devastated, Martin depressed and frightened. They returned to Broceliande and closed the door of their house against the world, keeping the shutters up throughout the summer, shadows living among the shadows of their home, cradling and nursing the beautiful, silent creature who was their son.

2

Rebecca was singing in her sleep. It was an odd sound, drawn out, a single note that faded as each breath was exhausted. It was enough to wake Martin, however, and he sat up, running his fingers through the heavy sheen of sweat on the woman's pale features. She stirred restlessly at the touch and turned away, curling into a foetal position, beginning to breathe more heavily.

Now that he was awake, Martin heard two more sounds: the tap-tap of metal on glass, and the same note that Rebecca was singing, except that it was higher in pitch, a single, sustained tone.

'Daniel?' he whispered, puzzled. 'It can't be . . .'

He wriggled his feet into slippers and went to the window. Two children were on the path, the Breques girl, Cathy, and her elder brother, a gawkish lad of ten. It was the girl who was relating to the invisible travellers, her raincoat swirling as she danced and spun around, exposing thin, naked limbs below. She was in a trance, her brother loping after her, his eyes wide with the wonder of what only they could see.

Again, the tap-tap of metal on glass, and Martin crept stealthily to Daniel's room.

The two-year-old had somehow crawled out of his high-walled cot. In pyjamas, hair awry, he was spread-eagled against the window, his arms stretched above him, his fingers, one with a metal thimble on it, rapping on the pane. His face was pressed to the glass, his mouth gaping and emitting with every exhalation the single, musical note. His eyes were wide, sightless, reflected in the window.

He jumped suddenly when Martin touched him, then turned and let his father cradle him. Small fingers traced the features of the man who lifted him into his arms. Daniel's chin was wet with saliva. He was smiling and silent, now. He was heavy for his age, dead weight as he curled into a ball, carried back to his cot.

Rebecca was suddenly in the doorway, dishevelled and sleepy. 'What's going on?'

'He was singing,' Martin said, his heart racing, his mind still unable to grasp fully that Daniel had made this sound! *He was singing!*

'I suppose you could call it singing . . .' he added.

She came over and brushed fingers lightly over the silent boy's brow.

'I was dreaming of him,' she said. 'We were sitting together below bright stars, on a wide, cool desert. It was a dream of Australia. Together we were singing up a path, rocking side to side, but aware of each other. He was an older boy in the dream, Daniel as a grown lad, with good sight and a vibrant life. We sang together . . .'

With a shiver of recognition, Martin said, 'You were singing together just now. You in your sleep, Daniel by the window. A single note, not very musical.'

Rebecca smiled sadly. 'There you are then. Mother and son on the same wavelength, the same line. What was he doing at the window?'

'Kids on the path. The Breques children. He was tapping the window as they passed with one of Eveline's thimbles, but he couldn't have been aware of them. Could he?'

'I'm sure he could,' Rebecca murmured. 'Christ, he's got to be aware of something . . .'

Exhausted, they took Daniel into their room, and as always the boy fell into peaceful sleep between them, even though his eyes were open.

The two years since his birth had been terrible, more for the failure to make a decision on Daniel's future than for the fact of his disabilities. Should he be sent to a home, nursed by professionals, where his blindness and deafness could be addressed at every hour of every day? Or should he stay with parents who loved him, but who could do nothing practical to improve his physical condition? Daniel was not difficult. He loved being outside. He walked with Martin, hand in hand, and seemed, oddly, aware of that which was surely beyond his senses: the forest, the rolling sky, the passing storms, the animals in the fields.

The boy never complained. His worst moments were at night, when sometimes he would howl ferally, or scream in an hysterical way, always becoming silent after a few moments in either of his parents' arms.

Father Gualzator had blessed him and prayed for him. Yvette Valence, the local herbalist who lived above the local post office, had prepared all manner of rubs and potions, from camomile to dogwort, from belladonna in honey to the crushed skull of an owl, whose night sight was the most perfect in the animal world. No amount of sympathy had allowed this sympathetic healing to have effect.

Yvette, like the priest, was from Basque country. After feeling 'called away' from the high passes and airy forests of her native land, she had followed the path that wound north, through the painted caves of the Perigord and the dense oakwoods of the Dordogne, to where Broceliande straddled the way to the coast, cutting across the ancient route. The place had felt right to her, and she had settled. She had been a close friend of Eveline's, and was a doting friend and helper for Rebecca and Martin now, but she became frustrated with Daniel, perhaps confused and distressed by the failure of even the simplest of her healing cures. It was as if, she said, Daniel was aware of the charm she used and was blocking it.

Even the wart on his left thumb – which ought to have vanished within two days – remained obstinately in place, until one day he dipped his hand into the well water, by the hazels, and the crusty excrescence disappeared within an hour.

Yvette's time with Daniel ceased abruptly when Martin forbade her to come back to the house. She had arrived in a lather of fury and fear, holding fresh herbs in black, cloth packets, and a cross made from the branches of a yew.

'The boy is dead,' she said in hushed tones. She would not cross the threshold into the house. 'I realised it suddenly. The boy is dead. A traveller is inside him. I can't help you any more.'

To Martin and Rebecca's fury, she didn't keep this information to herself, but spread it through the villages.

Daniel, however, was far from dead. Senseless, literally, he showed otherwise every sign of vibrant life. And he had started to sing, single notes but different notes, singing them until he was breathless and exhausted, singing them with gusto. Where the conception for such sound came from was not readily answerable, but Rebecca, who was giving classes in song at the local school, sang to Daniel at every opportunity. Perhaps he was aware of the melodies through some other sense, a synaesthetic appreciation of the creation songs of the Australian aborigines, and the corrupt creation songs – the folk songs – of old France and England, with which Rebecca was now very familiar. So the house was a musical place, although at times the double act of tuneful and single-note singing, an eerie sound that lasted for hours, was too much for Martin, and he was glad of his job, at a small design studio in a town an hour's drive away.

A second letter arrived for Rebecca from Flynn. The first had been a short note, transparently sad, yet filled with best wishes, received shortly after Daniel's birth. As ever, with Flynn, it was not so much a question of knowing more-or-less where he was as of waiting for him to come to the small town and check the post office for any mail. He wrote sparingly, using an old fountain pen that spilled more ink randomly than it dispensed in the tight lines and folds of the words he expressed. Rebecca savoured the two letters, as if they were fragments of a lost shroud. Martin saw this but did not interfere. He was never in any doubt as to her love for him, nor her loyalty, and try as he did, on one occasion, he simply could not arouse in himself any sense of jealousy for the outback-traveller, reaching through space and time for his once-love, the Live Alone Lady as he called Rebecca.

Rebecca had written to Flynn, describing the odd way in which Daniel sang despite profound deafness and the way in which he seemed aware despite his blindness. Perhaps she had been seeking some intuition or insight that she remembered from her outback-travelling days.

She was rewarded with a letter, certainly helpful, but far from what she expected.

Jesus, Beck, your letter frightens the fucking life out of me. God knows how long since you wrote it. Time never meant a great deal here, but I guess you're in the summer when this is happening, as you describe it, and that's a solid strand of time or so ago, so I guess you've walked the line a good way since then.

But don't you remember anything that happened around you on the songlines here?

Jesus! If this boy, your Daniel, is singing, then he's taking! So the first thing to do, Beck, is stop singing. Christ, I wish our times were crossing, but we're adrift by months, and that makes me concerned.

Beck, stop singing. Remember the Three Lady Macbeths, as you nicknamed them? Well, there's a lot to remember in what those three ladies were all about. I can't get to you, Beck, or else I would, and you know I would. I'm hurt inside, and I miss you, but you wouldn't be my old Live Alone Lady if you weren't sure that what you were doing was the right thing, and I guess you've found a new line or two to travel, maybe those old teeth-from-the-earth stones you always told me about, and the dreamtime songs of the Celts, or whoever the hell it was that lived there at the time.

Beck, when a Man Walking reaches a songline, he sits down for a rub or two, and chews some sweet wood, and listens to the wind, then listens to the song, and maybe sings up a little of the old line. But the song is big in the air, and it's too big to take away, so he maybe sings a bit of it, and chews off a bit before he crosses, but there's plenty left to get inside the next Man Walking.

But a Lady Macbeth is out to take the song that was born. She'll walk around a puddle, walk through a hut, walk around a sit-down place, and when she sings the song, someone loses the song. Because that's what she's all about, a gatherer, a collector. What she does with the song only the Dream knows, but I've seen children stripped of music, and a young man lose the song that he'd been born with, and an old lady, in rags and with sticks, walking out across the dry places, full, fed and bloated on what she'd taken and making patterns on the land that only the tribe could see. So you beware, Beck. I don't like the sound of this Deaf Son Singing of yours and this Other guy or no, song is soul, and where the soul is lacking, the taking game is strong.

I send my love to you, Beck. God knows I miss you, and for more than just the jumping up and down, although, Jesus! those were good nights in the old hut, you truly are magnificent, and never to be forgotten, especially for your spirit. But I know you'll come back if the lines turn right for us again. In the meantime, God Bless and keep you, and that lucky bastard who sleeps next to you. And keep writing. I need to know you're OK.

Martin folded the letter and slipped it back into the envelope. Rebecca had Daniel in her lap, and was rocking slightly as she watched the news on the TV. The boy waved his hands in the air, sightless eyes on the ceiling, a glistening of liquid on his chin. He seemed to be reaching for something, but it was simply a reflex action. Rebecca glanced across the kitchen to where Martin was tapping the letter against the table.

'I don't mind talking about it, if that's what you want.'
'The letter?'

'Are you upset by it?'

'*Upset* by it! Not at all. You know me better than that. It's these "Lady Macbeths". I don't understand the references to "Lady Macbeths" . . .'

Rebecca used the remote control to switch off the television. She hefted Daniel in her arms and stood up, then sat the murmuring boy on his home-made 'stimulus truck', a wheeled cart with dangling objects, some soft, some hard, some noisy. At once Daniel started to use his feet to move around the wide kitchen, batting at the shapes and making incoherent howling sounds. He never laughed.

'Lady Macbeths are both the destroyers and builders of the songlines, at least in the remote tribes that Flynn is studying, and which I visited for a while. There's a lot below the surface in any culture, and sometimes you just get hints about how the rituals are governed. It's not that they're secret — they sometimes are — just that they're obscure. You can think of a songline as a barrier, or as a marker for a moment in the dreamtime, or as a place perceptible only to a particular form of consciousness. If you take the example of a wall, you need to maintain the fabric of the wall, or it rots and falls away. If the wall is made by song, and the songs define both the land and the totemic spirits of that land, then that wall still needs to be sustained and maintained by new song.

'Where does that song come from? It's born, of course, born in certain children of the tribes. The Lady Macbeths scour the tribes for those songs, and they literally *sing* them out of the child, then take them to the line, and sing them out, sing them back, make the songline strong again.'

Martin considered this as he drank his way through a full pitcher of cider.

'Is Flynn suggesting that Daniel is stealing your songs?'

86

'He's afraid of that. I can't think why. The songlines work differently here . . .'

'Sing to me,' Martin said, and after a moment, perhaps recognising the concern in his face, Rebecca leaned forward on the pine table and sang.

Her words filled the warm space. The tune made Martin shiver with recognition until he, too, was joining in, two voices gently singing in the kitchen of the farmhouse, while Daniel was silent, his arms relaxed, his gaze fixed on nowhere, as if he, too, was listening to the melody.

3

But Flynn's intuition, from half the world away, had been right.

Martin had been up to Paris for the day to meet a small orchestra company interested in employing him to redesign their logo. He had taken the opportunity to buy artist's materials, then went to the Place D'Iena, to the Oriental collection of the Musée Guimet, seeking inspiration if not for the new commission, at least for future work.

It was after ten at night before he arrived back at Broceli-ande. He was surprised to find Jacques sitting, half-dozing by the wood stove, the television tuned to a riotously unfunny games show.

Daniel was awake but silent, curled up on the sofa, thumb firmly in mouth, apparently oblivious even to the sudden draught from the door.

Martin woke the old man, and Jacques stood up, walking stiffly to the lad and stroking fingers on the pale face. He smelled of brandy.

'I must have dozed off. He seems fine, though. Good

as gold. He's even been humming a tune. You're making progress, obviously.'

'Where's Rebecca?'

'I'm not sure. She was upset about something. Asked me to come and look after Daniel. I'll be off, now, if you don't mind. It's been longer than I expected. That's not a complaint,' he added hastily. 'Any time. You know that. It's just that my joints, these days, do seem to like bed by about nine o'clock. Goodnight, Martin.'

'Goodnight. And thanks.'

Jacques walked awkwardly to the door, closing it behind him. Daniel stirred and made sounds, reaching into the void. Martin lifted him and hugged him and the boy relaxed again.

After a moment or two, as Martin rocked him, holding the long-legged child to his chest, Daniel started to hum. It was not tuneful, but it was familiar. Martin felt a dual reaction: of delight, and of apprehension. It was the song Rebecca had hummed and voiced those few nights before, after Flynn's second letter.

'Enough, now. Enough,' he said suddenly, putting a finger on the boy's lips. Daniel squirmed, frowning, watery eyes unfocused. But he did not object when he was laid down on the sofa and covered with a blanket.

Rebecca came home at midnight. She was dishevelled and distressed, the hem of her skirt filthy, her boots caked with mud. There was moisture on her greying hair, and apple blossom, which Martin picked away.

'What's happened?'

'How was Paris?'

'Paris was fine. I have some work, not much, but something. What's happened?'

She went round to Daniel and kissed him. The boy shifted restlessly. She was whispering something to him and Martin stepped closer. 'What the hell's going on?'

Her look was one of fear and anger, a challenge to him to stay back.

'I'm telling him that I don't begrudge him anything, that he can take what he needs. What else can I do? He'll take it anyway.'

'Song?'

'He's taken it, Martin. It isn't there any more. Flynn was right . . .'

'One letter from the outback and you succumb to the suggestive power of it? How can he possibly steal a song? Maybe he's learned it –'

'He's stone *deaf*!'

'We assume that. But we don't know that he doesn't have some other way of receiving information! You can't have lost the song!'

'Well I have.'

'This is nonsense.'

'It's not nonsense to *me*, damn you.'

She began to cry, sitting by her son, her head in her hands. When she looked up, through moist eyes, she was grim. 'I'm frightened. For three years I've been willing life into this boy. It never occurred to me that he might take part of *me*. I offered it, but now that it's happening, I'm afraid of it.'

'He's not taking your life, Beck. Every child copies, learns by imitation.' He looked at the peaceful boy. He thought, *every normal child, that is*. How could Daniel absorb the experience of his parents, when he was so blocked off from normal sensory experience?

'Sing the song, Beck. Sing "The Unquiet Grave".'

'I would, Martin. If I could I would. But it isn't there any more.'

Martin sang it. At once, as if aware of the sound, Daniel

89

started to hum the tune, tunelessly, a ragged accompani-
ment. 'Join in, Beck.'

And she tried. She opened her mouth, she watched
Martin's mouth, she struggled to find the song, but the
song was gone.

Later she sang 'Frère Jacques', demonstrated that it was
not something affecting her language, she had not had a
stroke . . .

But almost at once, little Daniel began to hum the same
old French tune, the music behind the roundelay. Rebecca
kept singing, and Martin joined in, but after a few minutes
– and it was now very late – Rebecca fell silent.

When she picked up the boy, she was crying. She started
to carry him to his room, he was dozing now, but turned
at the door from the kitchen. Grimly, yet with some
humour, she said, 'I never did like that song. So it's no
loss. But it's gone, Martin. It's gone like "The Unquiet
Grave" . . .'

There was *life* in the boy. In his dark world, with all tests
suggesting that he had no sight at all, and no language
ability, he began to flourish. He began to sing, and in a
matter of weeks his thin voice was in tune, the sounds
crisp and haunting, even though no words accompanied
the melodies he vocalised.

Rebecca declined. After a period of fear she became
unnervingly complacent about the theft she believed was
occurring. 'He's my son. What's mine is his. What's a song
to me if it helps him break down his own walls?'

Next to go were the songs she had sung as a child, the
Christmas carols, the simple hymns, the nonsense rhymes,
the folk songs that Eveline and Albert had taught them.

The words remained Rebecca's. It was strange for

Martin to see the doting mother and the langourous, lean child draped across her lap, the child intoning 'Once in Regal David's City', while Rebecca spoke the words in rhythm with the infant's humming.

Where once Rebecca's head had been filled with music, now it was a wasteland. She could imagine Mozart, but not articulate it. She could give voice to a note, to a meaningless sequence of notes, even to a scale, but when it came to singing, she was lost. Her appreciation of music remained the same, in fact became a source of solace. In a state of melancholy she would lock herself away in the bedroom and play CDs, increasingly loudly, of Fauré, Mozart and Mahler, composers whose work could create in her heart a feeling of great strength. But she could no longer sing with the recorded sound, she could only hear it, gaining and maintaining a spiritual strength that allowed her to caress and adore her growing son. What truly concerned her was that she seemed to be suffering a sort of tinnitus – her ears rang, her voice echoed in her head when she spoke and her hearing was slightly dulled.

Daniel was more active than ever. At night, he would bang on the window, most particularly when there were people on the path. Martin took him out, one black, cold morning, leading the lad, well-wrapped against the chill, in a quick pursuit of the local children who were dancing through some spectre of their own envisioning. Daniel gave no sign of seeing that ghost, but he reached out to the source of activity, and babbled meaninglessly in his childish tongue.

The specialist in Rennes could well understand Martin's anxiety, when Daniel was presented for examination. 'Whatever is at fault with his sight, I'm afraid you'll have to live with it, short of a miracle. But the acquisition of language is a complex process, and it comes as a surprise, but not a shock to me, to discover that your son is approaching language through song. I'm quite certain that he'll begin to talk within a very short time.'

'The boy is deaf! He can't hear. How can he start to speak?'

'I know! This is what is so beguiling. As far as our tests are concerned he has no response to auditory stimulation at all. Nevertheless: he *hears*. And everything suggests he'll soon start to talk coherently.'

Indeed, the day before the boy's fourth birthday, Martin entered his room in the early hours to find again that his son was pressed against the window.

'Come on, Daniel. Back to bed, now.'

He lifted the boy down, then felt the tug of a fist on his shirt collar. Dead eyes stared vaguely nowhere in the half-light, but from the boy's mouth hissed the words, 'Put me back!'

'Daniel . . .' Martin breathed, shocked by the sound, instantly suspecting that he had simply dreamed the words.

'Put me *back*,' Daniel said determinedly.

'Can you understand what I'm saying? Can you hear me speaking?'

'*Back!*' hissed the boy.

'Back on the window? What are you doing there?'

'Put me *back*.'

Martin lifted the lad back to the sill. Daniel flung himself against the glass, his breath misting, his nose flattening, his fingers spread out like the suckered pads of a frog. He stood there, trembling, breathing gently, and every so often his head jerked, as if he was listening.

As far as Jacques and Suzanne were concerned, this was a miracle and to be celebrated as such. Father Gualzator came round and listened to the boy's sharp, staccato speech. Daniel sat back in the chair, his legs drawn up

92

against his chest, his eyes unfocused; he shouted words, random phrases, each uttered in a tone of delight: 'Eat! The woods! Bright water! Bubbling. The well. Keep him in. Here they are! Food, please. Falling, always falling. Hah hah!'

'This is quite remarkable,' the priest whispered. 'I've watched a hundred children start to talk – signals first, then grammar, slowly becoming coherent. Daniel seems to be using scattershot. His pronunciation is excellent. The words clearly have meaning for him, but no meaning to the rest of us.'

'Kill bird! Stone sinking. Into the sea! Storm coming. Keep him down. Shadows!'

'It's as if he's creating his vocabulary from scratch. There can be no meaning to these shouted words; it has a curious feeling of Tourette Syndrome, but he communicates a sense of understanding, which I find powerful and alarming . . .'

'The dell! The shaft! Drowning! Bread on the table. Cold home down. Getting free! Sing song, sing song. Hah hah . . .' a curiously knowing laugh and a body posture that suggested listening. 'Oh yes! The shadows! Dancing on the path! Almost out. Cheese!'

Daniel stumbled from his seated position and reached the table, scrabbling among the plates for the ripe brie, gouging it with his fingers until Martin eased his small hand away, led him to a chair and guided his touch to a slice of the food, with a soft piece of bread.

Daniel ate and laughed, bobbing on the chair, dark hair flopping about his pale face, as if sharing some secret joke.

He had also discovered the TV, now that he had acquired a rudimentary degree of hearing, and he laughed furiously at some of the programmes, even when the subject matter was serious or completely inane.

*   *   *

93

These were the weeks leading to Christmas, and it seemed that each day something new that was also odd occurred. The children who occasionally ran the path, dancing with the spirits, now took to screaming with terror, disturbing the early hours of morning with their fear as they scattered and ran. None of them would talk to their parents about the cause of the panic, but it was clear that the apparitions, once so benign, now seemed nightmarish.

This change for the worse didn't last very long. Soon there was just the drifting, dreamy dancing, again, and the sound of laughter and excitement.

Conrad became very ill. He would come to the house, wheezing badly, and beg food and medicines, but any attempt to take him in, to nourish and nurture him through these bouts of illness, was met by his instant departure. A pale man, his eyes hollowing out, his lips drawing back to expose the cold, blank skull behind his kindly, canny face, he would accept expectorants, aspirins, and vitamin pills, but not hospitality.

Elsewhere, near Broceliande, he treated himself with infusions of various herbs, bringing the petals and leaves to Yvette, who created the potions for him.

The man was dying, and Rebecca in particular felt a strong sense of loss as Conrad moved, edgy and remote, through the scrub wood, and along the lesser paths about the area.

For a year or more, Rebecca had earned a small amount of money, and gained a great deal of pleasure, by teaching two local children folk songs, and music in general, using the small piano at the farmhouse. These lessons stopped when she discovered she could no longer sing; indeed, as she struggled for the final time with one of the girls, she realised that she could no longer focus clearly on the music.

'I need glasses,' she moaned. 'Thirty years old, perfect vision all my life, and suddenly I'm getting short-sighted.'

4

With four days to Christmas, the church bell intoned the dawn hour to signal Winter's Deep. From all over the region, people came by car and cart to the church on the hill, arriving for midday, wrapped well against the frost. The sky was brilliant azure, the sun low to the south and west. The forest of Broceliande glistened whitely. Breath hung in the air, streamers of mist behind each walking human shape.

When noon came, the congregation, spread around the base of the hill, joined hands. Daniel, between his parents, laughed as the whole circle stepped carefully, with many a collapse, many a trip, much humour, once around the hill, while the priest lit the fire at the porch entrance and the flame streamed high into the crisp day.

At the end of the clumsy dance, the children raced up the hill, scrambling over walls and through the hedge to be the first to carry the fire to the villages. They set off, thirty mufflered shapes, torches held high streaming black smoke. The adults crowded into the warm church and gathered round the copper cauldron of warm, spiced red wine.

As usual, the talk was of presents, and the extortionate price of computer games, radio-controlled cars and the other sophisticated toys that the little horrors of the villages were demanding, from Saint Nicholas in most cases, or from Old Provider in just a few.

Old Provider had been Rebecca's choice of gift bringer,

with his one good eye, riding his black dog at dawn and with his wailing daughter stumbling after. He was an ogrish figure ready to take the child's head if the offering of fowl and fish at the doorstep was insufficient. Rebecca had always enjoyed the sense of terror associated with the gifts from Old Provider, and as a child had dismissed Saint Nick, in his white fur robes with his moon-chariot pulled by eight white harts, as just a fairy-tale.

Daniel had indicated that Old Provider was his choice. The gift he would risk his head for was a collection of Disney songs on disc – he was an avid fan of TV and radio, now, sitting with his left ear pressed to the sound box – with bendy models of some of his favourite Disney characters, Baloo the Bear, Dumbo, One Eye and Three Eyes, and the Seven Little Miners (he didn't want Snow White!).

The proper way to summon Old Provider was to write the gift-request on paper, wrap the paper round a black stone and throw it into Broceliande (or whichever was the child's local wood). One child in every hundred was supposed to be able to hear the Black Dog growl as it snatched the stone, before bounding through the tangle-wood to where its master, the one-eyed man, lay sleeping below a pile of stones.

Daniel enjoyed this ritual, although his first attempt to throw the rock almost knocked Martin unconscious, the shot, from the blind boy, being almost completely in the wrong direction. When the stone finally struck the trees Daniel clapped and laughed but a second later he screamed and turned away from some sound that only he could hear, holding his hands to his ears. He ran back to the path, and towards the farm. Martin chased after him, caught him and hugged him reassuringly.

'What is it? What is it?'

'Monster . . .' the boy whispered, shaking. 'Heard monster . . . Black Dog . . . crunching bone . . .'

'It's only a story,' Martin assured him, wrapping arms around the trembling lad. 'Nothing's going to hurt you. It's just a bit of fun.'

'I know! I know!' Daniel crowed triumphantly. 'Joke! Joke!'

And he squirmed away from his father, giggling and screeching, stumbling over a rock as he celebrated his trickery.

Martin chased after him, wrestling him to the ground. 'Why you little . . . you little *monster*! . . . I'll teach you to pretend that there's *monsters* in them there *woods* . . .'

The boy laughed hysterically as his father's fingers engaged with ribs and soft belly, tickling powerfully through the heavy winter clothing.

Then suddenly Daniel glanced away. 'Look at Mummy.'

Martin followed the glance. Rebecca was standing facing Broceliande, a hunched figure, arms tight around her chest.

'Something wrong. Mummy shadow wrong,' Daniel whispered.

Martin sat up, holding the boy. 'What's up, Beck?' he said to himself, disturbed by the dark figure, the motionless, living statue of the woman, everything about her suggesting that she was in distress.

And then he looked at Daniel, at the way the boy was staring at the distant figure. He moved an open palm across Daniel's gaze but the eyes never flickered, the pupils remained fully dilated as usual.

'What's Mummy doing?' he asked cautiously.

'Listening. Big dog,' Daniel replied.

'Can you see her?'

'I hear shadow,' came the quiet reply. 'Mummy shadow. Mummy shadow frightened.'

Leading Daniel by the hand, Martin went over to Rebecca, and put his arms around her, kissing her quickly on her cold, right ear. 'What's up with Mummy shadow?' he whispered. 'What's upset you?'

'Mummy shadow?'

'Daniel's words. I think he feels the fact that you're upset. What's upset you?'

'For a second it was like being a kid again, seeing the ghosts. I thought I saw the Black Dog. Seriously, it seemed to hover in the woodland edge, up on its hind legs, watching me, like one of those bloody great big dogs from Grimm. Or was it Hans Andersen?'

'The soldier? The tinder box? That story?'

'That one. Yes. Each dog was bigger than the last, and had bigger eyes, like saucers. I saw the biggest. And it was so real. But it was so shadowy, everything is so shadowy . . . maybe I need a stronger prescription.'

She took off her silver-framed spectacles and peered at them. 'My sight's really going. I find it so hard to read these days.'

'Then it's the optician's for you, my girl,' Martin said with mock severity. 'As soon as they open after Christmas.'

He looked at the wood, frowning. 'But maybe you really saw what you saw.'

'New lakes, wolf-girls and wailing men. Why not Black Dogs?' Rebecca smiled and reached for Martin's hand. 'There's something changing in the forest . . .'

Daniel was tugging at his jacket, staring up at his father. 'Dog's gone, now,' he said.

It hadn't snowed at Christmas for years and Daniel was disappointed, having heard all about snow from the poem 'Night of Old Christmas'. As far as Martin was concerned, it was too damned cold anyway, but they spent Christmas Eve in traditional style, with Jacques and Suzanne. The priest came by for an hour or so, taking a little supper and several glasses of the spiced wine that every house would have in abundance.

Daniel ran around the warm kitchen, a bat with outstretched wings, guided by sound, flawless in his negotiation of obstacles, such as the inebriated adults who sat around the wide table, the remains of Eve Goose spread before them. Christmas day itself was a day of fasting, not that anyone ever took much notice of that particular tradition.

'Night of Old Christmas! Night of Old Christmas!' Daniel chanted, as he realised Rebecca was trying to get him into his nightshirt, to put him to bed.

He was allowed to sit with the adults a while longer, warm, wrapped in a blanket. Martin read the long poem by the heir to the British throne, a parody of the Victorian classic by Clement Moore, watching the enthralled boy curled against his mother and feeling the shivers of his own childhood as some of the stanzas brought back memories of Christmas past . . .

'The Deep of the Winter was now in the past,
And the snow that had fallen looked fair set to last,
And deep in the heartwood a cairn of grey stones
Was shifting and stirring and full of strange groans

For down in the earth, all wrapped up and snug
Old Provider was waking, his mind in a fug.

The black dog was barking, away in the wood,
And the children were quarrelling, who had been good?
And whose head was forfeit, that dread time of dark
If the fish and the fowl should fall short of the mark
And the man in his rags, with his good gleaming eye
Should bring gifts for the three, but the fourth child
    should die?'

Before he went to bed, Daniel reached to the big bowl of
chicken and trout that was put out for the Odinesque Old
Provider. 'Feel plump enough?' Martin asked.

'I'm good!' Daniel said emphatically, adding, 'Is Old
Provider . . . hungry?'

'Very hungry. But there's enough fish and fowl here to
feed him, his dog, *and* his wailing daughter.'

'Why? Wailing?'

'Enough questions, young man. Daughters wail because
daughters wail, and presents come at dawn, because that's
the way it works.'

A simple way of saying, he had no idea.

'Head in sack, slung on his back,' Daniel murmured, and
shuddered, making a chilled sound as he curled into Martin's
arms and was lifted from the cold flagstones of the porch.

'But you've been good. There'll be no head in a sack on
the end of *my* bed tomorrow – *or* on Old Provider's back.
Just lots of fun toys, and funny songs. But only if you sleep,
now, and don't make any noise during the night . . .'

He used his foot to open the door to the stairs, and
glanced back at the group around the table, where Father
Gualzator was using a teaspoon to scoop the last of the
mulled cider from the copper tureen into his glass.

'Do we have any more holy water?' Martin asked with

a grin, and Rebecca grasped the signal, went to the wood stove and uncorked another flagon of the apple.

In his arms, Daniel murmured, 'Rest of my bones, under grey stones.'

'Why? Wailing? Uncle Jacques. Why?'

'*Because she was Old Provider's eldest child and favourite child, but she wanted gifts without earning them, and she wanted gifts that he couldn't give. So he took away everything that she had, except her sorrow, and made her run blindly after the dog, to pick up every gift that fell from his sack, especially the heads that he gathered from the greedy and the evil and the pretenders, and you know how many pretenders there are among the children of the world, so his sack was full of heads with their tongues sticking out, and their eyes crossed, even some still with their fingers stuck up their noses. Sometimes he put the head in a flour sack and left it on Christmas Eve for the parent. But sometimes he put the head on a small tree, and if the child repented the tree grew into a new body and walked home on its roots. If the parents took the tree-child back, they would have to cut a small piece of the skin, or bark, every year to offer to Old Provider with the fish and fowl. That's where we get the expression, a chip off the old block. You remember the song Auntie Suzanne and I taught you?*'

> '*A chip off the block,*
> *I'll live a full clock.*
> *A splinter forgot*
> *I'll end full of rot.*'

'*That's right. You do remember things well, young man. Well, sleep now, and in the morning we'll dance around the kitchen to Baloo's Song . . .*'

'*Saw Black Dog. Saw shadow.*'

'*You saw the Black Dog?*'

'*It's hungry. It wants Mummy.*'

'*Where did you see it?*'

'*It runs up the path. It eats shadows.*'

'*What do you mean, It wants Mummy?*'

'*Mummy shadow. Black Dog wants to eat Mummy shadow.*'

Old Provider duly provided, and Christmas Day passed with pleasure, leftovers, and a long walk over the fields. There was no more talk of Black Dogs and Mummy shadows, and Martin's frisson of excitement when he had thought, for that instant, that Daniel had actually seen something was soon forgotten.

The songs from Disney's Jungle Book became semi-permanent residents in the house until well into the Spring, when the weather, which until then had been abysmal, began to improve dramatically, heralding an early and warm summer and the opportunity for the family to spend time outside.

Resurrection Sunday was particularly fine, and Martin drove the family across to the megalithic site at Carnac, encouraging Daniel to touch the stones, describing the ranks of uprights, stretching miles towards the west.

Daniel made it clear that he wished to hear the sea, and they drove to a small bay and descended the steep path to the red sand. Here, Rebecca sat on the rocks peering gloomily through her thick lenses at the shifting ocean. Martin searched for fossils, and Daniel wandered in circles, laughing and shouting.

And it was here, about half an hour after they'd come to the fresh air and salt spray, that Martin saw Daniel pursuing a broken-winged gull. The black-headed bird was weaving across the sand and Daniel was following the creature exactly, reaching for it. When it suddenly jumped, half flying for a few yards before descending again, the boy followed it with his gaze!

Martin walked stiffly towards his son, his heart thundering. 'Daniel?' Daniel looked round and grinned.

'What colour's the bird, Daniel?'

'Black and white,' the boy said. 'Broken wing.'

'Can you see it? Can you see the bird?'

'See it,' Daniel whispered. 'Bird shadow. Like Mummy shadow. Like Daddy shadow. See it.'

'My God! At last!'

He waved a hand in front of Daniel's eyes and the boy followed the movement, gaze bright, breath sweet as his father kissed him, joyfully, ecstatically. Then he looked towards the rocks. 'Mummy shadow crying.'

Rebecca's head was in her hands. She was shuddering silently. Martin ran to her, sat next to her, lifted her chin to peer at the tears. 'Beck?'

'Christ, Martin. It gets worse. It keeps getting worse. I can feel it going. The world is shrinking. Oh Christ, everything is shrinking, everything's going dark, everything's starting to look like shadow.'

5

The boy played with his cars, running them across the stone floor using the small radio-control panel, his fingers working the switches confidently and accurately. He was getting tall for his age. He would soon be six, though he looked older, perhaps because he had grown fast in the last few years. He could not see colours, but he could see shades of grey. He was beginning to talk very coherently, almost gabbling, at times, as if catching up for lost conversations, though his conversation was self-centred, occasionally brutal, rarely questioning.

Martin felt very frightened of him.

It was hard, now, to deny that there was some close link between Daniel and Rebecca. He had dismissed Flynn's letter, the slow stealing of song, as quackery: the Australian had put crazy ideas into the head of a vulnerable, suggestible woman. Now, though, he regretted that impatience. Now he was afraid.

Rebecca could not bear to spend time around her son, and Daniel had noticed this. Sometimes he expressed concern in an ordinary and childlike way: he cried for his mother. She spent an hour with him each evening, rubbing her eyes, squinting as he played, telling him stories in a voice that was becoming hushed, using words that seemed to sit thickly on her tongue. She complained of a permanent headache and constant tinnitus, the sound of surging waves in her hearing.

Each evening, when she could bear no more, she made an excuse and went to her room, the third bedroom, now converted to her study since music no longer meant anything to her. One day when Daniel ran up the stairs and pushed the door open, calling for Rebecca, Martin heard her scream abuse and throw a heavy book. Daniel scampered into the living room and hid below the cushions on the sofa, crying softly.

She was ashen-faced when she came to bed that night, skin glistening with dried tears. She stumbled to the bed and stared vaguely at Martin. She undressed slowly. He thought she was drunk, the way she tottered, the way she held her head as she unbuttoned her dress, awkwardly, loosely, then sat down heavily to peel off her stockings.

'Beck?'

'Blind,' she whispered and started to shake. She crawled under the covers, a naked, cold body, trembling like a frightened cat. She clung to Martin, sought his mouth with hers, held the kiss urgently, eyes closed.

'Love me. Now. Love me.'

'Beck . . .'

'Love me! Quickly!'

Her hands were on him, stroking, tugging. Her touch was icy and Martin shivered, feeling unaroused and frightened by this blind and passionate urgency. He eased her fingers from his body, pushed her down gently and moved across her, cradling her face as he kissed her softly, warming the freezing skin below him.

'Hold me now. Hold me gently,' he whispered.

As they loved, her breathing became calmer. Eyes closed, she gripped him with fierce fingers, nails drawing blood from his back, teeth clamping on his shoulder as she made quiet sounds, then whispered, 'Can't take this. Daniel. Can't take this. This is us. Can't take this away.'

'Oh Beck . . .'

'Don't stop. This is . . . Good. So good . . .'

Someone was running along the landing. Hot and quite breathless, Martin paused for a moment, listening to the heavy footfall.

The door to the bedroom was flung open. He twisted in alarm, staring at the tall figure that stood there, dark against the glowing nightlight.

Angrily, Martin shouted at the boy: 'Daniel! Back to bed. Now!'

'What are you doing? What are you doing?'

'Daniel! I said back to bed! Now!'

Rebecca began to cry. The boy stood obstinately in the doorway. Martin kicked the covers off and walked quickly and furiously to his son, his hand coming up to strike the lad, who watched him defiantly.

'Yes. Hit me. Hit me hard. Why not?'

The boy's face was a mask of anger and defiance. Naked, Martin dropped to a crouch and held Daniel by the shoulders.

'What are you doing? Why aren't you asleep?'

'I don't like what you're doing to mummy.'

'None of your business. Go back to bed. Go to sleep.'

Daniel glanced across his father's shoulder and grinned. Then he suddenly hugged Martin, whispering in his ear, 'He's wrong. He's wrong. I can have it all.'

'What the hell does that mean? Who's *he*?'

But already Daniel had turned and was scampering back along the landing, to his room, to his own bed.

Martin closed the bedroom door. There was no key for the lock and on a vague impulse he moved a chair and wedged it below the brass door-knob.

In bed again, Rebecca was propped on her elbow, staring into the distance.

'Where were we?' Martin asked gently. She shook her head. Then, as if with great effort, she said, 'Stay. Close. Keep him. Away.'

'Beck, what's wrong? You sound as if you're drunk.'

'Words. Effort. All gone. Going. Knew it. Would happen. Flynn right. Oh God . . .'

She fell back heavily, crying silently. Martin lay down below the covers and held her close to him for the rest of the night.

In the morning, Rebecca seemed almost her old perky

self. She sat on the edge of the bed and peered around the room through her lenses.

'All grey,' she said matter-of-factly. 'No colour, now. Daniel has all colour now.'

She dressed easily and went downstairs. The boy was standing in the inglenook by the wood fire, leaning against the brick wall, hands in his pockets. As she bent to stoke up the embers he watched her silently. No words were exchanged. Martin watched this from the stairs, then came into the kitchen to make breakfast. Rebecca put on her coat and went to the back door.

'Where are you going?'

'Something,' she said and smiled, peering at him. 'To do,' she added. 'Alone.'

'Where's mummy going?' Daniel asked. 'I don't like mummy going off alone. What's she up to? Why doesn't she stay here and play with me?'

'What do you want for breakfast?'

'Anything and everything,' Daniel said loudly. 'I like lots of everything. Hot bread, eggs, melted cheese, oranges. Just give me everything.' Then: 'Where's Mummy going? She shouldn't leave the house.'

'Shut up. Sit down. Read a comic book. Eat when the food comes.'

'Don't be rude to me.'

'It's too early in the morning, Daniel. Shut up. Read. Wait for breakfast.'

'Where's mummy going?'

'Bugger mummy! Did you hear what I said? I've not slept a wink all night. Now be a kind and thoughtful son, and shut up, and wait for your eggs!'

'Two eggs. And fried bread and tomatoes. And bacon.'

'What are you, English? That's what the English eat.' He remembered quickly that there was an English boy attending the local school for a few weeks, and Daniel was fascinated by him. '*Very* unhealthy. You'll make do with what I give you.'

6

After he had taken Daniel to school, Martin went back to the house, but instead of working on his designs he prowled restlessly along the path, up to the church, then back again. All over Broceliande the flocks of starlings and sparrows were crowding the sky as they returned from the south to flow in great speckled floods about the canopy and the villages. The air was fresh, scented with new growth.

On impulse, Martin followed the forest road, and turned off along the track that took him to the old bosker's edge-wood mansion.

He stood by the fence, looking first at the grizzled remains of last summer's catch. There were no new carcasses here, and there were streaks of green on the iron and oilskins on the hut. No smoke rose from the chimney, and the path to the door was fresh with yellow weeds.

'Conrad?'

Martin called, then called again, waiting hesitantly at the edge of the shack before stepping forward to pull back the oilskin door and peer into the foetid gloom.

'Conrad? Are you here? I'm looking for Rebecca.'

There was movement in the shafting light from the only window, a sudden shift of body mass below the piled furs on the bed. As his eyes accustomed to the gloom, and his nose to the stink in the place, Martin moved towards the farther end of the habitation. It was cold in here, the fire grey with ash, long dead.

'Conrad!' The old man's face became clear suddenly, pale against the yellow of the pillows. He was like a skull, his eyes fully sunken into the bone, his lips no more than thin lines defining the grinning face of death. In hands that were like white spiders he clutched the wooden panel of one of his pictures, hugging it to his breast through the blankets, as if holding a lover.

'My God. You need help. You need a doctor.'

'Do I?' the ghostly figure wheezed, and then made a sound that Martin was sure was a laugh. 'Isn't she beautiful? Oh Lord, how I would love to see her now.' He peered with difficulty at the smudged crayon drawing.

Martin gently teased the piece of wood from the trembling hands. He cradled it and stared at the crude drawing of the girl in full face. The colours were scratched where nails had probed and stroked the slim and smiling features of the long-gone girl.

'I dream of her all the time,' Conrad said. 'But it's such a long march home. I don't think I have the strength. *Do* I have the strength? Please tell me. I can't be sure unless you tell me.'

The bosker was leaning up from the bed, his face a frightening mask of need, of questioning, of seeking – his eyes blazed with urgency, his mouth trembled. Martin was shocked, deeply saddened. He had realised suddenly that he was present at the end of the woodsman's life.

Quietly he said, 'No, my friend. No you don't. You don't have the strength. I'm sorry.'

'There's no way home for me?'

'No. I'm sorry. I don't know what else to say.'

But as if he had heard some welcome words Conrad's breath hissed from his lungs in a pleasure of release, and he lay back, his watery gaze upon the dust that spiralled in the light from the window. His fingers again clawed across the crayon face.

'Thank you,' he said. 'I'd thought as much. But I tried. Oh Lord, I did try. Not one minute of one hour of any day in all of my life since I marched here, since I walked the circle here, not one moment have I abandoned her, and I think of her now, and God bless her, she has certainly done the good thing and sustained me, although I don't suppose she knows it. I am so tired, Martin. I hardly have the strength to lift an arm. But I must go and listen to the boats. That is where I belong, now. Will you take me to the lake? Please? You asked about Rebecca. She was here. Yes. Will you take me to the lake? I'll tell you about Rebecca as we go. Will you take me?'

'Of course. I'll get your clothes. I'd sooner take you to the infirmary.'

'No. Please don't. It's outside the circle, else I would have gone there years ago. It would make me happy to hear the travellers' boats again, to hear the water. Thank you anyway.'

Some hours later, by the lake, Conrad crawled into his crude shelter, padded up the furs and the pillow he'd brought with him and settled back to die. Martin built a wood fire and stacked a good amount of tinder in arm's reach, below the hide canopy. The lake was very still, very quiet, dragonflies humming among the rushes. There was a chill touch to the air, in this sheltered place, even though the sky was bright, luxuriant and calm.

Conrad's gaze never left the far wood, across the mere.

'There's a battle being fought. You should have gone away, as Eveline was keen to tell you. If you hadn't stayed, the battle could never have been joined.'

Martin cast the line again, a hook with a grub on the end of a willow rod, watching the small weight splash as it struck the surface of the lake. He was determined to catch a fish and give the old bosker a taste of fresh food.

'What battle?'

'The age-old battle,' Conrad wheezed, half laughing. 'You know how it goes: I want the power that you have. I want to be strong though it will make you weak. Nothing has changed for thousands of years. Sometimes the battle is fought on whole landscapes, sometimes in the small kitchen of a warm and cosy house. Martin, you really should have gone away. Eveline knew what she was talking about. She was frightened for you, and for Rebecca, and all you have done by staying here is let the fight be fought again.'

'I don't understand –'

The weight was tugged, the line snagged. Martin jumped up and held the willow rod tightly, dragging it in against the pull, reaching out to wind the coarse line around his hand.

'Which fight?'

'The fight for magic,' Conrad murmured. 'Don't pull too hard.'

The fish struggled but was completely hooked. Silver and green thrashed on the scummy lake, eyes flashed angrily from jutting jaws. It was a pike.

'Greedy bastard!' Martin taunted from the shore. 'But you'll make food for three days.'

'It's quite a monster,' Conrad agreed excitedly, sitting up, grinning as the struggle continued. 'Let him have a little slack, give him a false sense of security. When he drags back he'll stop, hoping to be abandoned. Jerk the line and the hook'll fix deeper, right in the bone. He'll be lost then. You can let him die in the lake, or wind him in slowly, but not too fast. It's a strong line, but that fish has a kick like a mule, and a mule can break a line like this.'

'*Who's* fighting for magic? I don't understand.'

'Of course you don't. You're on the outside. The battle is not between Rebecca and Daniel – it's between enchanter and enchanter . . .'

Martin was stunned into silence for a moment, hearing the words, half understanding them, not quite ready to accept the deeper, stronger truth. Eventually he said, almost disbelievingly, 'Do you mean Merlin? You really think it's Merlin doing this?'

'He's trapped, across the lake,' Conrad said quietly, pointing vaguely to the distant shore where the trees crowded and the crows flew. 'His prison lies across the lake, just on the other side. When the lake came back into existence, it brought him close again. The woman too. Vivien! The screaming man, the wily enchantress. With the old enchanter's knowledge as the prize! I don't know how the strategy is working. All I know – don't pull so hard!' he snapped, as Martin's line was tugged. 'You'll lose him, and I want to taste this monster. Better . . . better! Ease him in, just ease him in . . .'

'All you know?'

'All I know is that *Broceliande* – the two warring lovers – is in your son and in your sister.'

'She's not my sister. No blood link at all.'

'Whatever she is. In Rebecca. Your mother sensed the possession all those years ago, when your brother died. I'm sure of it. That's why she sent you both away. But you came back, and now the wood has Rebecca, and her son. The power has them both. She came here, God knows why. Rebecca. She came here to the lake, then she came to my lodge and sat with me. She's blind, you know. And nine parts deaf, now.'

'I know.'

'She's lost song, she's lost story, she's losing language. It's all going into the boy. Or rather, to the traveller inside the boy.'

'To Vivien?'

'To Vivien.' The pike thrashed suddenly, then was still. Frightened by the ideas that the bosker had put in his head, tired of the struggle out on the lake, Martin jerked the line angrily. The fish – it was two feet long, and gleamed purple as it broke the surface – rose into the air then fell back, but a second jerk on the line, the line cutting into his skin now and drawing blood, that second jerk snared the beast and it fell quiet.

He wound it in, cut the hook out of its mouth, cut off its head and tail. He gutted the monster, scraped the scales and pushed two pieces of willow through the carcase, propping it over the fire on a crude spit.

'How do I stop it?'

'The fight? You can't. It's too late. You were a fool. You were warned.' And he added quietly, 'There's no way home for you either.'

'That doesn't help.'

'Nothing can help.'

'I don't believe that. There's a transference going on. Language, sight, song ... the boy is taking it from Rebecca. Or is he? Is it possible that Rebecca is just reacting in an hysterical way?'

'She sees shadows, now,' Conrad said. 'Only shadows. She hears only first words, hears only the oldest songs, the shadow songs. She's lost the first part of the fight. Daniel has drawn her out, he caught her unawares. Now she has a chance, though. This is only the middle game. Do you play chess? She has by no means lost. Leave them alone, leave them to end the struggle, one of them will win, one of them will be whole, nothing you can do will help shift the balance. So don't start choosing. You'll be left with one of them, and one only. If you interfere, you risk losing them both.'

I don't believe what I'm hearing! Oh God, this can't be real . . .

'There's something I don't understand, though,' Conrad went on in a hushed, weary voice. 'If the woman we think of as Vivien tricked and trapped the old enchanter, all those centuries ago – why is she still here? Why does he taunt her? Something must have gone wrong.'

Martin was hardly listening. He stared out across the blue lake at the heart of Broceliande, where the moans of a dying man could sometimes be heard, and the cries of a woman, and from which shore came silent boats, and ghostly travellers, escaping whatever evil lay at the heart of the wood.

I don't believe it! Merlin and Vivien still playing their tricks, their games . . . and in the process a family is destroyed?

But he *did* believe it. All his life he had believed it. All his life he had accepted that people moved up the path, to vanish below the hill where the church – even as a ruin – had tolled its bells of calling, and mourning, and feasting: bronze-ringing that signalled the changing of the quarters of the year, when the fires were burned in different ways, and the offerings were made in different ways, and the people of the land came to dance and talk and drink and remember.

Of course he believed it. But what was happening now was something beyond his experience.

I can't choose between them! Don't ask me to choose between them!

'I think we should go back to the edge of the wood.'

Conrad sighed and snuggled down among the skins, below the protecting umbrella of oilskin. The lake glimmered in the setting sun. It was close to dusk. The pike had been picked clean, the uneaten flesh wrapped carefully.

'I'll stay here, I think. A boat will be coming for me shortly.'

'A boat?'

As Martin understood the old man's point he felt again a moment of intense grief. 'I don't want you to die.'

'I'm already dead,' Conrad breathed, and chuckled through his parchment lips. 'Do you know the way back? Can you find the way back?'

'I think so.'

'Too bad if you can't. There's no way of drawing you a map!'

The bosker smiled again, then closed his eyes, drawing the skins around his neck as he lay by the lapping waters.

'Goodbye, Martin.'

'Do I just leave you here?'

'I won't be here for long. The boat's already on the lake.'

Martin stood and peered across the water. A wake was spreading, as if a water bird were swimming, but Martin could see no creature there.

He put more wood on the fire, throwing the bony remains of the pike into the reeds. When he looked back, Conrad's eyes were closed, his mouth gaping. There was no movement below the furs. He was probably dead.

Martin made the sign of the Cross and Wheel on his chest, then followed the path, away from the lake, through the crowding trees, running back to the hunting lodge, then the edgewood, and at last to the path and his own house.

7

It was early afternoon, now. He had spent too long in the forest and it had been difficult to find his way back to the edge. He had felt crowded and crushed. At times he had imagined himself followed, which had been a disorientating experience.

As he ran to the house to pick up his car – he was late for Daniel, who had to be fetched from school – he heard the terrible screaming from the kitchen, and for a second was stunned into immobility. Then Rebecca's terror resolved clearly and he broke into a breathless run, almost flinging himself through the door.

Rebecca was standing in the middle of the room, which was in chaos. She had thrown the table over, kicked the chairs, broken plates, cups and picture glass. Her hands were bloody, her face smeared with red streaks. Her hair was awry, her long dress torn and stained. She was turning where she stood, and screaming, and shaking her head, battering at her eyes with the raw horrors of her fingers.

Martin grabbed her and forced her still. 'I'm here! I'm here! Beck, what's happened? What's happened?'

'Shadows!' she wailed, then collapsed against him, weeping openly, clutching him in an embrace that said *never let me go!*

'What *about* shadows?'

'All round. Everywhere. Watching. Laughing.'

'Come on . . . let's get you cleaned up.'

He urged her upstairs. She stumbled, felt blindly, whispered, 'I can't see. Anymore. All gone. Shadows only.' In the bathroom he tended to the cuts on her hands, then undressed her and helped her into a warm bath. She lay back, her plastered fingers playing on his as he washed her, stroked her, comforting her as much as he could.

'Please,' she said quietly, through the steam and the heat. 'Don't. Let. Daniel. Home . . . *Please* . . .'

Even as she spoke, downstairs the back door was flung open. Outside, the sound of a departing car told Martin that one of the other parents had brought their son home.

The boy pounded up the stairs, came straight to the bathroom, bursting in to stand there, face glowing, breathing hard. 'Got a lift from Thierry's dad. Why weren't you there? What's up with Mummy? I'm hungry. Can I have some bread? It's all messy downstairs. Have you been fighting? Why weren't you *there*?'

'Go downstairs and straighten the table and the chairs. I'll get you a sandwich in a minute.'

Daniel stepped quickly to the side of the bath and looked at the pinkish water, at the rigid, naked body of his mother, her hands wrapped firmly, tensely around Martin's. She stared blindly at the ceiling.

The boy said, 'I love you, Mummy. Don't be hurt. I really do love you. I always did.'

Rebecca turned her head to the tiled wall, slipping slightly in the water. 'Away!' she hissed.

Daniel grinned at his father. 'I think I'm in the way. Shall I close the door?'

And with a suggestive chuckle he ran to the landing, pulling the bathroom door shut behind him.

* * *

Downstairs, the sound of noisy rearranging was testimony to Daniel's efforts to tidy up after his mother's period of hysterics. Martin led Rebecca to the bedroom, insisting she get under the covers. She was shaking, a terrified creature, confronting darkness saved for shadows – and no shadows that were cast by the warm and familiar sun. She had few words, now. She struggled to speak, resorting to a scrawled note as Martin sat on the bed, close to tears himself.

She wrote: *ask Jac and Suz to have the boy. Ask priest to visit.*

'You're going to stay with Uncle Jacques for a few days.'

'Why?' Daniel asked. He was sitting at the table, staring defiantly as ever, his face that of a ten-year-old, though only six summer suns had warmed his lanky body. He had cut a chunk from a stale baguette, toasted it and spread it with brie. He chewed slowly, arms folded on the table, eyes fixed firmly on his father. 'Why?' he repeated.

'Because I said so. Mummy isn't well and I need to look after her, and it will be easier if you stay with Uncle Jacques.'

Daniel shrugged. 'All right. When do I go?'

'When you've finished your sandwich. Pack some clothes and I'll drive you over.'

The boy did as he was told. He appeared downstairs, a small case in one hand, his New York Yankees windcheater opened to expose a Spookbusters T-shirt. Martin knelt down and pinched the boy's cheek. 'You don't mind, do you? It's only for a while, to help mummy get better.'

'I don't mind,' Daniel said, then dropped the case and flung his arms around Martin. He was fighting back tears, and when Martin pulled away slightly he could see how the boy's lip trembled.

'It's not for ever.'

'Are you sure?'

'Of *course*!'

'Mummy doesn't love me. She told me.'

'Nonsense. Mummy loves you *very* much. *When* did she tell you?'

'In a dream. She's frightened of me. She thinks I'm trying to hurt her.'

'She's very ill, Daniel. And I really want to do everything I can to get her better. But part of her being ill is that she behaves strangely, she says things she doesn't mean. I want you to go and stay with Uncle Jacques and Aunt Suzanne, and behave yourself, and do what you're told, and in a few days you'll come back here.'

And in his head, as he spoke these words, a voice whispered, *you liar. You liar. You're terrified of what is happening. You suspect your son. Conrad's words have frightened the life out of you. You liar . . . liar . . .*

Martin left the priest and Rebecca alone, the woman sitting huddled by the window, apparently staring out across Broceliande, the man, in jeans and track-suit top, standing behind her, talking quietly.

Later he came down and accepted a mug of coffee. 'She's made her peace,' he said. 'I hadn't realised her spirit was still so strong.'

'Is that why she wanted to talk to you? To make her confession?'

Father Gualzator nodded, staring into the mug. 'What are you going to do?'

The question unleashed in Martin the full burden of helplessness. What to do? What *could* he do?

'I have no idea. Specialists . . . speech therapists . . . psychologists . . . opticians . . . Rebecca says she can only see shadows, not even shadows of objects that are real. Like a kid round here, dancing through the people on the path, but they were never terrifying. She's terrified of these shadows.'

'There's something else,' the priest said, frowning. 'Her language –'

'Almost gone . . . ?'

'Almost completely gone, I think. I believe she has clung to these last few words to make her peace with God and the hill. Now, she has begun to speak strange words. Literally, strange words, but familiar. I can't be sure . . . I wrote some down . . .'

He came over to Martin and showed him the page of his notebook. He had scrawled Rebecca's murmured phrases phonetically.

'It's gibberish,' Martin said.

'I don't think so. There are constructions here that have familiarity. Look: iambathaguz. That sounds like *Mabathagus*, a particularly unpleasant entity from mythology, a sorcerer.'

'Never heard of him.'

'Of course you haven't. All you do is use your eyes to read. You don't use your eyes to *remember*. But then who am I to criticise? Here's something else: jingux. In Basque, that's almost the word for God, although not God as the church and the hill would understand it. Jinx.

'I think a lot of the rest of this is a deeper peace being made, but there is so much, she is speaking so much, and keeps laughing, as if triumphantly. I don't understand it. Not at all. But this fascinates me. I'm going to go south for a while, to find an old friend, someone who has a wider eye, an older eye than mine, someone who might see a little deeper into this, er . . .' he hesitated, searching for the word.

'Gibberish?'

'It's not gibberish, Martin. It's pain. Look after Rebecca. She's terrified.'

'I know she is. I'll look after her with all my heart.'

8

Almost as soon as the priest had departed for Basque country Martin took Rebecca to Paris, to her appointment with a specialist, André Benvenista, at the National Institute for Parapsychology. Suzanne accompanied them, while Jacques took care of Daniel.

The meeting, the observation on Rebecca, was unsatisfactory and distressing.

She lay in a room overlooking the Seine, her scalp covered with a fine tracery of electrodes and sensors. It was a bright day, and Paris, at least, was alive with activity.

Martin sat quietly by the window, watching the technicians about their business, aware of strange patterns on black video screens, outlines in three dimensions of the brain of the silent, shadowed woman. Colour flickered in the infra-red as she was tested – reds, blues, starbursts of yellow. Martin thought of turbulent or boiling water.

Everything was recorded and later he was shown the findings, understanding nothing. He watched the screens. Bursts of activity in the frontal lobe triggered sequential activities in the temporal lobe, limbic system and brainstem. This was as it should have been. But he listened, uncomprehending, as he was shown a 'furious' echo from the limbic system, an 'after-event' that spread rapidly back, insidiously setting off activity in other regions of the neurocortex, a pattern of response that was meaningless to the psychologists who watched.

This 'event' occurred when Rebecca spoke words in the strange tongue that Martin had listened to in the deep of the night. But each time she spoke in what Father Gualzator had suggested was some form of early Basque, a normal speech pattern could be observed, though once, when she was whispering at random, she suddenly murmured in the deep-of-night sounds again and set up what Benvenista called a 'standing field of bio-electric activity', a split-second in which her whole brain was illuminated, as if awakened at once, a terrible shock that caused her to gasp, sit bolt upright from where she lay, to stare and froth, a fit of tremendous power, but a moment only, a moment of ancient memory too strong for her sheltered twentieth-century mind to cope with.

Immediately after this there was nothing but darkness on the screen, but she whispered, 'Martin . . .' and a small glow appeared, a flicker of light, a guttering candle, a calm flame in the stygian darkness that was the web within her skull.

Finally, she spoke words in the sequence of lisps and glottal sounds that was the deep-of-night language, and there was no signal at all from the language centre of her cortex, only from the motor area, showing nothing more than that her tongue was moving. She spoke words from a darkness so deep that it no longer registered. Over and over these odd sounds whispered, yet among them came the name 'Martin', and when 'Martin' was sounded there was that comforting flash from the frontal lobe, but thereafter, just the gloom of visual silence until she was stopped and brought back to whatever consciousness she could experience through touch and sound and shadow.

'To put it simply,' Benvenista said, 'it's as if her learned language has been scraped away, exposing older forms, primitive forms – like a city, destroyed to expose the hill where the first settlers camped in prehistoric times. The core of our language is embedded – we build upon that core as we grow and experience communication. But the core of Rebecca's language no longer registers. It is either still there, but has been hidden somehow; or it has been destroyed.

'But there are no tumours, no areas of necrosis, no fibrous masses, no signs of a stroke, no abnormalities. Everything in physiological and anatomical terms is healthy. And it's the same with the visual cortex: show her a shadow and it registers. But the shadows she sees – at least, that she indicates she sees – do not show – except, of course, in the motor cortex as she follows the ghost with her eyes.'

'But you think her language might still be there? All of her senses? Somewhere – just hidden?'

Benvenista spread his hands and shrugged as he stared out at the bright day. 'In the absence of damage, I can't imagine an alternative.'

Martin almost said, *what if someone had stolen her words, her songs, her dreams*, but he refrained from speaking. Across the room, Rebecca was making incoherent sounds and staring in the direction of the voices.

Although Benvenista would have liked to keep Rebecca longer, she was signalling with her body, with her crude speech, that she did not wish to stay. Martin drove them all back to the farm by Broceliande and spent an hour ringing around for a full-time, live-in nurse. He eventually found someone to take the position as from the next day.

Suzanne stayed the night, but Rebecca, once in her room and seated by the window facing the forest, was relaxed. She could perform most bodily functions without assistance, but gave no indication of being aware of either Martin or the older woman.

Two days later, Father Gualzator returned.

Martin was walking along the path with Daniel, holding the boy's hand, talking to him gently. Daniel's behaviour at school that day had been disruptive, and Martin had been advised to take him home. He was coming down with flu, perhaps, was the diplomatic suggestion. As Martin had entered the classroom to take his son home there had been an almost tangible tension. Daniel was by the window, at a desk on his own, illuminated by the pale sun. The rest of the class whispered and wrote in exercise books. Daniel came quickly over to his father, and the teacher, a fair-haired man in his late twenties, smiled reassuringly as he closed the door behind Martin.

'I'm sure it's just a temporary upset,' he said.

As Martin led Daniel down the corridor, behind him the classroom erupted into the sound of baying, barking and cheering, only subdued after thirty seconds of the teacher's shouting.

On the path, Daniel suddenly stopped, clutching Martin's hand more tightly. He was listening against the light wind. 'It's the priest,' he said. 'He's hiding something.'

Martin scanned the land around, the dark wood, the hill with the sun setting, the scatter of houses. After a few minutes he saw the wobbling figure of Father Gualzator, approaching them on his ancient bicycle.

Smiling broadly, breathing hard, the priest dismounted. He was wearing his track-suit and a Redskins baseball cap. His smile, as he greeted Daniel, was transparently fixed, but he dropped to a crouch and embraced the boy.

'How are you getting on with Uncle Jacques?'

'All right. I miss Mummy, though.'

'I'm sure you do.'

'Uncle Jacques watches football all the time, and his computer can't play good games.'

'Oh dear. That *is* a tragedy. But he has a lot of books, doesn't he?'

'I suppose so.'

'Would you like to have a wobble on the bike? It's a bit big for you, but it's good exercise. Too bloody good,' he added with a smile at Martin, taking a deep breath. 'I'm out of condition.'

Daniel had grabbed the bicycle and was racing it away towards the church, hidden from view over the nearest hill. As he cycled furiously, he called back, 'I can hear everything you say!'

Martin shouted, 'Did you hear what I just said, then?'

Ringing the bell, Daniel called back, 'You didn't *say* anything.'

The boy was in the distance. 'How much is two and two?' Martin said in a normal voice. The bike skidded to a halt. Daniel laughed. He rang the bicycle bell four times then began to pedal furiously, riding perilously close to the ditch by the path.

Father Gualzator pulled a face. 'He has *very* good hearing, your son. Conrad had the same facility. Must be something to do with the air round here.' He gave Martin a meaningful glance. The priest, too, was aware of Conrad's encounters with the ghosts, and with his belief that Merlin was behind the new phenomena around Broceliande.

'Daniel's a very talented young man,' Martin said. 'As soon as Rebecca is better we'll all be going on a long holiday. Somewhere hot, with lots of sea and sand.'

Daniel had vanished. The two men stopped and stared at each other for a moment, the unspoken words between them signalling their unease with the boy, with the idea of being listened to. Then the priest shrugged, as if to say, 'What else can we do?'

Martin said, 'So. Did your Old Eye help at all?'

'Only a little. Let's go to the house, I'd like Rebecca to be with us when I tell you what I've learned. At least, what I *think* I've learned.'

Outside the farmhouse, the priest's bicycle was propped against the fence. Rebecca was at the window, a pale face in dark dress, staring out across the forest. She didn't move when the gate rattled shut. Martin stared at her in sorrow, standing on the driveway until a second face behind her resolved into Suzanne, who waved at him.

Inside the house, Daniel was playing a computer game in his room. Martin stood behind him for a few minutes, watching the way the boy manipulated the two 'mouse' controls, determining the three-dimensional action of the two mediaeval armies as they engaged on the wide land-scape. It always astonished Martin how so much information, so much awareness of what was off-screen, could be held in the mind of a child playing these complex inter-actives.

'I'm staying home, now,' Daniel said quietly, suddenly. Martin squeezed the boy's shoulder and was surprised when Daniel looked up at him, moist-eyed.

'That's what I want too,' he said. 'A nurse will look after Mummy. I'll look after you. Uncle Jacques will be sorry to see you go, though.'

'No, he won't.'

Ignoring the bitter words, Martin went to Rebecca. Father Gualzator was sitting with her, holding her hand. He had two sheets of paper on his knee.

Martin kissed Rebecca's pale cheeks, then brushed her lips with his, eliciting a response, a desperate hug, a shud-dering embrace that lasted for minutes. Then slowly

Rebecca relaxed, again becoming blank-expressioned and almost limp.

The priest mouthed the words written on the sheets of paper.

I am in hell now. So is the other.

The fire was put out. The swan drowned in ice waters.

The bronze thorn pricked as it was intended. The blood was quick. Love was quick.

Martin. Martin. The stag danced by falling water. Enchantment killed me. The god/ghost behind the mask is in the stone. ('That refers to "Mabathagus", I mentioned him before.') *The stone covers the pit. The pit consumes the bones. (But) the shadow ones are on the path.*

Love you. Love you.

The hemp knot is twisted twice. She has no breath. The trickster is tricked.

I am in hell. Let me out.

The ghost has been drawn from me. Martin. Martin. Help me.

Let me out.

I am in hell.

Let me out.

There was the sound of breaking glass, of smashed machinery. Martin leapt from where he was sitting, by the silent, staring Rebecca, by the frowning priest. He ran along the landing to the room where Daniel had been playing.

As he opened the door, the boy pushed past him, screaming as he ran to his mother. The VDU screen was smashed, the keyboard broken in half, the mirror in the room broken too, and all the shelves emptied of their toys and books. Daniel had thrown a fit of rage. Now he was screaming incoherently at the priest. Martin reached for him and dragged him away. Rebecca sat quite motionless, undisturbed, unperturbed.

The boy suddenly stiffened. He was white with rage. His eyes seemed to stare from his head, popping from below the lids. The breath in his lungs was hoarse and animal. Martin felt his skin tingle with an odd electricity.

'What happened, Daniel?' he asked quietly.

The boy fled past him, thumping down the stairs. Chasing him, Martin was only able to stand by the back door and see his son, hair flying, racing into the dense edgewood of Broceliande. Where Daniel had leapt over the fence, a bloody shred of his torn jeans hung limp and sickly.

Upstairs, for a brief and wonderful moment, Rebecca laughed; but it was just the rattle of a dying ghost.

The boy had vanished into the woods. Martin wanted to follow him, but he was frightened, he realised, frightened of the alienness, the anger, the incomprehensibility of the behaviour of the lad.

'Daniel,' he whispered. 'Whatever is happening, whatever rage is in you, you *are* my son. Rebecca's son too. Don't abandon us.'

Did Daniel hear? Was that movement in the edgewood, that shift of branches, the rustle of leaves?

In a state of emotional limbo, Martin returned to Rebecca. She was asleep, now, fully clothed, but covered with a thin blanket. The nurse said that the drowse had come quite naturally, as if the woman had been exhausted and just curled up for forty winks.

Downstairs again, Martin read through the meaningless words.

'Let me out. Let me out,' he quoted. 'A genie in a bottle?'

'There are two voices here,' the priest said, taking the sheets. 'There's the old voice, with its odd references – swans, stags, stone gods; and the phrase "let me out". And there's Rebecca's last message to you. Here, where it says the ghost has been drawn from me; and the use of your name, and the sentiment of love. And "help me". That's Rebecca. The other voice is what's inside her, the traveller, and the language is a lost one, and the references are to lost events. At least, that's the conclusion of my Old Eye in the mountains; but even so it was only an intuitive guess on her part. The language Rebecca whispered to me is older than the painted caves. Even to an Old Eye, it's like trying to reconstruct a burned city from the charred remains of its foundations.'

'Everyone who talks to me talks of ruined cities,' Martin said, staring at the forest.

Father Gualzator walked down the drive to where Daniel had thrown his bicycle. He picked it up and checked the tyres, then rang the bell. He was distracted and unhappy and before he cycled back to the church and the hill he walked back to Martin and took the man's hands in his, staring down, not meeting eyes. 'This will sound cruel,' he whispered. 'And don't assume it's true. But I don't think you can get *both* of them back.'

'Oh Christ! That's what Conrad said to me. But I can't accept it.'

'You may have to. The old bosker may have been touched, but he was touched by charm, not madness. I don't think Daniel and Rebecca can ever be together. The one so dead, the other so alive . . . but they're both of them ghosts, Martin. I don't know where you go from here.'

'Exorcism. That's all I can think of. Exorcise them.'

'Bronzebell, Book and Nightfire?' The priest shook his head. 'The travellers in your family are too old to be intimidated by the Church and the Hill. The exorcism needed in this case isn't something *I* can accomplish.'

For half an hour Martin walked briskly to and fro along the edge of the forest, calling for Daniel. The light was going, and a storm was coming from the west. The breeze was cold and beginning to stiffen.

He went quickly back to the house, called Jacques, then another neighbour, and when both told him that they'd seen nothing of the boy, he fetched his torch and overcoat and went out again.

It was beginning to rain as he reached the first of the old bosker's lodges, the ramshackle iron and wooden hut. The heads of the hunted foxes had vanished from their stakes, but the hanged line of squirrels turned and twisted in the wet wind, as did the torn oilskin over the door.

Daniel was sitting on the bed, a shadowy figure. He blinked as Martin flashed the torch in his face, but kept staring at the light. He was leaning against the wall, below the remaining pictures of Conrad's childhood sweetheart. His arms were limp by his sides, his gaze quite expressionless, save for his narrowed eyes.

'Stop shining it in my face.'

'Sorry.'

Martin set the torch's light to fluorescent. The stark glow illuminated the boy's pale features and set sharp shadows around the room. Martin sat down in the old man's chair.

'Why did you break your computer?'

'I don't know. Just felt like it.'

'Why are you upset?'

'I'm angry. Not upset. Angry.'

'Why don't you come home, Daniel? I'll make supper, we'll look after Mummy.'

'Leave me alone.'

'You can't stay here all night. The storm is going to be fierce . . .'

As if to illustrate his words, the whole structure shook and shuddered, the oilskin billowing as the rain and wind swirled and gusted.

'I need the storm. I need the darkness. I like the darkness. It helps me think.'

'Daniel . . .'

'Not Daniel!'

'Not Daniel?'

The boy stared through the white light. A smile touched his lips; he was otherwise limp, propped against the rough wall like a doll.

'Leave me alone.'

'Who are you? What do you want?'

'I've got what I want. Most of it. He thought he could starve me at birth, but I've taken what I want, and now he can't see anything but the shadows of lost forests. He's *skogan*. He can't hear anything but stone songs. He can't make any sound except running water . . .' Daniel laughed hoarsely, then looked away. 'Leave me alone. I have to think.'

'Let Daniel go. I want him home.'

'Too late. The boy doesn't want to go home.'

'But I want him to come home, and I'll take him home, and you too unless you release him.'

Daniel sniggered, his eyes closed as if with deep weariness. The storm raged through the forest, wind swirling through the eaves, sending skins and paper flapping in the cold shack.

'Don't threaten me,' Daniel said. 'I'm here for the duration. He's kept something back from me. He always keeps something back from me . . .'

Martin felt that the reference was not to the boy, but to the 'he' who travelled inside Rebecca. 'I intend to get it. But how? How?'

And suddenly, uncontrollably, Martin leapt at the limp human figure on the bed. The surge of rage had surfaced unbidden, and took him unawares. He just knew that he *hated* the traveller, that he was incensed at the so-calm dismissal of the human life in which it was a passenger. As he struck at the face, and squeezed at the neck, he was aware that it was his son's body that he was assaulting; but it was not Daniel who was the object of his attack. It was the enchantress inside him, who screamed, and laughed through her choking throat, used strong fingers to bend back Martin's, then kicked him powerfully, sending him hurtling back across the shack.

Daniel sat up straight, rubbing his neck, weeping from his left eye where Martin's first blow had landed, taunting. 'Daddy, Daddy, child abuser!'

'Get out of my son!'

'I *am* your son, you fool! This is how I was born. The body's just the shell. *Your* body's just a shell. We're all *travellers*, as you so quaintly call it. Now go away! I'm stronger than you by far.'

And Martin left, staggering back through the driving rain, leaving his son behind him in the darkened ruin, leaving his life behind.

He was weeping as he entered the house. Suzanne was there, and she drew him into her bosom, holding him very tightly as the rain rattled the windows, and upstairs

Rebecca shrieked and howled, her words incoherent, her footfall heavy as she stumbled about the room, the nurse trying to calm her, to ease her back to bed.

At about four in the morning, as the storm abated slightly, Martin woke from a deep, disturbed sleep. He was sprawled on a blanket, by the still-warm stove, using a cushion as a pillow. He became aware of someone crouching by him, a hand on his back, and he turned over quickly, looked up to see Rebecca, dimly lit by the night-light in the hall. She was wet around the eyes and lips, feeling blindly in the dark. When he reached for her she grasped for him and twisted below him, murmuring sounds.

'Oh Beck! Beck . . . you shouldn't be up . . .'

'Ssssh!' she breathed, and he drew back.

'Can you understand me, Beck?'

She had opened her dressing gown. He placed his hands on her breasts and she closed her blind eyes, covering his hands with hers, holding him hard. He leant down and kissed her and at the back of her throat she started to sing, her legs jerking violently, meaninglessly until Martin realised what she was trying to do. He reached down and undressed quickly, desperate to keep the kiss, desperate not to lose her.

Moments later, as she reached down to draw him deeply home, he felt a great fatigue. It was an irresistible drowsiness, and though he fought against it, he was helpless in its grasp; and making love he fell asleep, his last thought a silent plea for wakefulness.

In the morning she was gone. He woke, cold, half naked, to find the nurse in a panic.

'She's gone. Oh my God, she's gone!'

Quickly covering himself, Martin stood, blinking the sleep from his eyes, rubbing them furiously. *She put a spell on me!*

'Where? Gone?'

'I don't know. I don't know. The door was open. I only woke a few moments ago . . .'

'Call Jacques. The number's in the book. And the priest. Tell them that Rebecca has gone walkabout, and I need them to help search for her.'

Outside, in the grey dawn, the forest of Broceliande shimmered with the rain from the night's storm. It seemed to have grown, to have become heavier, to have leaned towards the farm, to have consumed a little of the path. The air was fresh. The milk-cart was rattling past. Up on the hill, the church was a black tower against the spiralling clouds.

'She's dead,' Martin whispered. He couldn't find tears. He remembered her touch from the middle of the night, the feel of her lips, the warmth of her sex, the touch that said how much she needed him, the touch that had said goodbye.

'She's dead . . .'

And he knew she would be at the lake. He walked indoors again and found his coat and rubber boots. He fetched a rake from the shed. The nurse watched him. He felt very calm. He felt dead.

'Where are you going? Where are you going to look?'

'She's in the lake,' he said. 'Tell Jacques. She's in the lake.'

'What lake?'

'The lake in Broceliande, by Conrad's grave. The lake in the heart of the forest.'

'Will he know which lake you mean?'

'Just tell him to follow the path.'

'If you're sure of this, then go. Now. Hurry!'

He walked down the path. After the storm, the wood was quite still. It was as if the world had ceased to breathe. He was cold inside, he might have been floating through the trees, not walking. The memory of the kiss, the memory of her body, these things were gentle pleasures, memories of a lost life that walked with him, accompanied him calmly down the path, past the bosker's cabin, through the silent forest of Broceliande.

And yet, as he passed Conrad's hunting place, the frame of wicker, the wooden igloo with its rough skins, a voice said, 'Hurry!' and he began to run.

And by the time he came to the lakeside, to flounder in the mud among the rushes, he was screaming for his lover – as if a spell had broken and suddenly there was hope after all. As if the drowned were not yet dead, and the water could be brought out through their mouths, their eyes, all the passages of their bodies, and the spirit returned to the flesh.

As he thrashed in the cold water, so the birds rose in flocks, to wheel about the lake, dark shapes in the dawn, circling and watching like hungry crows over the battle-fields of old, waiting for the spoils.

When he saw her he screamed. As he approached he stumbled, aware of the two shapes floating in the deeper water.

He rose with a howl, soaking from head to foot, the rake held like a weapon, waved angrily above his head. The rats that had been feeding swam away. The dawn breeze caught the spill of hair. The bodies, interlocked by arms, turned slowly as the waves began to break against them. Martin staggered through the lake, then swam to reach them, drawing them by the feet, drawing them back to the shore, back to the mud.

They were alike, so alike. They were asleep, their arms entwined, their hair entwined, their faces white and almost smiling. In death the travellers had left them, no doubt. The peace of lives released in death touched each closed eye, the corners of each wide, perfect mouth.

Martin kissed them both, and hugged them, standing in the lake, the wind chilling his body. Then he dragged them through the reeds and to the dry earth where the wood began, and when Jacques arrived, hours later, astonished by the sight of the lake, he found his nephew on his knees between the dead, holding their hands in his against his chest, as if the three were praying.

'Turn them over! Get the water out of them! Turn them *over*, man.'

'They've *been* turned over. Let them rest at last.'

PART THREE

The Vision of Magic

How from the rosy lips of life and love
Flash'd the bare-grinning skeleton of death!

From *Idylls of the King*

Opening the Tomb

'Martin! Martin! There are people on the path. Your people!'

The words, shouted from outside, seemed like a dream at first, but with the constant hammering at the door, and the rattle of dirt on the window, he soon came awake, stretching out on the floor, groaning as his deadened limbs came back to life. He was fully clothed and his mouth felt sour and dry.

Again, the boy's voice, 'Martin. Martin! Hurry!'

He peered out into the brightening dawn. It was Richard, the Lordez's eldest child, a familiar and cheery youth who kept his pony in Martin's field. The boy saw the man and beckoned, then pointed to where Clarisse, his sister, was cautiously circling an invisible spot on the path, astonished by what she was seeing.

He went downstairs and drank copiously from the water bottle, then walked outside, shivering with the chill.

Richard called to him. The boy, fourteen now, was frightened, or perhaps apprehensive.

'What is it? What have you seen?'

'People on the path,' Richard said, his voice a whisper, his pale eyes wide. '*Your* people.'

'My people?'

'It's Daniel. And Rebecca. They're walking up to the hill.'

It took a moment for the meaning of the words to register. Then Martin was running, gaining speed, all sleep gone, all alcohol drained from a mind that was suddenly racing. Rebecca? Daniel? And as he ran he murmured, 'Rebecca . . . ?' and his voice began to rise in volume until he screamed, literally screamed, 'Rebecca!'

He reached the suddenly startled girl and gripped her by the shoulders. 'Where? Where is she? Where's Rebecca?'

Clarisse looked terrified, trying to pull away from the unshaven man, her eyes a window into combined terrors.

'Where is she?' Martin shouted, shaking her. 'Where is she?'

'You're inside her,' Clarisse whispered and her face twisted into a sob. 'Please – let me go.'

He released the girl. She scampered away, then stood with her brother, slightly hunched, watching the path.

Martin turned, his arms outstretched. He could feel nothing. But he danced on the path, turning, turning, remembering Seb, desperate to touch the dead.

'Beck. Oh God, Beck. Are you here?' And loudly to the children, eyes still closed, 'Where is she? Am I still inside her?'

Clarisse's voice was a howl of sadness, 'No. You've danced in front of her. Just stand still.'

Martin stood on the path, eyes closed, trying to feel. There was the scent of dawn, and a gentle breeze. He could hear the girl making noises, like a kitten, frightened. She was crouching, now, her brother with her, watching the man as he embraced the empty path.

'She's passing through you again,' Richard called, and Martin closed his arms around his body, trying to hold the ghost.

'What about Daniel? How does he look?'

They walked together up the path. The children described what they could see, and Martin tried to remember how it had been when he had been a child. Rebecca was walking slowly. She was dressed as she had been dressed when he had dragged her from the lake. Daniel was looking back, looking worried. Why was there always one person on the path who looked back, as if haunted, as if hunted?

They came to the church and Martin began to cry. He could feel nothing! He ran to the frightened children, grabbed at Clarisse. 'Dance inside her. Please! Dance inside Rebecca. Tell me what you hear, tell me what you feel!'

'It's too dangerous,' Richard said, but he hesitated. The girl shuddered, gripped by Martin's hands. Her eyes filled and flowed, but she remained silent, blinking nervously.

Martin was desperate. 'Please? Clarisse, will you?'

'*Dangerous!*' Richard said earnestly. 'Our parents always told us – not inside people we know!'

Screaming, not hearing those odd words *not inside the people we know*, Martin implored the girl. 'Dance inside her! I must know how she feels! For Christ's sake, do it! Clarisse – do it! Please! For me!'

The girl burst into tears, but nodded. 'Look after me,' she wailed as she tugged free and ran in pursuit of the invisible people on the path. Richard stared icily at the man, terrified. His sister's sobs turned to screams of fear as she slowed to enter the ghosts, looking back.

And at that moment Martin realised what he had done. He raced after the girl, grabbed her, swung her round and hugged her as she cried out and sank down with relief. 'I'm sorry. Clarisse, I'm so sorry. I was forgetting how dangerous it is. I'm so confused, so frightened. I'm so sorry, love. Of course you mustn't dance inside her.'

Richard suddenly screamed, 'Be careful! Clarisse! Watch out –'

The girl's eyes had widened and she smiled. Somewhere, a long way away, the sound of someone running . . .

Martin held the girl, noticing how she seemed to melt, how her eyes glowed. Richard was running towards them.

'Get out! Get out!'

They were inside the people! Rebecca and Daniel were passing through them!

Martin dragged the girl to the side. Richard thumped him hard on the back, a small man, furious. 'You let them into her! You shouldn't have done that!'

'I didn't know. I thought they were ahead of me. I can't see them, Richard. I can't see them. Only you can see them. Christ, I want to *see* them! Where are they now?'

The boy hesitated, fury calming, then he looked towards the hedge around the cemetery. 'Passing through. Rebecca is looking back at you. Do you think she knows you're here? Did she feel something?'

'I don't know.'

'Did you feel anything?'

'Nothing.'

They both looked at Clarisse.

'Sis? Did you feel anything?'

'Let me out,' the girl said quietly. 'So close, now. So near. Let me out!'

'Who's saying this?'

'The old man. The old man in Rebecca. Let me out. I'm nearly out. Let me out!'

'I don't understand.'

But all Clarisse would say was, 'Stuck in the shaft. Trapped in the tree. Let me out. Let me free!'

Her brother Richard took her home. A few hundred yards down the path the huddled pair broke into a run, holding hands, racing against the rising of the sun to return to their house.

Martin swung on the iron gate, imagining the way that Rebecca and Daniel were now descending below the hill, to pass through their own gate into a world beyond his understanding.

Let me out? Trapped in the tree. Trapped in the shaft . . .
I'm nearly out. Let me out . . .

And Martin remembered Sebastian's drawings, made years ago, shortly before the boy had died.

It took him two hours to find the faded paper, the scrawled sketches that Sebastian had made. Eveline had kept them safe, of course, as she had kept everything that her sons and daughter had drawn and written. They had been locked in one of many boxes, and the boxes stacked in orderly array within the attic. It was volume and security that made the task of discovery so difficult, but at last, from the filed and ordered memories of his mother, Martin found the sketches of the 'vases', the odd drawings that his brother had produced shortly before his death.

By the time he reached the church, Matutinus was underway, the priest, in his black robe, singing the words-of-morning to a congregation of two (the Delbondes, who never missed Matutinus). Candle smoke filled the church. Martin sat quietly at the back, and when the Delbondes scurried out, ready for breakfast, Father Gualzator snuffed the candles and came quickly down the aisle.

'I was watching you. I saw everything. This morning.'

'Richard and Clarisse?'

The older man nodded, taking the papers from Martin's hand as if already he had intuited their content.

'My old eye didn't fill in the figures, but the children could see the ghosts of Rebecca and Daniel. And I heard the old man's voice: Let me out.'

'You heard it as an old man's voice? It was the girl who was speaking.'

The priest laughed drily. 'Old eyes do see, old ears do hear. It was an old man, speaking through the girl. He's trapped, like the genie in the bottle. Except that he's close to getting free. He's been close to getting free for nearly two hundred years, now. These sketches are fascinating. They confirm something I've half suspected since I came to Broceliande. Come into the vestry.'

'I wish you'd shown me these before. Look here . . .'

Father Gualzator produced a box file, opening it to reveal yellowed parchment, vellum, torn pages from note books, schoolbooks, even the blue tint of quality writing paper from earlier in the century. He spread the sheaf of paper on the table. On all of them were sketched, in childish hand, bottles and vases, all with bits of tree and bone inside them, each stoppered with little hats, or caps, consisting of round blobs.

But they weren't vases. They were shafts into the earth, and the stoppers were:

'Stones. These are votive shafts, dug deeply into the ground and capped with stone cairns. Do you see? The image was confusing for the children who glimpsed them from the ghosts, and they've always drawn jars, or vases. But they're shafts. It's a familiar device from pre-history, running on into late Celtic times. The shafts were filled with bones, stones, trees, whatever, and there is no reason why a shaft in one area of the world should necessarily function in the same way as a shaft from another. But they are clearly an attempt to commune with the earth, perhaps to mollify the earth. Sebastian, like all the other children whose drawings I've managed to accumulate, has shown a shaft with a tree inside it. That was very common. The deepest shaft I know was dug about two hundred years before Christ, and was one hundred and forty feet deep, and very narrow. A whole tree had been thrown down it, plus pottery and bones, a dog, a stag, some bits and pieces of gold and bronze. Right at the bottom, below everything, was the corpse of a child, a deformed child, mind you, its skull neatly divided by a single blow.'

Martin leafed through the drawings. The similarities were astonishing. Each of these had been drawn by a child after dancing through the people on the path. Yet the oldest was from the early eighteen hundreds. The proportions were so much the same. The lopped off tree, its branches cut, all showed the same number of stubs: six, six for the stubs of a dismembered male human body.

'Then this is the evil at the heart of the wood. Conrad knew it. He told me, just days ago. Merlin *is* trapped in the heart of Broceliande. His grave is there. Just across the lake, according to Conrad. It's always been there, hidden from prying eyes, but no longer hidden, I think. We can get to it. We can dig him up!'

Father Gualzator smiled and leaned on the table. 'This is the *pain* at the heart of the wood. And yes, it's Merlin, or whatever it is that we've come to call Merlin. A vague memory of the killing in ancient times has survived as a legend of Merlin trapped in a tree, in a shaft of air, accessible only to Vivien. But it's an *earth* shaft. And probably very deep. And he, or it, is down there. And it wants to be let out. It's been creeping out for ages. It's been trying to tell us where it's buried. That sounds dangerous to me.'

Martin let the priest's words flow into and over him. All he could think was: perhaps he can help. If I let him out, perhaps he can bring back Rebecca. Perhaps he can give life again to Daniel. There is old magic in song, as Rebecca discovered. I must try. I must try . . .

But he couldn't do it on his own.

Martin watched as the priest filed the drawings, adding Sebastian's own sketches to the collection.

'I'm going to dig him up.'

Father Gualzator shrugged, frowning. 'Most of me wants to counsel against such an act. It should have occurred to you that you stand to release not just Merlin, but to revive Merlin's tormentor again. They're both down there, although how and why Vivien was trapped is beyond me. Something went wrong, all that time ago. She has been a vengeful and violent spirit for two thousand years, striking from the grave – possessing, using, destroying . . .'

'Nevertheless . . .'

Martin hesitated. The priest was in a cold sweat, his hands shaking as he tied the ribbon on the box-file.

'Will you help me?'

'I suppose so. I'll try. I'll help until I can't. Then you'll have to forgive me, but I'll not help if I feel the people in this parish are threatened. Do you understand that?'

Martin understood and said so.

They moved through the woodland for hours, following the path by Conrad's first home, by his hunting lodge, dragging the canoe on its makeshift sled, lowering it down the rock faces, hauling it across the marshy ground, around the giant oaks, through the sun-bright glades, shifting their packs as they sweated on the path. Breathless and hot in the humidity of Broceliande, the priest in physical distress despite his fitness, they listened for the sound of the lake.

The canoe could carry two. Martin had driven to Bordeaux to buy it. It was made of fibreglass and was styled like the canoes of the North American Indians. It should easily transport them across the lake, from home-shore, to heart-shore.

Towards the end of the day they were moving still, dragging the long canoe along the path, but at dusk, just as the sun was blinking out of sight above the trees, they found the quiet water and the old bosker's ruined fishing lodge. The body of Conrad lay there, drawn deeply into its skins. The cross above the grave where Martin and his uncle had buried Rebecca and Daniel was dark in the tree line. Father Gualzator went and blessed the hump of earth before coming back and watching the mist rise on the water.

'Did you wrap them in linen?'

'Very carefully.'

'In one piece, I hope –'

'I'm no butcher.'

'Good. We should stay overnight here, I think. Cross the lake at dawn.'

Martin hauled the canoe to the reeds, pushing it half across the mud so that it was taken by the lake. He heaved the two packs into the middle of the craft, then came back for the shovels and the winch.

'No. Let's cross now. I'm impatient to go, impatient to be there.'

Without a further word, the priest clambered into the prow of the canoe, picking up one of the paddles. Martin pushed the boat afloat, splashing through the muddy shallows, then flinging himself aboard. The mist parted before them, even as the sun dropped from view and the whole lake, the whole wood, became grey and silent.

It took less than fifteen minutes to float, rowing gently, to the farther shore, pulling the boat onto the bank and turning it over, to make a crude shelter for the rest of the night, close to the thin trail they could see leading inwards.

*　　*　　*

The stone cairn had spread under its own weight and, of course, the weight of time. Perhaps it had once been as high as the man whose dismembered corpse, represented in blue-stone, now probed obscenely from the spill of boulders, earth and weeds. The cairn, now, was no more than a hump, half-filling the curious glade with its eight confining oaks, its single stone, a piece of grey stone, fallen, resting heavily against the broadest of the spreading trees. There was room, in this clearing, to sit, to camp. The flowers were yellow, the thistles high, the branches draped with old, old rags. The canopy was heavy, but left a clear space to the sky and the light, as the day began, gleamed on the blue torso of the stone statue.

'Are you feeling fit?'

Father Gualzator grinned as he rolled up his shirtsleeves, responding to Martin's question with a shrug. 'Soon find out. Statue first?'

They scrabbled the stones away from the broken statue. The eyes in the sharply carved face stared blindly; the mouth gaped as if in death. It was made of green and white marble, and the skin of the naked form was covered with tiny marks, a complete tattoo of designs and symbols which the priest examined with fascination.

'Everything, from cuneiform ... see? Here, the little wedges ... to ogham, over here, over most of it. These are a sort of rune, these ... only the Lord knows. Interesting man, below, our Merlin.'

Together they managed to prop the statue against the leaning greystone. By day's end they had cleared the cairn to expose the stone slab that covered the shaft and fixed up the winch, which made the tree sigh as weight was taken. The stone slab was a foot thick, and the metal hook could hardly grip it, but as the last of the dark birds returned to their nests, and Father Gualzator's small fire, with its jug of coffee began to signal the end of the first day's work, so Martin got the stone to rise, exposing the compacted earth below. The priest came to lend a hand and they pushed the slab away from the shaft. It fell heavily. The earth felt as cold as ice.

'Come out, come out, wherever you are,' Martin whispered, digging his fingers into the hard soil.

But the genie below remained quiet.

In the morning, Martin discovered the priest sitting shivering, terrified, cold and puffy-eyed. The man had not slept during the night, or rather, he had fallen asleep, only to be woken by the sound of terrible screaming.

'Whilst you slept, I saw the murder. She used an axe and a great knife. He was a small man, young, dark-haired, dark-bearded, trim and tidy, like a prince. He lay motionless, as if helpless, as she hacked off his limbs, then blinded him. I have never seen such fury, such triumphant fury. This woman, like death in a white and green robe, raced into the wildwood, came back with a tall thin tree and lopped off its branches. She sharpened the point of the tree and drove it through the body in the glade until a full four feet extended from the skull. She made a pit, the air around her was filled with spinning earth, and into that pit she flung the body.

'And then she screamed, and the vision faded, save for the sound of fury and despair.

'When the screaming passed away there was an hour or more of silence, but there was movement here, movement I can't understand. Even my Old Eye wasn't sufficient to show the process by which the people came to be on the path. But they came, I know it. The wood, while you slept, became alive with activity. I heard children's voices, I think I counted seven in all, and a man's voice intoning in a lost language. At last a man appeared, the ghostly white image of a man, who seemed at first bemused by the glade, then behaved as if he had been struck, holding his eyes, his head. For a while he had walked normally, despite his ethereal thinness. Now he began to flow, that sublimely delicate movement which you will remember from your childhood visions and which I can still see at times. He left the glade towards the lake. I followed him along the trail. He became immersed in the fog that sits on the water, but flowed away from this glade, across to the path by Rebecca's grave.

'After he had gone I couldn't sleep, and about two hours ago I began to be tormented by a voice, and by the feeling of pain in my ears and eyes, as if fingers were gouging at me. I'm not wanted here, Martin. Whatever lies in the shaft, it doesn't want me here. I don't belong, and it will not let me stay.'

Martin comforted the older man. The glade was dew-wet, webbed with silk, quite silent. He pushed wood onto the fire and set light to a wax block, pouring coffee grounds into the jug, with water, and setting it to heat in the flames that crackled from the wood.

'I need you to help me dig. When the digging's done, then go, by all means. But please stay till then. I need you to help with the digging. If you get attacked again, refer them to me.'

The priest laughed, pushing his hair back and shaking the moisture from his hand. 'Don't take on –'

'More than I can handle? I'll try not to. Just stay. This thing wants to be let free. It will understand that I need you to help that process.'

'You're very confident, all of a sudden.'

'I'm desperate,' Martin said with a glance across the glade. 'I've got less than thirty days to bring them back –'

'Forty days before the spirit leaves the corpse? That's Church-lore. We're outside those rules, now.'

'Maybe. Maybe not. How can I tell? All I know is, I want them back, father. I want them back.'

'I know you do, Martin. And I'm sure they want to come back. But you are aware, of course . . .'

'What? Aware of what?'

'That they can never come inside the hill again. They can never come inside the church.'

'Yes. Of course. Of course I'm aware of that. The sacrament must come to them. I know that.'

'As long as you do remember. It's the first time I've been faced with such a possibility. It will be very hard to deny Daniel. I don't relish the thought. But of course I'll stay and dig. When the digging's done, though, please let me go.'

'When the digging's done, I may not have any choice in the matter.'

Six feet into the shaft Martin's shovel struck against wood, a thick cut of oak, a round sliced from a wide tree. It was sealing the shaft below. He scraped the black soil from one small arc, then an arc on the opposite side. The lid was six feet in diameter and the winch should lift it easily. The wooden platform was set upon more earth, from the dead sound it emitted when struck by iron.

With the winch hook in place, Martin gouged the earth from the rim of the wheel, then ascended to the grove to assist with the hauling. The wheel came up, an undecorated piece of oak, and the stony soil below was revealed, as was the pointed tip of the tree that was buried there.

As he dug down, so he found the evidence of offerings, from fragments of pale red terracotta figures to carved wooden animals and bits of metal. Gold flashed, a thin crest with holes for a chain; then silver, beaten into the now battered shape of a boar with long legs and a delicate filigree of spines along its back.

The tree was a tall, thin hawthorn, its limbs lopped short.

His own length below its tip, Martin found the broken skull of the man impaled upon it, the jaw broken where the thrust of the trunk had carried it through the mouth. He passed the skull to the priest, then excavated as much of the skeleton as he could, noticing as the bones were brought to light how all of them were delicately carved with just the same signs and symbols, runes and letters as the skin of the statue. When at last he had found the long bones of the leg, and the yellowed game tiles that might have been the feet and toes, he tied the winch hook to the tree and clambered out of the shaft.

'Bring her up!'

The tree came out of the grave. Father Gualzator had dug a hole in the clearing to receive it and they planted it anew, then arranged the bones at its base, with the bits and pieces of gold, silver, stone and wood that had been resurrected during the excavation.

It was late, again, and the grove stank of mud and fresh earth. The priest gathered up his pack and Martin went with him to the lake, helping him to the canoe.

'I'll go home and wash, then come back with a second boat. It's by far the easiest way. I don't mind waiting for you, by Conrad's grave, but you might be some time and I have the hill to think of, the church and all.'

'If I need you, I'll tie a white flag by this landing place.'

'If you remember . . .'

'Don't cross unless you see me, or see the flag.'

'We'll see. Goodbye, Martin. I'll be praying for you. To Old Provider . . .'

'Thanks for your help.'

He watched the priest paddle away, soon lost by distance and vapour.

He returned to the grove and sat by the open shaft for a while, smelling the earthy stink of time. Then he crawled to his shelter and blew fire into the embers below the pot of coffee.

Merlin

The bottle had been uncorked, the genie loosed.

In the dead hours of the morning the darkness around Martin became filled with the sound of children. If there was a moon it was hidden behind the heavy overcasting of clouds, and only the dull glow of embers gave a touch of light in the gloom. He sat up and listened to the dancing in the grove, the laughter, the language, the curiosity of these creatures who explored him from another realm.

He sensed a particular excitement in the grove of trees, and watched the tall thorn, and caught glimpses of the bones that he had arranged about the tree. If his ear was tweaked, it could easily have been a breeze, an insect or his imagination. He had long lost the sight of the ghosts that were shed from this place, but he was delighted that he could hear them.

At length, they withdrew into the forest, although the sudden flight of herons, away towards the lake, and the sudden splash of wings on water as a duck was disturbed suggested to Martin that something, someone, had gone that way.

Then with dawn came the feeling of being breathed upon, closely scrutinised. As light turned the canopy to a series of stark branches, the grey stone to a wraithed figure leaning against a tree, as dawn brought the sense of old sight to this grove, so the smell of stale breath, the presence of an old man in front of him, grew more strongly.

'I know you're there,' Martin whispered to the grove.

The sour breath was still heavy in the air, the almost-sound of breathing, as if a man crouched before him, trying to keep as quiet as was possible.

'I know you're here,' Martin repeated. 'I need your help.'

The presence went away.

An altar bell was ringing, a thin tinkling sound but quite insistent, coming from the direction of the lake. Martin stirred from sleep – he had been two days here, now – and trotted through the forest to the reedy shore.

The priest was there in the larger canoe, but he had hauled across a kayak, which was pushed into the mud. 'It seemed like a good idea,' he said from the water. 'And I've brought you more coffee, some fresh bread, cheese, various things. Here. Catch!'

He flung a rucksack which Martin caught easily. There was the clink of full, glass bottles. 'Thanks.'

'Has he come?' Father Gualzator asked, wobbling unsteadily on the lake.

'Yes. I think so. But he doesn't want to talk. He hasn't talked yet, anyway. I'm going to stay on.'

'For your information,' the priest called finally as he rowed the heavy canoe away, back to the village, 'the body of the old bosker is no longer in its shelter. I don't know what that means, exactly, but there is no sign of an animal having dragged it away.'

The dead body of the woodsman, Conrad, came across the lake in the late afternoon. It was slumped forward in the canoe, an oilskin over its shoulders and lowered head like a shroud. The corpse was not rowing. The thin craft glided silently on the grey water, pulled by unseen hands, and by the time it reached the rushbed, Martin was back in the grove, huddled and apprehensive.

Whatever he had expected to see next, the thin, youthful, naked man who walked quickly among the trees and came across to him did not meet that expectation. And yet, for a moment as the vibrant figure stooped to touch his eyes, Martin saw the grimace of the fleshy skull, the faded eyes, the yellowing flesh of the old bosker. It was a glimpse only, and it was a reflection of the dead man that would haunt him through the days, when the light was just so, perhaps when the enchanter's glamour faded for a second.

The traveller in the corpse said, 'I don't know how much you loved this man, and if it disturbs you to see him like this, then say so. I can change its look.'

'No. No . . . I'm not disturbed.'

'The body of the woman was more tempting to use, but I think you would have been more disturbed . . .'

'Yes,' Martin murmured, watching as Conrad walked easily to the bones, squatted and fumbled among them. 'Conrad?'

'Not Conrad. The harder you try to see him, the more you'll see the decay. Concentrate on the conversation and the . . . what do you call it? Glamour? Charm? The charm will help. It's a simple magic, but I'm still quite weak.'

Martin shivered with a growing understanding. 'From the way you speak I suppose you must be . . .' he glanced at the shaft. 'Are you the spirit from the tomb? Are you . . . Merlin?'

Conrad seemed to be amused, but all he said was, 'Thank you for releasing me.' He looked round sharply, saying softly, 'Why *did* you release me, I wonder? No doubt you expect something in return.'

'I don't expect anything. I have a hope, a dream, that's all.'

156

The 'glamorous' body was crouching, again facing Martin, Conrad aglow with life, despite his years, holding in his hands the yellowed skull that Martin had lifted from the pit. Gaze met gaze, curious, searching, considered.

Then Merlin smiled, glancing away to where the path led to the lake. 'The drowned woman. The drowned boy.'

'Her name was Rebecca. She was adopted by my parents when she was thirteen or so. We loathed each other as children. At first. Then . . . didn't. No-one ever knew, but we were each other's first lovers. We came to love each other very deeply when my mother died. We had a child, Daniel. They both died by drowning a few days ago. It had been a terrible few years. Daniel literally drained her, took all her sense and senses. I found them in the lake, on the other side of the lake.'

After a long while of curious watching and thinking, Merlin rose and walked to the pit, where for two thousand years he had been entombed. The robust flesh of the glamour was like a halo around the racked and shrivelled corpse, and Martin remembered Conrad's tale of Rebecca, wolf-shadowed and shimmering.

Merlin said, 'And you believe I was a part of this?'

'Yes. It's all I can think of. The man in whose body you are travelling thought so too. Some part of you was in Rebecca. You fought against an enchantress who travelled in my son. The battle was fought to the death. You both lost. But I implore you, since I've found you, if you can do it, bring them back to me.'

'How?'

'Rebecca *sang* to her dead lover. He'd been drowned. The water left him and he recovered. That singing magic was a part of you, wasn't it? If she could do it, you can do it. Sing them back to me . . . both of them!'

Merlin turned quickly, frowning. He moved back to the

157

fire, head low. 'But what you don't understand, when you ask something so reasonable, is how much damage would be caused. There would be a great deal of damage done! I don't think so. I don't think it would be wise to help you.'

'I beg you. If it's possible . . .'

'But the damage. Singing magic, as you call it, is very powerful. It has always been the hardest magic to control. I repeat – I don't think it would be wise to help you.' He shook his head, crouching and prodding at the flames with a small stick. After a moment he smiled, still staring at the fire, and whispered, 'It was the hardest magic to deny the woman, I remember. She wanted it so much!'

'The woman?' Martin echoed. 'Vivien?'

Merlin glanced up at the name, thoughtful for a second, then amused. 'Vivien. Yes. Vivyana . . . ivanyavok . . . evunna . . . evye . . . The name has always been attached to her, always means the same thing.'

'The Lady of the Lake? As in the Arthurian Romances?'

Again the man had to think, then seemed to comprehend some connection or other. '*Vision of magic*,' he said. 'Her name approximates to that: the vision of magic. But the word that stands *behind* her name was often used to mean whirlpool, or sucking waters. Yes. She was often associated with lakes. But The Vision of Magic goes closer to the heart.'

'Is there more than one Vivien, then?' Martin asked.

Merlin laughed, genuinely amused, now. The sparks flew from the fire as he prodded the embers. 'It depends what you mean. Is there more than one of you? Apparently not. And yet there's a line inside you that connects you with the past and the future, a line running from your fathers to your sons, your mothers to your daughters. All different from you. All of them you, though, just as you are all of them. But each of you is short lived. For the likes of Vivien and myself, the line runs along a path that is *outside* ourselves. It is the path that changes, not the spirit. We live a lot longer than you. Why are you frowning?'

'Your words: lines, paths: it's the language that Rebecca used. It brings back memories.'

'The land is criss-crossed with lines, paths, channels and hollowings. The people who live among those lines are crossed and criss-crossed also. I am not unaware of Rebecca . . .'

Hope surged furious: 'Then can you bring her back? You travelled in her, you were there when she died. Can you bring her back? Can you help me bring back Daniel?'

'I don't know. I've been trapped a long time. When you say I travelled in her . . .' Merlin shook his head. 'You're right, yet you're wrong. You don't really understand.'

Martin collapsed forward, tears surfacing, despair in control again. 'How do I make it *clear* to you? I had a life. Now I'm in hell. I loved a damaged boy. I watched him get better. I loved him more. I watched my lovely Beck decline. I couldn't love her more, I just felt helpless. Then I realised . . . Not Beck, not Daniel . . . not them at all.' He raised his head and stared at the impassive corpse. 'You! You and your own tormentor! You fucked with my life! You used us for your games!'

'They were not games . . .'

'I don't care! How can I care? I had a *life*. You and your tormentor took that life from me, took it from the two people I loved, left them dead, drowned in the lake.'

He had started to cry, missing Rebecca so much, missing the sweet boy, terrified of what was happening, aware that he was in a cold glade talking to a dead man, aware that his hope was no more than a dream, that waking dream to which one clutches, not wanting it to go away, holding on for fear of the coming light, because for a moment, just for a moment, there *is* a little hope.

After a while he ceased to cry. He was shivering. The fire had burned low. He looked up, rubbing hands against his eyes, and the cowled form of the young-old man was there, head low as if thinking.

'Help me . . .' Martin whispered. 'If I can have them back . . . help me . . .'

'How long are you prepared to wait?' the woodsman asked quietly. 'Two thousand years?'

Martin's hopes had risen, but he collapsed again when he heard those taunting words. *Two thousand years?* 'No,' he said. 'You know I can't.'

'Two hundred, then.'

'You're playing games. You know I can't.'

'Twenty years? Can you wait that long?'

'That's the worst of all! That's like being in hell. No. I can't wait twenty years. I love them. I want them *now*, not when I'm a husk.'

Merlin laughed below the cowl, but it was a sinister echo of despair and frustration. 'Then twenty days.'

Martin sat up quickly. 'Twenty days?'

'Time enough to talk to you. Time enough to warn you. Time enough to decide what I can do for you. You *did* let me out. But you're asking something very damaging. I have to think. I have dreams too. I have needs. You find it hell to wait twenty years, yet I've waited two thousand.'

'You live longer.'

'I die more slowly. Anger has time to flourish. But you *did* let me out . . . but where is Vivien? In the boy still? Or has she found another place? What to do? Which one to help? What to do with you . . . ?'

Martin said nothing, waiting desperately.

'We'll begin tomorrow. I think I'll talk to you. I think

I'll tell you something about the path, and something of the magic that Vivien lusts for. We'll begin tomorrow. We have twenty days. But at the moment, the shadow is going from the wood.'

It seemed that Merlin drew for his strength upon that time of change in the forest when the sun was descending, leaving behind a swirl of its own power, which circulated freely and randomly for a while and was a source of energy. Soon after, the earth took control again, and at that moment Merlin could not exercise his will. The 'window of opportunity' – an expression that Martin had learned as a child from watching the various shuttle launches into space – varied according to the brightness of the day, the conditions of the atmosphere. Magic was in this way barometric, and Merlin's ability to coat the corpse of the old bosker with glamour, and then use it to communicate, was severely limited.

'We'll begin tomorrow.'

Vivien

Shortly before dusk of the following day, glamour came back to the stiff and shrouded corpse of Conrad, and Merlin came from below the tree to the fire, where Martin huddled, cold and afraid, his thoughts drifting between his need for Rebecca and his son and the clear reluctance of this ghost to help him in their resurrection, and the spiritual presence of Merlin himself, a fearful effigy which he had accepted and to whose whim he was now committed.

For a while Martin sat within the hard and shining gaze of the old woodsman; then Merlin whispered, 'Listen . . .'

The path that passes through Broceliande is circular, stretching from this western coast a vast distance to mountains in the east, in the very depths of the land. It winds its way through valleys to the south of here, through caves, then east along the sun-baked coast of an inland sea. North of the far mountains it cuts through dense forests, lakes and rivers. Much of it is now drowned below the ocean. But when the path was first walked, the land in those places was above the sea. Time and the pull and tug of the moon simply changed things. The path is still there below the ocean, but it takes a special concentration to walk it.

It was neither I, nor the woman of magic vision that you call Vivien, who first walked the path, although I have an inkling as to the nature of that long forgotten traveller. I came later, much later, although I am earlier than the legends with which you associate me.

My first encounter with Vivien was where the path passes among the lakes and blue forests of the north, in a place of grey and white swans, red wolves and reindeer. The insects in those forests were a trial to any voyager. The lakes were so cold that in each and every one of them a hundred human bodies floated, half-way down, dead yet still alive, suspended from the process of living by the ice. The magic men of the region, the shamans, swum among them naked, feeding on the faint echoes of memory in the drowned, learning past truths to aid their own journeys to the underworld. They surfaced for air at regular intervals, screaming with the cold, then plunged again, almost dancing with the slowly turning bodies in the deep.

On the surface of the lakes, the swans glided, and Vivien swam among them. She had a light fledge of black feathers on her arms and the red and blue shapes of an owl and a salmon on her breasts and belly. She was a child at the edge of womanhood and otherwise quite pale.

As this sprightly juvenile swam and dived among the feeding swans, playing with their shapes – adopting their shapes – amusing herself with the inner and outer forms of the peaceful birds, I knew at once that the girl was an enchantress.

She was so young, though, that her power was unfocused. She was like a baby, clutching at new things, half inclined to destroy, only gradually discovering the need to be gentle. The mosquitoes which swarmed about me, drawn by the scent of the reindeer on my body and the aroma of the hawk on my head, were a tribulation to me. Yet she, with the swiftest of movements of her left hand and clutching a small talisman of nothing more than birch twigs shaped as a circle and a cross, banished the voracious creatures from her pale skin, crouching in the reeds, preening her feathered arms with a long, white comb.

She knew I was watching, of course. No doubt she'd been aware of my stink from the moment I left the birch forest to walk along the rushy shore, looking for a place to fish.

Like a cat, her head kept turning up to sniff the air. She watched me by sound not sight, but I'm familiar enough with the glance of light on the keen eye that tells that sight has been briefly employed. Oh yes, she was aware of me, and I was wearing the skins of the beast, bird and fish, so she knew I was kin with the Vision of Magic. But as the grizzled men of the villages floundered in the ice waters, listening for the tunes that would guide them to the past, so in me she had detected a different breed of conjuror.

Her interest was as pointed as the breasts on which she gently splashed cold water, as bright as the light on her long black hair. I moved slowly through the tall rushes and like a trout swimming in shallow water I was alert, fully aware of the taste of the fly, but half aware of the bait, of the trap, of the hook.

As if to further tease and entice me, this pristine, nubile creature flew suddenly above the reeds, the action of the flight like that of a dragonfly. It was a brief flight, high above the lake, a short dance in the air with outstretched wings. Whatever charm she had used, however, wore off quickly and with a slight cry, the sound of irritation, she plunged from the height into the mud, where she floundered and spluttered, her wings now filthy.

But it had been a moment of exceptional magic, and charm in every sense, a waif-like body, pale and slender, perfect and unbroken, hovering, then swooping above the blue lake, slim legs kicking in the action, a moment of control – the wile in the woman – then the moment of chaos – the impetuosity of the girl.

She was proud and angry as I hauled her from the mud. She didn't resist, despite the indignity of the moment, which told me instantly that this had in part been designed for me.

Almost at once she was laughing. Her hands were over me, parting the folds and creases of my furs and skins, looking for the skin within the skin, finding first the rank, torn wool of my vest, then the marks, scars and tattoos of my trade. But made curious by these patterns her fingers tried to read them, like a blind man reading the marks and gnarls in hardened clay of the Babylonians.

'They mean nothing to me!' she cried aghast, then covered the slip. 'They're fascinating,' she added, with transparent caution.

'Fascinating?'

'What do they mean? What do they do? Where do they help you travel?'

'Marks of my birth, signs of my tribe, nothing more,' I said, but she tugged the thin hair of my beard.

'Liar!'

'Prove it.'

'I will.'

It was a tease, and there was a smile on her face. And anyway, I was young then. You may not be aware of it, but there is a bone in every human body which, when broken, begins the passage of time. For most of you, this bone is broken in the womb and soon dissolved. Rarely, it remains unbroken for centuries without end. My bone in those years was unbroken, although I was certainly cautious of too much vigour, too much of the hunt. My beard was black, my hair strong, the muscles in my body like whales below the grey sea, firm and powerful. They had to be — it was just as well — since I was travelling great distances, and existing on precious little, save for fish.

It is always the fish that betrays us.

The trout, splendid in so many ways, can never learn to tell when there is a hook inside the juicy fly. And the trout is the great weakness of all hunters. It is itself a hunter of superb prowess, but it is incapable of swimming anywhere other than into the flow of the river. It feasts blindly and voraciously through that flow, only to die, surprised, on a sharpened bone.

At some time in our lives we all will be caught. And young though she was, when I first met her, I am certain that Vivien was aware of this simple, ageless truth.

I was about to say more to her when one of the shamans ran naked and screaming from the lake. Wild, frenzied, and blue as if starved of air, he shivered past us, his hands encasing the grey, winter buds of his sex. He danced and cried, a man older than his years, patterned on his arms for flight, I noticed, but not yet on his face for travel through the earth, nor on his legs for the great running, the hound running.

He saw me, and saw my furs, and came bounding over to me, huddling inside the reindeer skin, so physically strong that I couldn't detach his icy hands from my flesh, where they sought my heat, and so the two of us fell struggling and yelling into the mud, the one in search of warmth, the other in a desperate escape from cold fingers.

Now it was Vivien's turn to laugh, and she hauled us up. The shaman, bereft at this moment of any power worth his drum, began to flog the warmth into his body with a handful of rushes, running back to the village and the long lodge, where the fires burned continually.

This, it turned out, was also Vivien's village. The raven-feathered girl dressed herself in a simple woollen skirt, a bright blue shirt and wolfskin overcoat, then led me to her home.

It was here, choking on the smoke from the fires on which fish and small game were being cooked, that Vivien demonstrated her second piece of magic, an entrancing act again, and one which was a sinister portent for the future, although I was not aware of this at the time. It was simply an interesting piece of magic. But I should certainly have understood the significance of the performance, and that I failed to do so, I am still convinced, is because she had put her first hidden charm on me.

The longhouse was crowded, mothers and fathers grouped around the fires, each watched over by a *loki*, a heavy tree whose animal faces grinned across the room. There was the constant sound of laughter and raised voices, and of song, accompanied by reed pipes and small drums.

The shaman who had so frigidly and irritatingly fled the lake waters, and the memories of drowned men, paid particular attention to me for a while. He brought me soup, then the raw cheeks of salmon, and flat cakes of bread in which the resinous and delicious taste of birch was abundant.

He talked nonsensically of his experiences in the lake, and showed me drums and stretched skins that reflected his visits through what he called the 'swan's neck', visits to the places where the shapechangers lived. Everything in this land of lakes and forests was defined by animals, and each journey described as a voyage: to higher worlds through the gullet or crop of a bird, to hidden forest worlds through the heart or gut of the reindeer; to worlds below the water by passage through the gills of a pike. It occurred to me in a moment of humour to ask if the longer the bowel the more difficult the journey, but to the *Pohola* it made no difference. In any event, the food tasted wonderful, despite the fact that recently each limb or cheek or sausage had been the channel to another realm.

Vivien had been conspicuous by her absence for some time. There was an air of apprehension and humour in the longhouse, and I was aware that an entertainment was being prepared for me. These people, the Pohola, were of a generous nature, if inclined to melancholy (their songs and stories were remorselessly depressing, a fact I attribute to the harshness of the land and the extent of darkness that subdues their spirits).

Vivien entered suddenly, causing the smoke to swirl. She was wearing a dress of white wool, which flowed about her as she turned, her feathered arms extended. Her face was painted black, but like a bird. Behind her, six small girls from the village entered quickly, all equally simply dressed, and each with the severed wings of swans tied to their arms, which they flapped awkwardly. Their hair, waist length and amber, flowed as they twirled and laughed. They were not normally permitted in this lodge, and were both nervous and thrilled to be within the fish-smoke.

My friend, the shaman, laughed noisily, pointing and making comments that I couldn't interpret. The mothers clapped, the fathers smoked, watching the small dance, watching me for my reaction.

By *their* reaction to what followed I can only assume that they had seen no such event before. It happened like this:

The seven dancers formed into a circle, wings outstretched and touching, dancing slowly round the fire. People moved back where they sat, towards the walls, throwing cushions and rugs between them in a wonderful display of relaxation. I was pushed back too, and only just rescued my bowl of salmon cheeks. These were a rare treat for me and I intended to eat until I could eat no more.

Then Vivien moved into the ring, her steps and movements timed to the steady chant of her companions, who still danced as they giggled, firelight making them glow.

To my astonishment, Vivien lifted her skirts and crouched down suddenly on the fire, throwing back her head and screaming. Smoke billowed from below her dress and somewhere someone cried, 'She's burning. Stop her!'

But at the same moment she flung herself aside with a high-pitched laugh. Instantly the air was filled with a ghostly shape, a huge translucent apparition that towered to the rafters, filled the centre of the lodge, a swirl of white, a touch of amber, that at once *hardened* – and became a swan of vast proportion, a bird whose wings, when stretched, filled the longhouse from end to end.

And now it beat those wings and screeched. The movement threw the people hard against the turf walls of the lodge. The swan's neck, thick and powerful, thrashed a boat's length this way and that, its huge head sweeping over us, the beak opened to emit its pain, a mouth that could have swallowed a child.

Wings struck against the rafters, and the rafters broke, the thatch fell, the turf crumbled. Fires went out, wooden pillars cracked as the beak struck; the whole place was mayhem. Everyone was screaming as the beast struggled to escape the confines of the house.

It was tied by a tether to its leg. It fought against the tie, and I felt tugged myself, as if responding in sympathy. As the beast struggled and flexed, so did I. I caught a glimpse of the girl. She was watching me from behind the biggest of the wooden *loki*, the huge totem that guarded the centre of the lodge. She was grinning, she was out of control. She had terrified the people. I knew then that she, like me, was a stranger here.

The swan suddenly broke through the roof. It beat its wings frantically, shedding feathers, breaking feathers, straining its massive neck towards the sky. As it started to rise, the wind catching its wings, so the tether tightened, and the unseen loop around my foot tightened too.

The wretched girl! She had conjured not just this apparition of the swan, but a link between the swan and me, tied by our feet, tethered by magic!

The swan flew and I was dragged across the floor, as if carried by those spirits of the hearth called *fyjulga*. I had an instant only to reach for my bone knife and 'cut' the cord, falling back upon the cold embers of the fire that Vivien herself had extinguished earlier, when she had used its flame for the magic to make this apparition.

The girl laughed, then fled. Starlight shone, and the swan died, somewhere out among the blue lakes. It was a creature fabricated by a young, fierce mind; it died a quick and cold, wet death, but that is appropriate.

There was a cut on my ankle, no less deep than if real wolf-gut had gouged into me. The blood flowed and I bound the wound carefully.

Angry though I was, all I could think of was the girl's laugh of surprise that her trick had worked, the glint in her eyes and the sudden apprehension that followed as she knew that she would be punished for causing the longhouse rafters to be broken.

And if indeed she were punished, then no doubt the sting of the wet birch branch sharpened and heightened her power. I don't know. I could think of nothing from then until the moment, early in the first spring dawn, when

I slipped away along the path at dawn, nothing but the girl and the way she had tested me, and teased me.

Yes. I wanted her fingers on my body again.

Yes, I wanted her to read me, though she would have understood nothing.

And yes, I was determined that it would never happen. I knew that if she touched me, now, I would be dead before too long.

She may have conjured a giant swan, and dazzled guileless eyes. I was more aware that she had squatted down and smothered a blazing fire without harm, using the searing heat for magic!

As if exhausted by this recollection of an event so long in his past, Merlin sank down inside the cowl and fell silent. Martin stoked the fire and sparks swirled among the spreading oaks, to dim and die below the black but starbright void of the night sky.

Abruptly, the grim figure sat up and drew a wheezing breath, which Martin thought might have been a chuckle. Merlin whispered, 'It all comes back to me. I can see that time again as clearly as a fish can see the fly—'

When I left those tribal lands in the far north, Vivien followed me. I'd known she would. Since she was young she was trapped in the place by her own inexperience, but at length she learned of the existence of the path, and she used her skills to enter the long walk, the movement around the path that is endless, that is its own world.

By the time she took her first faltering step – no doubt aided by the wings of birds, her favourite manifestation – lifetimes had passed, and I was in the land of the Pretini, which you probably know as Albion, or Logres – the place has many names. My bone had still not broken, but the fire that she had extinguished during that simple illusion among the Pohola burned within me, forming a link across the ages.

I constantly dreamed of fire. She burned into me from the years lost.

She ran like a wolf across the land. She swam across the ocean. She slept in caves and moved through the sap in the trees. She came close to me, then found her form again, a powerful woman, now, still seeking to understand the marks upon my body.

The truth is that there is a great attraction in the moment of touching. The moment she touched my painted, patterned flesh, the moment that she felt the carved bones *below* that flesh, she was not just intrigued, she was seduced. The shaman with his cold hands suffered a similar seduction, but was easy to deny. Vivien was wilier by far, and had the talent of time, the ability to play her strategy across more than a single lifetime's span.

She knew that she had touched power, touched secrets that could be of great use to her. She intuited that having touched my power she could either have it, or live in its shadow, but that we could not share it. How could we?

If Vivien was to have my skills, she would have to wear my skin. She would have to age by wearing my own age; all beauty would have to be sacrificed to wear the scarred skin of an older man.

Her exuberance, her youth, prevented her from pursuing this until the bone in her body broke. She was clever enough to hold the break, so that though the years passed for her, she aged slowly. As I remained a wolf, seasoned, skilled and always lean, she aged steadily; but she had her charms, and her wings, and there is nothing so youthful as the first flight of a bird at the breaking of dawn.

Old, then, yet still young, Vivien pursued me for the secrets in my flesh.

To confuse her, I created a shadow of myself and sent it back along the path, back to the northlands, travelling towards the sunrise.

It was my intention to meet the shadow again as our paths crossed, and take it back, but I never found it. It still wanders somewhere; perhaps it was seduced from the path, perhaps it faded. It's hard to know these things, although I have heard of a land bridge in the far east, where the ice makes a thick bridge between this and another world, so perhaps it strayed further than I realised. It was a small shadow, possessing small magic. More charm than substance, you understand, and though its life should have been long, it would have been at the whim of all creatures.

Nevertheless, the trick worked at first and I was not aware of Vivien again until after I had stayed for many years in the forests of the Caledon.

One day I sniffed her presence. The air in those mountains is very clear. I have always believed smell to be a form of substance, invisible to the eye, continually shed like skin from the body. I knew she was in the land, though still distant, and I packed my things and walked south.

In any case, it was time to leave the Caledon. There was very little of interest in the forests, although the game was good, the game is always good. I had been there for far too long and I was tired of the cold, tired of the flight of gulls, which could take me out across the wide sea but show me only rocks. The ocean to the west is a forbidding place. If there is a magic beyond it, it defied my eyes to see it.

I rested for a few years or so in the land of the Parisii, near a large town called Eboracum. The distress of dogs, one day at dusk, told me that they had smelled the small enchantress and again I fled.

I passed time in high hills, in deep woods, and confronted passing horsemen, often solitary princes or low kings, seeking this, seeking that, the mind of the warrior king in those days was singularly triumphant, and discovering the lost arms and armour of forgotten heroes was all they seemed concerned with.

In each act of confrontation there was a moment – the moment of surprise, as they saw this wild and hairy man screaming at them from the tree – when their thoughts spilled out like sun through a sudden break in clouds. I fed upon these fears and thoughts, and in this way kept abreast of change as I slowly travelled south.

At some point I sent a second shadow north along the path, but this time the trick failed. She found it and turned it round, and I let it pass me by. She pursued me, then, with energy, running through her lives with the agility of a cat. And in time her persistence was rewarded.

Our paths crossed in the fort of Caerleon, one bitter autumn evening, when the cattle and sheep were being drawn back behind the high walls as the light faded, and the fires lit to show the land. There was a raiding party on its way and the stronghold's warlord, Peredur, was to make a chariot charge against them. Fire and fury was all about me as I stood within the gate and watched the nightland, the confusion and fear of imminent battle. The air was filled with prayers and charms. The blood in the horsemen and the farmers was a sour stench in every corner where they crouched, drinking deeply, waiting for the onslaught.

Vivien came running through the heavy gates just as they were being closed, her red cape flowing, the cowl back from her long hair and pale, beautiful face. She saw me and ran to me, breathless. 'Got you! At last.'

She tugged my beard and frowned, then smiled. 'Still black, still strong. It isn't fair. You look no different now than then. Are you using charm? Do you need charm?'

I replied as ambiguously as possible. 'I use charm occasionally. I never *need* to use it. And you?'

'I use it!' she said directly, staring at me as if daring me to comment. 'Oh yes. I use charm.' Then more immediate concerns occurred to her. 'Where do I get food? I need water. Will we die? There's no need for us to die, my feathered arms can carry us both. I'm so glad to see you again. It's been a long hunt. But where do I get food?'

'I'll take you.'

And she fell against me, no longer the enchantress, simply a refugee, exhausted and in need. I led her through the fires and cattle to the heart of the fort. I had pitched my tent here, above a hidden well. This bubbled briefly through the ground and satisfied her need.

Her performance on arrival at the stronghold, her behaviour, I am certain was not a guile, simply the last defiance of her long journey in search of me.

The enemy had built no fires, their warriors scattered in discreet bands from the river to the higher land, north of the fort. Their tactic, clearly, was to invite a night attack. Almost certainly there was a larger band waiting to fire the gates and pillage the stronghold.

I counselled the warlord as to this, but found that his own seers, by reference to their local augurs, had perceived the same eventuality. They could not, however, locate the bigger army, a task I attended to with as much phony ritual and simple illusion as possible (I was earning my keep, you understand) and discovered them hiding in the overhang of the river bank, a force of horsemen some sixty strong. I could see as well that most of them had come by boat, and that they were unused to the stolen horses with which they had been supplied.

They would be ferocious, then, from the land of the Eriu, probably, but they would have the disadvantage of the night, unfamiliar trails and restless steeds.

This was the sort of language the warlord of Caerleon understood. He divided his horsemen at once, carefully allocating them to two attacking forces.

The lightning raid on the group of men by the river left them shattered. The horses were driven off — twenty recaptured and led back to the fort — and skirmishing along the woodland edge left honours even and the dead paired-up.

The hostiles licked their wounds and marched north-wards at dawn, seeking smaller prey. Vivien taunted them for a while with ravens, which she was adept at summon-ing, while in the fort there was a feeling of the feast and celebration.

But Peredur was furious.

In his eyes he had treated the raiders with honour, he had paired-up the dead, he had won the skirmish. The fact that the Eriu had stayed in his land was an insult to his name.

Grimly, then, he picked his ten best warriors. They put on black cloaks, black armour, black helmets, armed themselves with feathered spears, knives, but no shields. At dawn they rode from the fort in silence, eleven against forty.

Later, near dusk, seven of them returned, Peredur lead-ing the bloody troop, two heads slung by their hair across

176

the neck of his horse, forty sword hands tied to the spears, the four dead knights tied to their flagging mounts.

He sent boats to the twenty Eriu who had survived the second battle and who were now by the river again, to take them home.

For seven months or more, well into the winter, which was fortunately mild, Peredur strengthened the ramparts of the fortress, a tremendous task, filthy and exhausting, but one undertaken with great enthusiasm by the people who sheltered on the hill.

Such was Peredur's command and authority that only the sourness of the ale was ever complained about, a fault which he addressed at once by sending a raiding party across the wide river to the islands in the marshes, where apples and honey were produced in abundance.

He was a great man, this one, and in the presence of great men, magic is enhanced. As such I was able to move the heavy tree trunks used in the re-construction, and even aid the transport of new gates, heavy blocks of blue-stone that would eventually be hauled down and used as grave markers.

Peredur affected my magic more than any other man. I put wings on his shabby little horses, or so it must have seemed to his knights, since they were able to ride at the canter for half a day and the horses were as fresh at dusk as at dawn. In this way Peredur patrolled the land to the east as far as Camulodunum and north beyond the seven totems that marked the edge of Eboracum. This was a vast distance for any man to be recognised by name and to have the pattern on his sword known too.

Peredur was truly the offspring of the wolf.

Behind the new walls, the warlord built new houses, as if to say this is my final place; this place will endure.

He enlarged the forges and the bakeries and built new

grain stores. He described the house that he wished to construct for me where my tent was pitched, but I refused, tempting though it was. But as if he needed to demonstrate his gratitude, he surrounded the tent with a wicker fence – which made it hard to walk out by night, since he'd included only a single gate. But his need was stronger than my irritation, and Vivien and I inhabited a skin house on a birch frame, behind a wall of willow.

We had wanted to be left alone, but we became a place of homage. We were plagued with effigies in straw, with limbs in coarse clay or bread, with painted wood and feather charms. These things accumulated, slung and strung to the wicker, thrown into the tent, buried just around the edge. At night we would gather them in, but by the morning there were twenty more. Some had power, and these we acknowledged and responded to. Most were simple dreams, and we discarded them as quickly as we could, taking them by the sackful to the deep woods at the bottom of the hills. Vivien dug a shaft there, faster than I have ever seen – I found nothing ominous in this at the time – and plugged it with stone in such a way that we could open it at leisure to deposit more of these charms.

I imagine the shaft is there today, rank and sour with hopeless dreams.

If the scouring of that pit did not disturb me, Vivien's water magic did.

I had never shown her how to conjure water from the earth – this is a strong magic, and must be carefully applied – but she must have watched me from afar, or spied through the eyes of a bird. I caught her out when I saw her at the forge, bringing water in a bucket. I fled at once to the tent and felt the ground. It was damp. The filling cup was wet as well.

She had found out how to tap the source!

But what was she doing at the forge? I feared the worst, and devised charms against iron, bronze and tin. I was already protected, by my nature, against bone and wood, but in any case these substances were not easily controlled by fire, only subject to its heat.

Discreetly, I watched her. She was fussing at the bellows, shaking her head at the ironworker: not right; not that way, this way. Do it again. And again.

At length a small shape appeared from the coals. Vivien watched as the ironworker tempered it in the water from our well. Steam billowed and she saw me, smiling quickly, perhaps with embarrassment, or guilt. She reached into the bucket and brought the cooling object to me. It was not iron at all, but bronze, bright as the sun. It was in the shape of three leaves of the May tree, with four berries and a single thorn. I could not believe this exquisite work to be the handicraft of the man who worked the forge, but the talisman was so enchanting that I took it and turned it.

The thicket itself could not have produced as perfect a twig in such perfect detail.

'What is it for?' I asked Vivien. She laughed and kissed my cheek and chin.

'It's for you.'

'What does it do?'

'It shines,' she said, still amused.

'What does it give me?'

'Shining!'

'What does it take from me?'

'Nothing but darkness. A touch of darkness.'

'But I like darkness. I need it. I *walk* with dreams and darkness. I thought you knew that.'

'It doesn't touch the shadow. It's not a *taking* thing. It's a *shining* thing. Like you.'

'Why are you giving it to me?'

'Because I love you, idiot. Because we complement each other.'

'You spied on me to learn how to make the water rise.'

'Not at all. I thought about the water, and how it might rise by magic. I constructed the magic myself. I didn't spy on you. That would have been wrong. You either tell me, teach me, or leave me to my own devices. Don't be jealous.'

She punched my chest, hard! and walked past me back to the tent. The thorn was sharp – I was careful not to draw blood. The shining leaves felt soft, the bronze soft. When the sheen of the metal bloomed, when the leaves began to green, they would be powerful indeed.

I reciprocated the gift almost at once. We went away from the fortress and found a place of isolation, high on the hill, with a view, further to the south of Lyonesse and the ocean that was consuming it.

'I hate to see the world drowned,' she said one day.

'Why? What makes you sad?'

'When it drowns it dies.'

I knew, then, that for all her charm, all her skills, she was simply a chancer, that is to say, a dabbler, without true insight. She thought that as Lyonesse drowned, it was gone. She had no understanding that as it drowned here so it was surfacing, reshaped, regenerated in another place. She could not feel that *connection* through the hard places of the earth. She saw only the sea and the rock, and the battle that was fought between them.

By now she was intimate with my body, and I with hers. She could feel the patterned bones below my flesh, but had no understanding at all of their meaning. Truly, I felt my age, even though I was younger than her. The bone in her body cracked further, on occasion, and the skull in the beauty grinned at me as she tossed about me on the summer heath, wild hair flying. Sometimes I slowed time so that I could watch that raven hair flow dreamily against the white of cloud and the intense blue of sky.

The day came when she caught me at my tricks and broke the charm, leaning down to bite my lip, murmuring, 'Pay attention, you old trout! This is costing me!'

Her words were a shock to me. She leaned back against my knees, disappointed, rather frightened, trying to squeeze the unsqueezable.

'You've gone.'

'Not for ever. What do you mean – costing you?'

She glanced away, then pulled away, curling her body against my thighs, her dress drawn over her shoulder, her fingers and lips gently caressing the disappointing member.

'I'm not as strong as you,' she said. 'I want the pleasure, but I have to guard against the consequences. I want to give you pleasure too –' she phrased it precisely in this way '– but you don't seem bothered by the consequences. I'm using magic, when all I want to do is use my body. You seem uncaring.'

How deftly she had covered the slip. Did she really think I hadn't noticed those inadvertent, angry words?

This is costing me.

Of course it was! She was trying to work herself below my skin, to draw out my skills. Realising the slip, she had covered quickly with concerns about childbirth.

But it was a wonderful lie. And she was a wonderful lover.

For all my skills, I am as blind as any other man to the way that others see us. Vivien was ageing, aged, and because I was experienced with time she seemed as luscious to me, as we loved in various private groves in Albion, as the black-feathered swan-girl of the Northlands who had aroused me by the lake. But to those around us, she was older than me, a woman in her prime, and I was still a man in firm, wisp-bearded youth. Talented, yes, but still, by appearance, a son. Our liaison, the congress of which was often heard and seen, was not hailed with the same enthusiasm when otherwise the first sign of the White May was celebrated.

The time came, then, to leave this land, this chieftain, to follow further round the path, the long path. I mentioned it before. I was progressing south, and almost at the place on the loop of tracks and ridges that marked my own beginning.

There was an ocean to cross. Lyonesse was gone. Boats would be needed.

A greater difficulty was that I was loved by Peredur. He had, in that naïvete that comes with power, depended upon me because I was dependable. He was not threatened by betrayal, simply with withdrawal. It shook him deeply, but like the man of stone he was, he turned to stone for his thanks and his parting kiss.

'You can't leave! How will I move rocks without you?'

'Try ropes.'

'All very well to say that, but how will I test the ropes without you?'

'Stretch them between horses.'

'And the necks of horses? How can I possibly test the necks of horses without you?'

'Do what you do best. Ride them. Ride them till they drop. Some will never drop.'

He laughed. 'If I ever find such a horse I'll *marry* it. And when it dies I'll follow it to the cairn! You can't leave. How will I remember you?'

'On a stone, tall and grey. Nothing else. Not if you really care for me.'

'Don't insult me. I don't carve rock for pleasure! Far too much hard work. That's why I employ the likes of you,' he added with a mischievous smile. 'Where will I put this stone? *Should* I make it.'

'Somewhere where not even your horses can find it.'

'In the heart of the forest, then.'

'Yes. And near falling water. That's where my own heart will be.'

'I forbid you to go.'

'Have you ever tried to hold a shadow?'

'But our shadows are always on the road. It just takes sun and fire to see them.'

'Exactly. I was here before, I'll be here again. Endlessly.'

'But I shan't see you, shall I?'

'If you pass your eyes on wisely, who knows?'

How could I explain the endless, ageless circulation of time and the path?

How could I explain to him that I not only had generations of trail *ahead* of me, but unfinished business in past cycles that I would constantly – that is to say, every four generations or so – return to? His life was a function of birth, fighting, lovemaking and death. Mine was all of these things too, but without end, without end.

I simply kissed him. I promised him that I would remember him, and this is the end of this particular conversation, because I have done what I promised to do. I've remembered him.

Peredur was a great man, but that is all he was when it comes down to it. A man. And of importance. Like a stone broken into pieces he has become known to you in many forms, by many names.

It would dismay you to know what a simple man of strength and weakness, wisdom and humility, lies at the core of your romances.

Slow Ghosts

The long day, the longest he had ever lived, was almost ended, and Martin left his vigil at the lakeside – his long watch, across the water, over the graves of those he loved – to return through the forest to the ancient grove of trees which breathed with the life of an old enchanter, a broken stone, known by many names, but to Broceliande as Merlin –

As dusk grew close, the body in the cowl sat up, and without a word beckoned Martin to the fire. 'And so . . .'

With Vivien at the helm, the sail in my hands, we crossed by boat to the coast of Gaul, gaining the beach at Uxorum, north and west of here. I picked up the path to the south without much difficulty.

Within a few days we had reached Broceliande and Vivien became anxious. The forest was then as deep and entangled as it is now, and she felt herself cut off from some of her magic. Nevertheless, she hugged me close and followed in. She could tell, I imagine, that my own powers were closer to the surface, sustained by the wildwood. She imagined they would now be easier to draw out.

When we came to the waterfall we bathed in the deep pool, cleaned our clothes and built a shelter below the overhang. Vivien hunted in the deeper glades for a few hours, quite successfully as it turned out, and I found enough clay to make the vessels and pots in which to cook, consume and store our sparse supplies.

I had always liked this place, with its misting air, the strong, relentless fall of crystal, icy water, the crowding oaks. I had been here twice before, although no trace remained of those much earlier visits apart, perhaps, from a mark or two on stones, but the grey lichen was so thick it was hard to tell. Everything, otherwise, was the same, these sons-of-the-trees that had previously sheltered me being no less immense, no less embracing.

I was relaxed enough, secure enough in this place, to instruct Vivien in the essential nature of the magic that I carried. This is not to say I told her how to *work* that magic, but if she had talent (and I knew she did) then in due course – the passage of many generations – she could work it out for herself.

I quickly created a garden for her, a joyous place, full of song and wonder, fixed at its centre by proud ruins of hard-packed earth and heavy wood, in which she played and danced, delighted with the labyrinth of cold passages and high, rotting turrets. She was aware that I had drawn on memories of a city from antiquity, burned and sacked on the southern shore, a place of wonder that had long ago fallen to a siege by many hundreds of single-sailed ships. She was fascinated by the story.

'I want those ships!' she cried, standing in the ruins, green-daubed, slim and nude, feathered arms outstretched, eyes closed. 'Send them for me! Send them to fetch me. A sea full of ships, all for the love of me!'

And always, as she indulged in such fantasy, she ended with laughter and a wild dance in the wildwood.

Now I talked to her about the seven things that I could control, to a degree at least. All magic, you should understand, is developed from seven essential powers, call them talents. Different minds approach them in different ways, so there are no fixed rules. The first and oldest is the power of song, which is inborn in all of us, but only shaped by exceptional minds. You already know something about this talent, you've heard of its most dangerous usage. Song can create life and landscape. But there is a terrible price to pay. Vivien hungered for this knowledge, but I dazzled her away from it.

Secondly, there is the moving of stones by the power of the flow of hidden water. This did not interest Vivien at all. She could not see how such talent gives control over the shape of the land.

She was entranced, however by the third power, that of flying to and from the hinterlands of the Otherworld. It is impossible to enter the Otherworld completely, but the hinterlands are many, varied, and often quite accommodating.

The fourth power is connecting the parts of beasts, both hard and soft.

The fifth is an understanding of the human spirit as sustenance for mind and body. There are four guardians associated with this power, but they are too complex to describe, let alone explain.

Sixthly, the movement of awareness between the hard and soft forms of life; a dog to a stone, for example; a tree to a fawn. This is a very useful talent.

The greatest talent of all is this: to control, to contain and to employ the vision, hearing and dreams of children.

When a child is born it moves through the seasons at the same rate as everyone around it. But to the child, time is slow. Only in adulthood does the time *inside* catch up with time *outside*. To harness the time of children is to control time as much as it can ever be controlled. It is a form of *imaginative* time. If there are forces beyond our

186

understanding governing time, and I feel there must be, they are less in control when exercising their reach through a child.

Vivien, ageing steadily, slowly, still beautiful, still child-like, was using that very talent to stay as fresh, as keen, as quick as the lamb. She knew, however, that she must learn how to carve the knowledge of the child onto her bones if she was to step fully aside from time, and only I could supply her with that knowledge. Since I refused to give the knowledge to her she resorted to seduction, playing upon my need to rest, drawing out those shadows within me that are least circumspect, most guileless, despite their talents.

She addressed each shadow with a display, a vision, that enraptured me, enchanted me.

A song caused the water in the fall to pour in the opposite direction, exposing channels and passages in the rock from which odd, slow melodies cooed and wailed. This was a simple illusion – her talents were largely confined to illusion – but it suggested things to me that I had not thought of. In this way she entranced me. I have always been nervous of song, its power is deep, and yet is common; I have never been fully comfortable with the song in magic, but for a year or so after this illusion I played with melody, and harmony, and effected change upon nature. I came closer to the first song, although that is well guarded. It would take a greater mind than mine to go so far, so deep into the first songs.

She teased me and tickled me by bringing stones which cracked open, egg-like, to release lifeforms that are not bound by parents or offspring. Things that spring unbidden from the dark are fated only to amuse and die, since reproduction, as you or I would understand it, is not part of the life that exists within them.

She came to me in animal forms. She was especially exquisite as a vixen, dancing for me, leaping high to snatch bright birds in her crushing jaws. Somehow she could entwine herself with the language of animals – no illusion there! – and our conversations were fascinating. Animals have no greater sense of themselves, they run and live by certain stinks, by sight and by the deeper urges. But they have memory – although it is short lived – and with Vivien, as fox or fawn, as stoat or boar, I was able to hear those echoes of the animal mind, and gained a sense of how close they are to the Otherworlds. They occupy hinterlands that are denied to men. The animal realm is greater than instinct, but confusing. Vivien brought that confusion to vivid life, and for a while, through her illusions, through her visions of magic, I ran with creatures, *as* creatures, that until then had been denied to me.

She used charm to transform herself into the strangest, wildest, most alluring of creatures. She showed me, by illusion, how it would seem to live in fast time, then in slow time. She fashioned the earth into dolls and made them dance. I had seen nothing like this. It was pointless, in its way, but it was so amusing. I had taken magic seriously. I had long since forgotten how to *enjoy* the gift.

Eventually she took me home, a vision in the night of the remote past.

The man who danced wore the skin of a chamois around his shoulders and the broken horns upon his head. His face was painted and pierced with the features and feathers of an owl. The water-filled member of a horse, tied with leather about his hips, slapped at his legs like an obscene growth. His tail, stiff below the short cloak, was horse-hair. Clattering stones were tied around his ankles. His body was a swirl of painted blue and red as he danced before me by the water, half visible in the mist and spray, illuminated by a fire that cast his shadow on the trees. Sometimes he was upright, sometimes on all four legs, like the creature that possessed him.

His song was simple. He called to me to remember him from my birth in the deep caves, the animal caves. He called to me to paint again, as once before I had painted the smooth surfaces of the hidden stone, deep below the mountain. He called to me to dip my fingers in the cold, coloured pastes, to daub, to design, to reflect the life of creatures on the sensuous curves of the cold, moist rock, in the caverns, among the hands of my ancestors.

Vivien had seen my earliest memory! I was shocked, surprised; yet still entranced. She had drawn from me my first sights as a child, the Ghost Animal, come to greet me, and in so doing she had managed to go deep into my bones.

I think I knew then, as the sorcerer danced, as he had danced at my birth, I think then that I knew she would have me, she would kill me. She would tease me apart as a weaver teases apart the coarse wool fibres of a fleece.

To know that you are lost, yet to know that you have time to hide yourself, is a time of great pain. Around you, everything is normal, everything a joy. The anticipation of the moment of death is a voice that laughs from behind your head.

Vivien was laughing at me, even as she hunted for me, cooked the game, ate with gusto, ravished me with her body, and whispered in a way that meant: I need you.

She plotted the culling of my magic.

I planned its safe dissemination.

It was the final Vision of Magic that taught me the lesson I should have learned long before.

At the edge of Broceliande, in the west, is a wide clearing, ringed by twelve great oaks, tall trees on which have always been hung the trophies from the combats fought within its space. For as long as I can remember, warriors and champions have come to ring o'trees field to fight for honour, or for kings. Such a tournament was occurring there now.

Vivien came running through the forest. She had heard the squeal of horses and the rattle of wicker chariots. She came to fetch me and we returned to the forest's edge, coming to the clearing between the broad oaks, and standing back, behind the crouching forms of the defeated knights.

In the bright sun, seven chariots remained. They were circling the field, light wicker with small wheels, each pulled by two breathless horses, some grey, some black, one magnificent pair of whites. A charioteer in each, breech-clouted and grey-cloaked, spattered with blood, tugged and turned the restless team. The knight behind each of them was naked but for leather shoes and a sparkling torque around the neck. These grim-faced men, their hair spiked with white clay, their beards stiffened like quills, carried spears and small, curved swords. Each chariot had its shield, tall and thin, decorated with the clan totem, but these were not for protection. They were the trophy.

In the trees around hung battered shields, and broken spears. Two heads, still dripping, were slung in dishonour from one bough. The smell of the dead was upsetting the horses.

They attacked, each chariot facing left, picking its prey, then charging. It was chaos and terrifying, for they were all enemies, and there was no strategy, no sides taken. It was bloody mayhem.

A chariot turned over, and the shield was taken, a naked man limping from the field, crying with disappointment.

'I've seen this before,' I said to Vivien. 'Many times.'

'Watch,' she whispered, then ran a short way forward, glancing back with a mischievous smile, crouching low, staring out across the field.

The light suddenly changed, the sound of horses changed, the earth at the edge of the field began to shake with a different hoofbeat.

As the chariots withdrew to the edge of the field, to circle again, so, to my astonishment, they transformed. No chariots, now, nor small ponies, but horses of gigantic stature, draped in coloured cloth, their faces bright with metal. Armoured men rode them, turning and charging these huge stallions, tugging on leather reins that were draped with flags. Long, loose hair flowed around hard, beardless faces; metal rattled, and the swords that caught the daylight were long and straight. With much snorting from the steeds and screaming from the warriors, a savage attack occurred across the field, but this time in two armies, each of about eight. Metal balls, hideously spiked, clanged off long shields painted in bright colours, striking designs in gold, red and green.

When a man fell or was struck from the saddle he threw away his sword and stood quite still as his vanquisher plucked the shield from his horse or from his arms, then tossed it below the trees. Here, as in the time of the chariots, a boy scampered with the trophy into the branches to tie it, hanging it, triumphantly.

Where had these warriors come from? What transformation had occurred? Tall tents were pitched between the great oaks. Fires burned. Spears of great length, and plumed, iron helmets, hideously featured, were propped on poles.

As fast as the transformation had occurred it had gone, and once again the chariots rattled, small ponies whinnied.

Naked warriors, gleaming with sweat and blood, slashed, stabbed and struck in chaos.

Vivien was watching me hungrily.

And I realised with a moment of shock that I had opened my mind to her as easily as the minds of those knights whom I had surprised in the wilder woods of the north!

She had tricked me! She was breathless with the effort of her charm, but she was delighted too. Did she think I couldn't see what she had done? She asked me, 'What did you think of that?'

'How did you do it?'

'I saw it in a dream,' she said. 'I made the dream come back from then to now. It was to amuse you, nothing more. The next time you pass by this field, the next time you walk round the path, those horsemen will be here too.'

The long-to-come! She had touched the long-to-come. Not just the long-gone, then. Her fledgling power could reach through time in both directions.

But more importantly, she had crept into me through the gaping mouth of my mask. I had been as vulnerable in that moment of astonishing vision as was a charioteer to a stray blow intended for the knight he carried.

I was lost. Instinct told me that. When the Ghost Animal, my life-guide, had danced for me, stepping out of my first mind, stepping out of the long-gone, I had known I was lost. What needed to be saved was the magic I contained. Vivien must not have it.

I spent a season thinking. I defined Broceliande by my restless pacing. I hid the lake to stop her drawing power from it. It was a risky thing to do, because of course it drew attention to the fact that I was making changes.

I blamed age and confusion for the act: too many water

sources were interfering with my own vision, and quite soon, within a hundred years or so, I would have to start the next phase of my journey round the path.

Did she believe me? It's hard to tell. Her own mask was now firmly set. Have you ever looked into someone's eyes and seen not the loving heart but ice? Like the great ice that controls the land in the far north, that ice in the eye is a wall, a barrier, too cold to live beyond, too cold to cross, too slippery to even try to climb.

I had to get rid of my magic. I needed to hide it, to detach it from me. But I needed to hide it in such a way that I could gather it in later. The only answer was to turn it into shadow and send it on the path. I decided to send it south, travelling down the right side of the long trail, keeping its right side outermost to the ring. My intention was that I would then return north, retracing my journey – my life lived backwards – to meet the entities at some point along the way.

Vivien, I knew, would be looking for some escape to the north. She would be watching for me to turn in my tracks. She saw me as an animal, and knew the ways of clever beasts.

I knew that she would suspect the creation of shadows. I counted on her not expecting the creation of children.

It takes time and a great deal of concentration to fabricate even a single *infantasm*. I drew on the long-gone and that part of the long-to-come that I could reach. My difficulty was that Vivien's business, concerned mainly with providing for us, seeking the herbs, earths and waters that would enhance her own powers, did not take her away from the waterfall for very long. Even though I fashioned a Castle of enchanting visions for her, a place to explore, to stimulate her intellect, I was lucky if I had a full day to myself. I therefore chose my moments carefully.

I created seven children to carry my seven powers. I shall not concern you with the process of drawing the bones from the wood, the flesh from the wormy soil, the skin from leaves, the bloom from flowers, the blood from water, the bowels and other internals from killed animals – hares for the essence and spirit, of course, polecats for durability, boars for aggression, birds for most other things.

Finding flowers that were not illusion-born was the hardest task, since flowers are a rare presence in the season, whereas leaves only shrink from us in the time of Deep, or winter. But my time in the northern wastelands, where Jack Frost has been created to serve the needs of the reindeer people, had taught me how to control frost and ice to maintain the bloom of life, like those crushed insects in amber shards, which when released sing briefly yet exquisitely about a time in the long-gone that not even I can comprehend. To decipher those fleeting songs will take a greater power than mine.

Flowers could be kept vibrant as long as ice could be kept hard, and I found a way of keeping ice even in the sun. It was a simple trick, but Vivien did not know it.

And in this way I hid my magic.

Song went into the first of the *infantasms*, who was a boy from the beginning of the world, because song, as you know, came before words. He chattered from the bough of an old oak for the first few hours following his creation, but at last I drew him to my breast, and soothed him. He would have been about five years old. The flowers and leaves that formed his skin were hard to smooth down, but after a while they blended with the earth. He looked a little patchy; he was an odd mixture of colours. His fragrance was confusing, but then so is song. It comes from very deep. I sent him into the forest, protected by a simple charm. He would hide for a while, then walk south, and in due course, after many generations, we would meet on the path again, and I would take him back.

I decided to hide stone-moving in a girl, since I was certain that this would confuse Vivien, and in any case, the frustrating of people's expectations is something in which I delight. It is a simple form of control, but can be quite effective. I shaped the girl from the long-gone, from my memory of a place where the rock, below baking deserts, is vastly hollowed to make a labyrinth of tunnels, all designed to conceal the body of a king or queen. Vivien, of course, had touched upon this magic, when she'd made the shaft, but she had only scraped a single shard of knowledge and there was a great deal left for her to win. And so it continued.

Whenever I could, I summoned a child from the past or future, from different lands along the path, gave them body, gave them substance, gave them spirit, gave them charm, then carved my secrets on their bones. One after the other they went into the wood to hide, awaiting their chance to escape the forest and travel southwards on the path, that long walk through the valleys, along the shores of the sea, then through the mountains, the journey that would eventually re-unite them with me, their source.

Seven in all, shapechangers all, I sent them on their way, and soon there was a *hollowing* inside of me, a sublime yet painful vacancy, as much to do with the scouring of my magic as with the sense of vulnerability that now possessed me.

I had kept a few charms back, of course, and just as well.

Vivien, a vision of the huntress, soon after dragged a fawn into the clearing by the falls, her bloody knife held between her teeth. Quickly, she opened and emptied the creature, then dug shallow pits for the storage of excess meat before butchering the animal.

She was naked, she always hunted naked, and as she crouched to her work – inviting, vibrant flesh working on the sweet, dead haunch – my raven spread its wings.

'Aha!' she said, noticing my hungry stare, the flush on my skin. She grinned, putting down the knife, coming to me first to preen and then to pluck my feathers.

The mist was in her hair and on her skin as she flew above me, her voice loud, her grip strong as she hunted me to the finish.

Stretched out upon me, listening to the fall of water, she said, 'I enjoyed that. But I have to finish off the beast.'

'The beast *is* finished. Believe me!'

'The beast we'll eat!' she laughed. But at once I saw the shadow, the hint of understanding. She had sensed something wrong. She had touched the *hollowing* inside of me.

She was suddenly cold. 'I have to joint the kill. I shouldn't have taken it. It's too much for our needs. But what could I do? Old Provider should have created smaller deer. If I kill, I kill for a month. You can't simply kill a *tenth* of the beast!'

She was wrong about that, but I kept the knowledge to myself. 'I'm hungry.'

'So am I. Lie back and let the moisture cool you.' She stroked my languid flesh, relaxing me, then hardened her grip, staring carefully into my right eye as I squirmed with the sudden shock.

'There's something wrong.'

'There's nothing wrong.'

'Are you quite certain?'

'I'm quite certain that I'm tired. I'm quite certain that I'm hungry, that you're hurting me. What else do you feel is wrong?'

'You weren't as close. You didn't feel as close. But perhaps I'm being foolish.'

'I'll make up the fire, then.'

She looked down at me, still holding me in her hand as a cook would hold the heart of a slaughtered pig, looking closely, looking for signs of the worm.

'I don't know that I believe you,' she whispered.

She rose to her feet suddenly and jumped, legs tucked against her chest, into the icy waters of the pool below the fall. Seconds later she had scampered out, screaming with the cold, laughing, signifying her understanding that the action had been foolish, yet had been wonderful to her senses. She had banished her suspicions.

'Make that unholy fire! Quickly! *Quickly!*'

The children were all gone. It had taken several years, but the last had left the forest and they were alone, now, pursuing for a while their own lives, their own adventures.

I was vulnerable. I felt my age. I took to dreaming, which is to say, to flying, and became the haunter of battlefields, spying from above, or from the past at the strange ways into the Otherworlds. I was not recognised. I learned nothing I didn't know already.

Dreaming, I became weak. Weakened, Vivien saw her chance to take what she did not yet know was lost to her.

Quickly, quickly, then, she made her preparations.

*　　*　　*

I was in the sky, in cold but brilliant sun, aware that the first snows of this Deep were gathering to the east. Below me, five men had gathered by a lake and the lake waters swirled about the centre. Something was rising, either summoned by these men, or coming to attack them. They seemed quite nonchalant, crouching with their horses, and I circled lower, casting an inadvertent shadow.

I had been seen in that moment, and sling-shot was loosed to drive me off, but these travellers in the long-gone (yes, I liked to fly into the past as much as hunt the present) were less interested in a falcon than in the *hollowing* that was opening before them, the way through the water to a deeper place than the scrubby land around them.

Who they were is of no relevance; if you must know, they were five brothers, Kyrdu's sons; they were in many ways the scourge of the long-gone, they were adventurers, mercenaries, sorcerers by acquisition. Their stories – their adventure was immense – may have been remembered after them. Somehow, though, I doubt it. They went too far. If you're interested I can tell you another time.

What is important is that as I watched them, I felt my right wing crack, as if twisted by invisible fingers, and knew at once that my death had come.

I found the right winds and swooped, looped, glided and struggled back to Broceliande. I came above the falls and saw Vivien above my dreaming body. She was dressed in green, her black hair flying as she raised the axe and struggled with her task.

I dropped upon her, clawed and scrabbled in her hair until she backed away, allowing me to come back home.

It was too late, of course. Dismembered, spitted on her special thorn, I could do nothing as she danced her swirling dance, nine times round my corpse, throwing up the earth, holding it there, using the magic she had stolen from me, burrowing into the cold-earth home, then gathering stones and slices of fallen trees to make the traps.

She had not yet reached below my flesh to steal the magic; she was not yet aware that my bones were smooth again.

She danced through Broceliande. I could still hear, through my dislocated pain, the way she laughed.

'Fool!' she called me. She shouted it loudly.

She swam in the cold waters, climbed trees to their precarious tips, chased down game with her bare hands, tearing the swirling fabric of her green dress as she haunted the wildwood in her ecstasy.

Bloody, muddied and triumphant, she came back to where I lay.

'Fool,' she whispered tenderly, then kissed my dry lips, touching my eyes with raw-skinned fingers before, in the last act of her imprisonment of me, she put them out.

'What have you done? Where has it gone?'

The words, screeched like the scald-crow, were as sweet to my ears as song.

I had few charms left, but I had kept one back, a special gift.

I had been dreaming by the waterfall when she'd killed me, but my bed was a grey rock, and I shaped this, now, into the precise form of my broken, severed body. And on its mossy skin I carved the signs and runes of all the magic that I knew, but in a garbled form, sufficient to understand with the right wit, with time, with imagination, but certain to be incomprehensible to the lovely woman, the sinister woman, who had been a joy in my life – truly, the best of companions, the best of lovers; who can blame her for her more primal needs? – but a lovely woman who must now come to hell with me.

'Where has it gone? Where has it gone?' she shrieked.

I would have answered her, had I been able.

In her earlier moment of frenzied triumph, pursuing an older magic, she had devoured my tongue.

She threw me, head down, into the shaft she had fashioned in the manner of those shafts designed to conjoin with the Otherworld. She found – I have no idea from where – amulets and metal shards that would bind me to the earth; chalices and clay jugs that had once been buried with the dead; moonshards in silver, some in crystal, that would keep me forever in the shadow.

She let the earth fall back from its wildly spinning column, burying me. As it fell, she sealed the shaft at the four prime points with rounds of oak (she had learned *well*), then topped it with stones, topped these with the statue, whose nature and secrets had defeated her; and this she covered with earth, sprinkling the dirt with seed so that it would grow green.

Grow green and keep me down!

Then, in one moment, she put forth the charm
Of woven paces and of waving hands,
And in the hollow oak he lay as dead,
And lost to life and use and name and fame.

I wonder how long she embraced the statue, exploring its marks, working her fingers into every line and every shape and every crook and cranny of that broken stone, a lover sifting the cold ash of dead passion for some longed-for, warming ember?

The writing is tantalising because like a maze carved into the heart of a mountain it keeps on *almost* coming home, but never quite. And once she had engaged with those tantalising signs, once the first clues and hints of hidden power had embraced her fingers and her eyes, she was trapped, her spirit trapped, she was bound to me, tied by need, by greed, by a magic that was unfurling more slowly than the winter storm can level a snow-capped hill.

Each of us, then, was trapped by the other, and perhaps we both deserved the fate. If I had truly wished to keep the woman away from me, I could have done so. Lust, intrigue, the need to control her vibrancy, all these things perhaps had made me evil, and I can say this now because I have paid the price, and so has she. Eventually, because that bone was broken at her birth, her flesh succumbed to time. Her bones, still smooth, lie at the bottom of the pool, by the waterfall.

As for the broken man himself, murdered that cruel time in the long-gone, I began to dream again. It was all I had power to do.

The damage was too great. I had nothing left to do but wait.

Vivien, for the time she lived, was as tied to Broceliande as was I. My children, carrying my magic, rounded the path time and time again, passing through the forest. Vivien was aware of them, but not of what they meant.

Yet somehow, as they walked through this old place, close to the murderous shaft, they sent off shadows, little echoes, shaped by experience, memories of the murder, raised by the pain that still survives within this grove. I was helpless to stop this process by which slow ghosts began to walk the path, moving southwards in the wake of my seven children, my eternal children.

Each ghost was a restless creature, a fragment of magic, magical to the short-lived children of Broceliande, and you danced within them, age after age, and shadow magic was yours for a while, odd powers, small talents, a moment of

control, lost to each of you when the child in your heart
was lost.

The ghosts moved south, then east, then north and west,
following the path; echoes dogging the tracks of hidden
wisdom. And time and time again they passed this place,
my life in circles, never-ending circles.

Then crying 'I have made his glory mine,'
And shrieking out 'O fool!' the harlot leapt
Adown the forest, and the thicket closed behind her . . .
And the forest echo'd . . . 'fool.'

PART FOUR

The Spirit-Echo's Promise

When shall we meet again, sweetheart
When shall we meet again?
When the bright thorn leaves on broken trees
Are green and spring up again,
Are green and spring up again.

From *The Unquiet Grave*
(folksong, variant)

The Spirit-Echo's Promise

A heavy mist was rising in the glade; it began to obscure the leaning stone, the shaft, the cowled shape of Conrad, who was whispering in a voice that was becoming hoarse and faint.

Martin prodded the fire, placed wood on it, shivered with a sudden cold. He realised he was becoming drowsy, a striking, irresistible tiredness that he recalled from his last night with Rebecca.

Merlin was watching him darkly. 'If it isn't already clear to you, let me make it clear: I have very little of my old skill left. Having put my talents outside of me, in the children, it will take time to gather them in again.'

'Did you travel in Rebecca? The priest thinks you did. You've been escaping the grave-shaft for centuries, he said . . .'

'The prison has been weakening, certainly. I could tell. It occurs periodically when the second shadow I released along the path to deceive Vivien – the one that failed – passes through Broceliande. As it does so it draws me up, it draws her out, it gives us a brief fling at life, a fling at each other, it gives me an opportunity to taunt her . . .'

'Costing the lives of families!' Martin shouted angrily. 'Costing the lives of children . . . My family, my child!'

The hooded figure lowered its head. Martin fought against the weariness that was draining all strength from his limbs.

Merlin said, 'When we use a human body, it certainly dies. It becomes a spirit on the path itself –'

'Always looking back. Always frightened.'

'They are all frightened. My children too. I *made* them frightened. I made them cautious.'

He hesitated, thinking, then went on, 'Oddly, a spirit-echo of Vivien must have stayed in Rebecca after that incident in her youth which the woodsman witnessed; when she murdered your brother. Later, when she was carrying Daniel, the echo slipped through to the child, and Vivien had a second chance.

'But before Vivien was born again in the boy, I dreamed of Rebecca coming to the lakeside. I was as free as I would get, a shadow moving among shadows, not really free at all, but able to move away from the shaft. And Rebecca called to me, though of course, it wasn't Rebecca calling. It was the enticement of the Vision of Magic. Your son was inside her, but all I could sense was *Vivien*. I was on the path for a while, a brief freedom, a spirit-echo only, and Rebecca was a warm shell for that dreaming spirit, and I passed into her. It would only be for days . . .

'Once inside, realising the danger in her womb, I took away all of Vivien's senses, all the senses in the boy Rebecca carried. It seems Vivien was stronger than I'd guessed. From what you say, she won them back.'

'That was a cruel thing to do. The act against the boy.'

'So it transpires. As I said, I *was* in a dream.'

'So will I be soon. So I'll ask you again – before I fall asleep: bring them back to me. Please! Can you bring them back to me? Or has all of this been nothing more than an opportunity for you to excuse yourself through story?'

The face in the glamour-mask round Conrad twisted with indignation, but Merlin said, 'When I referred to damage, when you first brought me out of the shaft, I meant the damage to your family.'

'Christ! They can't be more damaged than they are!'

Merlin nodded kindly. 'In the way *you* think, I suppose that's true. But to bring them back risks bringing back the enchantress. And besides, the singing magic has gone. I told you this before. I am almost powerless. I can perform a few simple tricks. This body only seems alive because of glamour, and I'm quite sure that you don't want *that* for your wife and son.'

'No,' Martin said quietly, frightened by the thought.

'I can't help you. I can give you illusion. Of comfort perhaps. I don't think . . . I don't think I can do more. You seem very tired. Go to sleep. I shan't harm you.'

Martin struggled against the charm that was closing down his mind. He thrust his hand into the fire, the pain bringing brief life to his cry.

'No! I won't sleep! I *can't*.'

'You must.'

Merlin's grasp on his wrist was irresistible and his fingers were taken from the dying flames.

'Give me some hope, then. Just give me a little hope . . .'

'Hope?'

Martin stared hard into Merlin's eyes, and the corpse-grimace of Conrad showed for a moment. 'All I can give you is a vision. A small vision – of how it might end.'

'Anything.'

'Then go to sleep.'

Martin sank down into the cold mist by the guttering fire and half closed his eyes. As he began to dream, he was aware that Conrad had risen to his feet and was looking thoughtfully, almost curiously towards the lake.

*　　*　　*

An altar bell was ringing.

'Martin!' came the cry. (Again! . . . he had been half-aware of being called for some minutes.)

It was very cold. He sat up and stared around him, at the empty glade, the long-dead fire, the moisture on the grass, the scattered stones of the cairn, the trees. *Where was Rebecca?*

Again, the tinkling of the bell from the lake, and the priest's call. Martin looked at his hands, suddenly shocked to see the shallow scars, the still-sore cuts and patterns. As he stood inside clothes that were damp and rank, so he felt the pain of cuts from neck to groin. He looked quickly to the tree where the bones of Merlin lay. The yellow shards were scattered, fox-struck, batted and played with as the marrow was found to have long been sucked away. Of Conrad, of the corpse, there was no sign.

Something was wrong. *That damned bell!* And the priest sounded frightened as he called. And the silence . . .

And the beard on his face.

Martin touched the thick stubble. It was wet with dew, an abrasive beard, now, a week's growth perhaps.

Where was the waterfall?

He was hungry, his hands shaking. He called, 'Rebecca? Daniel?'

His trousers were saturated with his own urine. Around him, where he had been curled up, were the remains of bread, some rinds of cheese, the picked bones of a chicken, a china flagon that might have contained cider or water.

And the dream broke! Rebecca wasn't here – she'd never

been here — just a dream, just as Merlin had promised, but nothing more . . .

'Rebecca!' he cried aloud, then let his disappointment surface in tears, hugging his body, rocking where he sat as the anguish came through, and the brief touch with his family was taken away from him by the cold dawn, by cold reality.

When the despair had quietened, he left the grove of Merlin's tomb and followed the path to the lake. Father Gualzator saw him and stopped ringing the small, brass bell.

'I was worried about you,' the priest called from the canoe. The boat drifted sideways on the still water, just beyond the rushes. The man frowned, peering hard.

'Martin?'

'I saw her. I saw them both . . .'

'Who?'

'Rebecca. And Daniel.' The dream flowed through his mind again. He stared into the distance, remembering. 'I ran for so long, Father. It was such a wilderness — nothing but forest, and rivers. I ran across hills, I ran through caves, I felt the strength of a hound in my legs, I kept running. I was so lost, but I kept running — I could hear them, ahead of me, always just ahead of me. And then I found them, by a pool below a fall of water from the high rocks. They were crouching, drinking with cupped hands. For a while they didn't see me. I stood across the pool and watched them. Then I called to them and they seemed to hear me. I was very tired and I lay down by the pool and watched them. Rebecca lit a torch. It burned green. She waded through the pool towards me, apprehensive and curious as to who I might be. And then she said my name. The fire burned green and she leaned down to kiss me —

'She kissed me. And for a moment I was home. I had come home . . .'

* * *

'Martin!'

The priest's voice was harsh in the stillness of the new day. Martin looked at the man and frowned. 'Father . . . ?'

'Is that you, Martin?'

'Of course it's me.'

Father Gualzator seemed unsure, his face reflecting his confusion, his uncertainty. 'I've brought you what you asked for. Dressings for wounds, antiseptic, plasters, some more food.'

What I asked for?

'When did I ask for this?'

'Two days ago. You came to the church. Don't you remember?'

'No. I fell asleep by the grave shaft. I'm cut all over. Christ, I'm cut from head to foot . . .'

The stinging began to be unbearable and he tugged at his shirt, feeling it peel away from his skin, wincing as shallow but raw wounds opened. And as he collapsed through weakness and distress, the priest shouted distantly, 'By the Good God! What have you done to yourself?' and rowed through the rushes, to make the shore.

He bathed Martin's naked body with stinging antiseptic, then brewed a pot of coffee and insisted he eat the bread and coarse pâté he'd brought from the village.

'These are marks similar to those on the statue we excavated. You've mutilated yourself, copying the old man you say you saw.'

'When did I tell you about the old man?' Martin whispered. 'Christ! It hurts.'

'I should have brought fresh clothes. I'm sorry. You made me very nervous when you came from the forest. I haven't been thinking.'

'I don't remember . . .' Martin whispered. He tugged his jacket round his shoulders, pulled on the reeking trousers, the muddy shoes. 'Where's Conrad?'

'In his grave,' Father Gualzator said, grimly, pointedly. 'Where he belongs.'

'Rebecca? Daniel?'

'Back at the house. Where you brought them. You don't even remember that?'

Back at the house?

'Are they . . . oh God . . . Are they . . . ?'

'Are they what?' the priest prompted.

Martin grabbed at the man's jacket. 'How are they?'

Father Gualzator closed his eyes for a second, his head dropping as he realised Martin's misunderstanding.

'Drowned. They're drowned. You resurrected them and brought them back to the house. I'd assumed you wanted to see them properly to their cold-earth homes.'

'No!'

Shocked by the violence of the scream from the bleeding man, the priest stepped quickly back, stumbling and falling in the shallows among the rushes. As he picked himself up he was staring at Martin with a strange expression – part fear, part anger.

'I should have guessed! It's so obvious, now.'

'What is?'

'Who are you? Or do I even need to ask?'

'I don't understand.'

The priest laughed sourly. 'What have you done with Martin?'

'What do you mean by that? What do you *mean*, what have I done with Martin? Don't you recognise me? *I'm*

Martin. You fool! It's only a beard. Only some cuts. I haven't changed.'

'No!' Father Gualzator was defiant as he brushed water and mud from his jeans. 'I *don't* recognise you. And Martin wouldn't call me *fool*.'

Martin watched the older man, felt the cuts on his body sting as his muscular response to the priest's attack made the skin part painfully. *What had he just said?*

'I'm sorry, Father. I don't know where that came from. I'm very confused, that's all. I can't remember coming to the church, asking for bandages . . .'

'Of course you can!' Father Gualzator growled, smiling grimly. 'It doesn't matter. What are you going to do with him? Don't look so uncomprehending, you don't fool me for an instant. My eyes are too old! Are you going to kill Martin like you killed Daniel?'

'I don't remember coming to the church,' Martin said weakly. *What was happening?*

'*Martin* doesn't, I'm quite prepared to believe that. But *you* do. And you killed Daniel . . . If I'm not mistaken. Stop pretending! *I know who you are.*'

Merlin allowed a quick smile on Martin's face, then whispered, 'Go back,' and Martin, still confused, retreated to listen from within as the priest and the resurrected sorcerer confronted each other by the lake.

Merlin said, 'I stopped the enchantress. I had to. In the boy she would have had fresh life. She would have been very damaging. She had learned many things – mostly illusion, but certainly some things more than that – but for all she had learned, she never learned the suppression of desire, or need, or of the senses. She never learned control, and that frightens me now as much as it frightened me then. Which is why, I suppose – it's so long ago, now, I've had so much time to make my excuses – which is why I let her destroy me. It was the only way to destroy her.'

Father Gualzator formed mud into a ball, murmuring words from the *Bronzebell, Book and Nightfire*, drawing on the forest to make a weapon that might *hurt* this raw and resurrected spirit, stalking up the bank towards the stooped body of his friend, the hiding place of evil.

'And now it's Martin's turn. Is it?' he challenged. 'Another life taken. Another death. And I'm helpless, I know it.' He hefted the mud ball pointedly, he tried to show that he understood its small significance, its possible power, its restraining power. 'But I'll stop you if I can . . . believe me.'

'I do believe you,' Merlin said. 'And I don't believe you're as helpless as you claim.' He frowned at the lump of faith-blessed mud, then shook his head. 'Although I'm not quite sure I'm right about that. Then again, I'm not sure about very much at all. I'm too new to the world. What I *am* sure about is that Martin let me out. You were there to help him, I seem to remember, but I didn't want you around. Martin let me out, then asked for my help. I'm free in one way, of course, and relieved to be so. In another, I don't quite know what to do, where to go. I'm new to the world. I don't recognise it.'

'Let him go!'

'No. When Martin let me out, he asked for my help, and there was no fear in the request, no expectation of agreement, and no fear of retribution. I was surprised by that. I tried to warn him of the damage, the possible damage, but he seemed certain that it was a risk he would take, and who am I, who have I ever been, to argue against a man who is prepared to take a risk? What other function do I have? Why else was I born on the path? I can give you the small magic that can arm you against an unknown enemy. I don't *make* things happen, I can simply help in older, different ways.'

'Let him go!'

'Martin asked for my help, and he convinced me to help him. But I can't help him unless I travel in him. For a while at least.'

'And how long is "a while"?'

'In fact I'm nearly finished. I'll give him back to you quite soon. But if you want to help your friend, you should go to the church and watch him safely beyond the hill. And you should not interfere. He has a journey to make.'

'Where are you sending him?'

'To fetch back the singing magic . . .'

The priest shuffled uneasily by the lake, his gaze on the body of Martin, his ears attuned to the words, so civilised, so calculated, the words of a man dead two thousand years.

'The singing magic? Who stole it?'

'Nobody stole it. I let it go. An echo of it was captured by Rebecca. She used it once, she never lost it. If Martin can catch up with Rebecca he can find the singing magic, he can use the singing magic, he can do with it what he likes, and the consequences will all be his, because I'm still not sure what has happened to the enchantress. But he has a chance. It's a risk he must take.'

Puzzled, Father Gualzator looked back across the lake, back to the village, to the farm, beyond the excavated graves. To Merlin he said, 'Rebecca's body is in the farmhouse. Daniel's too.'

'But only the bodies, only the flesh and bones. Martin saw them on the path. The essential part of them still lives, still walks the circle. He only has to catch them. He has to dance inside them. He tried it once, a few days ago. But he wasn't looking. You know how important it is to *look*.

They passed right through him! He missed the chance.'

'How long, then? How long will it take for Martin to find the singing magic?'

'Six months, six years, six thousand years . . . It depends on how you look at it. He'll catch up with them eventually, and they'll come back to Broceliande, and life will go on for them.'

For a moment Father Gualzator was silent, his white, lined face showing grief, a desperate sense of loss. When he spoke, his words were scarcely audible. 'But I'll not necessarily see them. No-one here, no-one who loves them, none of us may see them again.'

And Merlin laughed. He was thinking of the long-gone, of the warlord Peredur, a brave man, a shining man, who had expressed the same wish that all things he could imagine should happen in the short, futile span of a single human life.

'That depends how well you pass on your eyes. With such Old Eyes as yours, Father, with such *long* sight – you should know that very well.'

'I suppose I do,' the priest said, all resistance going. 'I suppose I always have.'

Merlin came down the bank and took the ball of mud from Father Gualzator's hands. Without comment, without rebuke, without expression, he tossed the simple weapon out across the lake, then took the priest's muddy hands in his, embracing them with his fingers.

'Then why are you fighting me?'

'I don't know. Because I'm frightened . . .'

'Frightened of what?'

'The way you play with people – with their lives. And deaths.'

'Better to play with them than let them limp through

215

time, warm home to cold home, birth to grave, no twists on the path. Don't you agree?'

Father Gualzator twisted away from the other man. 'No! How can I? It goes against everything that the church believes in —'

'And the hill?'

'The hill too. The path is not straight, but it goes forward. It was never meant for us to play tricks with the path.'

'How do you know?'

The priest was shivering as he stared from the water's edge at Martin, his friend, at Merlin, enchanting him.

'I don't, of course.'

'Of course you don't. You've forgotten how to play with toys. A toy is lifeless, but you give it life — you make it do things it could never do on its own.'

'Our lives aren't toys!'

Merlin laughed. 'Of course they are! And like toys, you can keep them to look at, or you can twist them and torment them, and give them the *illusion* of life. But one thing's for sure, Father. All toys wear out no matter how well you look after them. *Dance* them while you can. It's the only thing to do with toys. *Surely* you agree.'

Suddenly weary, Father Gualzator looked away across the lake.

'Yes . . . somewhere inside of me . . . I suppose I do. I do agree.'

Merlin laughed quietly. 'Then I'll say goodbye. And I'll let Martin go in pursuit of his Vision of Magic. And as for you, Father. Hurry home. There's a storm coming from the west.'

'A storm?' The priest looked up, looked round. 'Are you sure? The winds seem quite still.'

'Ah,' Merlin said with quiet humour, 'but you don't

know the wildwoods of Broceliande as well as I do.'

'No. I suppose I don't.'

'Go home. Go back to the hill. There's nothing more, now, nothing that you can do that will make a difference. Go home.'

Other Tales

Earth and Stone

The sunshine is a glorious birth;
But yet I know, where'er I go,
That there hath passed away a glory from the earth.

Wordsworth, *Intimations of Immortality*

Carrying loudly across the rolling grasslands the *crack* of transmission was almost indistinguishable from that *crack* which follows the splitting of the great boulders, the megaliths of the tomb-builders who had lived in this land for seven hundred years.

The man, riding on a stocky, black horse, appeared as if out of nowhere. He was well wrapped in skins and fur leggings, and wore his hair in tight, shoulder-length plaits. His beard and moustaches were curled and stiff with some reddish paste. His saddlebags were anachronistic in this third millennium before Christ, but were at least fashioned crudely out of leather; their geometrical bulkiness was unavoidable since the equipment they contained was essential for the man's ultimate return to his own age. Like the horse, the leather bags and what they contained would be destroyed as soon as they had served their purpose. Of that there was no doubt in the man's mind at all; but his conviction was for the wrong reason. He had no intention of ever returning to his own time. He was going to remain here, among the people of the Boyne valley with whom he had become so involved – in an academic sense – during the short span of his life.

His name was John Farrel. He was nearly thirty years old and in this time of earth and stone he expected to be able to live another ten years.

As he came through the transmission field he turned his horse and peered into the blur that was the future. It started to fade and the last air of another time leaked five thousand years into its past, bringing with it a sour smell – the smell of machines, of artificial scent, of synthetic clothes; the odour, the stench, of successful adaptation.

Cold winds, the winter's last voice before the sudden warmth of spring, carried the smell of the future away, dispersed it across a land wider than Farrel had ever known. Machine, perfume, plastic, drained into the earth, were sucked down and away, lost from the grassy crispness of this age of rock and blood.

Farrel rode up the small hillock that lay immediately in front of the transmission field, turned again as he reached the summit, and peered down into the valley. The river Boyne wound across the landscape, a silver thread meandering eccentrically between the low hills until it passed out of view. Farrel's mind's eye felt, for a moment, the lack of the sprawl of red brick dwellings that would one day supersede those ragged forestlands of the wider curve. For a moment he thought he saw a car flashing along a main road: sunlight on speeding chrome. The illusion was just the gleam of fragmentary sunlight on the spread wings of a gull, riding the winds above the river, back to the sea.

Where the transmission field was slowly dissolving, the river was a blur, the land a green haze that came more and more into focus. Wind caught Farrel's hair, cooled the sweat on his cheeks and made him blink. The grass beneath him seemed to whisper; the wind itself talked in an incoherent murmur. It droned, distantly. Grey clouds swept across the pale sun and shadows fled across the valley, were chased away by brightness. The transmission field finally faded and was gone.

For a moment, then, Farrel imagined he saw a woman's face, round and ageing; blonde hair perfectly styled, but eye-shadow blurred and smeared with tears and bitter, bitter anger. *Why you? Why you? Why you?*

Her remembered words were only the gusting winds and the animal sounds of his horse, restless and anxious to be given free rein across this wild land.

How loud the silence after hysteria, he thought. He had not known how haunting another's heartbreak could be. *You'll never come back! Don't lie to me, you'll never come back. I know you too well, John. This is your way out, your means of escape. My God, you must really hate me. You must really hate us all!*

Last words, lost in the roar of street traffic. The stairs had trembled beneath him. The outer door had slammed, an explosion finishing them forever.

I'm here now. I'm here. I got away from them, from all of them, and they think – most of them think – that I'm going back when my job is done. But I'm not! I'm not going back! I'm here and I got away from everything, and I'm not going back!

The ghosts of the future faded, then, following the transmission field forward across the centuries. The land about Farrel came sharply into focus. His mind cleared. He breathed deeply, and though for a second he felt the urge to cry, he stifled that urge and looked around him, staring at the unadulterated landscape.

Small mounds were scattered in clusters down the hillside and concentrated along the river itself (thus being nearer to the river goddess, or so Burton had implied in his last transmission). The oldest tumulus was possibly no more than two hundred years of age. The youngest? Farrel searched among them: four hundred yards away there was a mound, perhaps twice his height, perhaps fifty feet in diameter. It had a kerb of grey stones which separated the dull greenness of the hillside from the dark earth mound, not yet fully covered with its own field of grass. A grave, perhaps no more than half a year old; new, with the cremated remains inside it still heavy with the smell of burning.

He felt dizzy with excitement as he associated this new tomb with the low grassy bump that it would become during the next five thousand years, a tomb so crumbled and weathered that only the discovery of its fractured kerbstones would identify it. A handful of carbon fragments, preserved in a natural cist between two of the chamber stones and identified as human remains, would raise a thousand questions in the minds of those who were fascinated by this enigmatic neolithic culture. And a year ago those splinters of charred bone might have been alive, walking this very countryside.

A flight of starlings wheeled above his head, spiralling at the mercy of the winds. A lone magpie darted among them until the starlings turned on it, and then the bigger bird dropped away down the hill to vanish against the sheen of the river. The shrill bird song was a brief symphony of panic and Farrel reined his horse around so that he could look towards the distant forest and the rolling downs of what would one day be his home county.

From behind a low, rain- and wind-smoothed boulder, a boy was watching him.

I have arrived in early spring, and as far as I can determine, seven months later than anticipated rather than five months early. I don't blame Burton for not being here to meet me. He must have rapidly become tired of hanging about, especially with something 'fantastic' in the offing. Whatever was about to happen that so excited him, there is no sign, now, of either him or the Tuthanach themselves. Correction: a single Tuthanach . . . a boy. This is the strange boy that Burton mentioned in his last transmission, and he is the only human life I have seen in these first few hours, apart from some invisible activity (in the form of smoke) from the direction of the hill of Tara. The boy was not overly curious about the horse, and has shown no interest in its disappearance. He ate some of its meat today and never commented on what must surely have been an unusual flavour. I'm very grateful to everyone who made me bring the horse, by the way. I'd never have caught any of the wild life, and I had to travel a good two miles to find a satisfactory hiding place. The village – I suppose I should say *crog Tutha* – is deserted and shows distinct signs of weathering. I confess that I am somewhat puzzled. The burial mound of Coffey's site K, by the way, is very new, something that Burton failed to report. I had a frightening thought earlier: could Burton be buried there? There is no sign yet of tombs on sites L or B, but there are so many others that are not detectable at all by the twenty-first century that I don't know where to begin. Burton hinted as much, didn't he? I wonder why he didn't go into specifics? The tumulus at site J is already well weathered, which suggests our dating was a little out –

say by four hundred years? And as Burton reported, the site of the giant Newgrange mound is still barren. I actually came out of the transmission field on the very spot the great tumulus will occupy. I didn't realize it for quite a while, and then it made me feel very strange. Further details will follow in my second transmission. For the moment, since my fingers are aching: signing off.

For the first two nights Farrel and the boy slept in the spacious shelter afforded by a deep rock overhang and the entwined branches and roots of several stubby elms that surrounded the cave. By the third day Farrel's interest in the unexpectedly deserted crog began to outweigh his reluctance to actually camp in the decaying village. He remained uneasy. What if the Tuthanach returned during the night and took exception to a stranger setting himself down in their tents? Burton's report had not indicated that this particular Boyne people was in any way warlike or violent, but this period of the neolithic was a time of great movement, populations succeeding populations, and axe and spearhead used for drastic and final ends. The megalithic tomb-builders of Brittany, especially, were familiar with this part of the Irish coast. In their massive coracles they hugged the south coast of England until the confused currents around Land's End swept them round the Scillies and up into the warm flow of the Irish Sea. From there they up-oared and the shallow seas carried them automatically to the Irish coast north of Dublin, along just those picturesque beaches that had seen the original settlers putting into shore, seven or eight hundred years before.

In one of his transmissions, Burton had given a single, brief account of a small 'rock-stealing' party that had raided a crog further south, near Fourknocks (crog-

Ceinarc). The raiders had killed and been killed, not by the Ceinarc, but by wolves.

Wolves were what Farrel feared most. In his own time wolf packs were quite timid and easily scared. In this age, however, their behaviour was altogether different – they were fierce, persistent and deadly. Better, he thought, to believe in the non-hostility of the Tuthanach than risk the teeth of such wolf packs. Provided he kept clear of the rocks and stones in the territory of crog-Tutha, and in no way 'stole' them by carving his own soul spirit upon them, he imagined he would be safe.

He explained his plan to the boy, whose name was Ennik-tig-en'cruig (Tig-never touch woman-never touch earth). The boy put a hand to his testicles and inclined his head to the right. Uncertainty? Yes, Farrel realized – a shrug, but a shrug overlain with anxiety.

'Would this Tig's people kill us if they returned?' he asked, hoping he had said what he meant to say . . . (Man-woman this Tig and this Farrel on the wind – tomorrow, more tomorrow man-woman close to this Tig this Farrel?)

Tig darted to the entrance of the overhang, peered out across the windy downs, looked up to where the branches of the elms waved and weaved across the drifting clouds. He spat violently upwards, came back to Farrel grinning.

'Death (– wind –) has no room for this Tig. If this Farrel stranger will be my friend (– lover? – earth-turner? –) death will spit at this Farrel too.'

'Did death make room for that Burton?'

Tig sat upright and stared deeply into Farrel's eyes. For two days the boy had declined any knowledge of Burton, pretending (obviously pretending) not to understand. Now Farrel pushed his advantage home.

'Does this Tig want this Farrel stranger as a friend? Then

this Tig must tell this Farrel where that Burton lives or dies.'

Tig curled up into a ball, burying his head beneath his arms. He wailed loudly. Farrel was about to ask again when Tig spoke:

'That man-stranger Burton is touching earth. All Tuthanach are touching earth. Not this Tig. Not this Tig. Not this Tig.'

Farrel considered this carefully, not wishing to distress Tig to the point where the boy would leave. He knew that 'touching earth' was something immensely important to the Tuthanach, and he knew that Tig was forbidden his birthright of touching. He could not touch women, he could not touch earth. No love, no involvement with the land. No children for Tig, and no spring harvest as the result of his love for the earth. Poor Tig, denied the two most wonderful consummations of this early agricultural age. But why?

'Where does that Burton touch earth?' he asked.

The boy looked blank.

'Where?' pressed Farrel.

Tig again crawled to the cave entrance and spat into the wind. 'This Tig is just a beast!' he yelled. 'That man-stranger Burton said this Tig is just a beast!'

And with a loud and painful shriek he vanished, running across the downs, a small skin-clad figure, clay-dyed hair sticking stiffly outwards, fat-greased body shimmering in the weak sunlight.

THIRD TRANSMISSION — FIFTH DAY

Still no sign of the boy who ran off three days ago when I questioned him about Burton. I suspect Burton upset

228

him in some way, possibly as simply as calling him names. Burton is 'touching earth' apparently, but I have a suspicion that he is dead and touching it from a few feet under. I hope I'm wrong. But Tig – the boy – has said that *all* his people are touching earth. What can it mean? I see few of the expected signs of agriculture in the area. My hunch is that they are either farming at some distance from the crog, or raiding other neolithic settlements. Time will tell. I confess that I am worried, however. There is no sign of any equipment or any message or record discs of Burton's. I shall continue to search for such things and also for Burton, whether or not he is alive.

I am now encamped in the crog itself. A pack of dogs terrorizes me, but they are sufficiently diffident at times that I suspect they belong to the village. They have one useful function – they help keep the wolves at bay. I have seen wolves prowling through the cemetery, near the river. They seem to scent something and occasionally excavate a shallow trench in the earth, but always they leave in apparent panic. They also prowl around the skin wall of the crog, but the bones and shrivelled carcasses of their own kind that hang suspended from tree limbs have some effect of discouraging their entry. The dogs chase them off which concludes the process, but they always return. I am not myself safe from the obviously starving mongrels that are sometimes my guardians. If only Tig were here, he might be able to control them.

My H.Q. is the largest hut, possibly the headman's house. The inner walls are daubed with eccentric symbols that are identical to the rock carvings in and around the many tumuli. These paintings are absent from other huts, and I may well be in the local shaman's hide-out.

I keep saying 'hut'. I should say tents. The material is

deer skin, sewn together with leather thongs. No evidence of weaving, though mats, door edges and lightholes through the tents have been made out of leather threads interlinked in suspiciously familiar ways. Wigwam style, four or five shaped wooden poles hold the tent upright. Each tent has a fence of carved bone points standing around it, and in the centre of the crog is a group of four low tents, skin stretched over bowed wooden frames making four rooms not high enough to stand in. These have been separated from the rest of the community by a deep ditch. Carved boulders, showing circle patterns, stand both sides of a single earth bridge across the ditch. Is it a sacred enclosure? An empty grain store? I don't know. I've explored the tents thoroughly and there is nothing in them save for a few polished stone beads, some maul-shaped pendants, spirally carved, and a skin cloth containing five amphibolite pestle-hammers, unused I think. Maybe you can work it out. (Ironic, isn't it . . . I'd normally jump to all sorts of conclusions!)

Imagination is the worst enemy still – I'd thought that particular frustration would have stayed behind when I left the future. Ah well. Incidentally – the ditch is probably that small enclosure between the trees at strip-site 20. We're in that sort of area, as I said in my second transmission. Other features along that strip are not in evidence, and may well not be neolithic. I am fairly convinced that this is the Newgrange settlement. There are no other communities in the area, and this one settlement will probably be responsible for all three major tumuli, even though several miles separate them. There's nothing but small burials on the Newgrange site as yet. I wonder when building will begin?

Artifacts? Thousands of drilled stones, pendants; axe and arrow heads; several bows, very short, very limited range; slings, leather of course – two tents used for pottery and some marvellous Carrowkeel pots all lined up ready for firing in small clay and stone kilns. Most of the weapons and stones are clustered inside the skin wall – ready for action? The skin wall itself is two layers of hide, suspended from wooden poles. Human heads have been sewn between the two layers and the outer skins have been drilled with holes so that the dead eyes look out. Although some of the heads are fairly recently severed (both sexes) I can't see Burton's. Hope still flickers.

Head hunting seems to have started even earlier than the pre-Celts, unless these are sacrifices. But no carvings of heads, so perhaps it's just a small part of the culture at the moment.

God, where *are* they all?

It's a marvellous spring. I've never seen so many birds in my life, and the insects!

At dawn of the day following his third transmission, sudden activity among the already noisy lark population of the deserted tents on the western side of the crog brought Farrel running. He recognized the darting grey shape as Tig and called to him. The boy furtively crept out from his hiding place and stared at Farrel, lips slack, eyes dull.

'Glad to see you,' called the man. Tig smiled and slapped his hands together.

'This Tig hungry.'

'This Farrel hungry too. Can this Tig use a sling?' He waved a leather sling he had been practising with. The boy rushed forward, lips wet, eyes wide, snatched the weapon and lovingly caressed the leather. He stared up at Farrel.

'Lark or hare?'

'Which is the tastiest?'

Tig grinned, slapped his stomach, then dropped to his knees and kissed the soil. Jumping to his feet again he ran off out of sight behind the wall of skins, and ultimately out of earshot down a tree-capped slope. He returned after half an hour, blood on his knees, dirt on his face, but carrying two fat white-chested hares. Farrel started a fire in the small outside hearth that seemed to serve as a fire-pit to all the tents in the vicinity. As the wood fire crackled and browned the pungent flesh, Tig threw tiny chips of stone onto the embers. Retrieving one of the fragments Farrel saw it had been scratched with zigzag lines. The patterning, which he recognized as a standard rock-carving of the Boyne Valley area suggested flame and Tig confirmed this. We take fire from the earth, he explained, so we must make the earth complete again with a small soul-carving.

'But this Farrel didn't carve this. Nor did this Tig. Is that the way it is done?'

Tig immediately became worried. He crawled away from the fire and sat distantly, staring at the smoke. Farrel drew out his mock bone knife, scratched a zigzagging line on the same piece of stone, and cast it onto the flames. Tig grinned and came back to the pit.

'This Tig can't carve. This Tig can't touch earth, or carve soul. But this Farrel is a good soul-carver.' He pointed up into the air and Farrel noticed the smoke rising straight up since the wind had suddenly dropped. He didn't understand the significance, but soon forgot to question it as the meat cooked through. The fats sizzled loudly as they fell on the flame and rich odours brought both man and boy crowding to the tiny spit, eyes aglow with anticipation.

*   *   *

'Ee-Tig, cranno argak ee-eikBurton en-en na-ig?' *You knew Burton?* (This Tig eye-felt wind-felt that Burton man-stranger?)

Tig spat a small bone onto the dying fire. He eyed Farrel suspiciously for a moment, then rose up on his haunches and passed wind noisily. He seemed to find the offensive action very funny. Farrel laughed too, rose up and repeated the action. Tig opened his mouth wide and shrieked with laughter. Farrel repeated his question and Tig spat onto the fire. The saliva hissed and steamed and Tig laughed. Farrel asked for the third time.

'Kok.' *Yes.*

'Ee-eikBurton 'g-cruig tarn baag?' *Is Burton dead and buried?* (That Burton eats earth, skin cold?)

Tig hesitated. Then his hand touched his genitals, his head inclined. He didn't know, but he was uneasy.

'Ee-eikBurton pa-cruig pronok dag?' *Is he alive?* (That Burton kisses earth, urine warm?)

Tig said he didn't know.

'Ee-Tig ganaag ee-Farrel olo ee-eikBurton ee-Farrel ka'en ka-en?' *Are you afraid of me because you think I was Burton's friend?* (This Tig afraid of this Farrel because that Burton this Farrel were not not-strangers?)

'Kok.'

'Ee-Farrel cranno orgak ee-eikBurton. Ee-Farrel en-Burton. 'n nik Farrel.' *I knew him but I didn't like him. I have a woman.* (This Farrel eye-felt wind-felt that Burton. This Farrel not touch/never touch that Burton. This Farrel close/touch woman Farrel.)

What would she think, he wondered, of being used as a sex object to a twelve-year-old moron? Joke. How many thousands of years would it be for the joke to be appreciated? To the Tuthanach, to all the Boyne peoples, denial of friendship to a man had to be coupled with a declaration of friendship with a woman. It seemed so unrealistically simple to believe that a man with a woman whose sexual appetite was high would not have a close male friend . . . (*nik*, woman, implied a sexually aggressive woman; a woman or man without any such desires was called *crumkii* – stone legs.) It was a bizarre piece of nonsense and yet it appeased. Like the beast that presents its hindquarters to an attacker – submission. The name of the game.

Tig was much happier. He clapped his hands together repeatedly, pausing only to chew a ragged nail on his left index finger.

'Ee-Tig en-Burton. Ee-eikBurton en-Tig. Ee-Tig tarn ee-eikBurton baag na-yit.' *I didn't like Burton either, and he didn't like me. But I killed him some time ago.* (This Tig never touch that Burton. That Burton never touch this Tig. This Tig skin Burton cold several yesterday.)

'A-Tig tarn ee-eikBurton baag?' *You killed him?*

'Ee-Tig . . .' eyes downcast, voice lowering. 'Ka-kok.' *I hope so/I wish to do so/I think so.* Which was it? Farrel felt infuriated with himself. What *had* Tig said?

'Orga-mak ee-eikBurton m'rog?' *Where is Burton's body?* (In all the wind Burton's head?)

'Ee-Tig-ee-Farrel Tig cranno na'yok.' *I'll show you now.* (This Tig this Farrel Tig eye feel high sun.)

FOURTH TRANSMISSION – SIXTH DAY

The simplicity of the language is deceptive, I'm sure. I talk easily with Tig, but have an uncomfortable feeling that he is misunderstanding me in subtle ways. Nevertheless one thing seems sure – Burton is in trouble, and possibly dead, killed at the hands of the backward boy who is now so important to me (while he is in the crog the dogs don't come near). Everyone who should be here is 'touching earth'. You might dispense with that as something unimportant – tilling the ground somewhere? Planting seeds? Nothing of the sort.

Tig led the way across the hills, some miles from the river. The forest is patchy across the downs, never really managing to take a dominant hold on the land – trees in great dense clusters hang to the tops of some hills and the valleys of others so that as one walks across the country there appear to be bald knolls poking through the foliage on all sides. Tig himself is inordinately afraid of the woods and skirts them with such deliberation that I feel some dark memory must be lying within his poor, backward skull.

After about an hour we waded across a small stream and ran swiftly (Tig covering his head with his hands and wailing all the time) through a thinly populated woodland, emerging on the rising slope of one such bald hill that I had seen earlier. Boulders probed through the soil which was perhaps not deep enough to support the tree life. There were shallow carvings on many of the boulders and Tig touched some of these reverently. Most noticeable about this hill, and most puzzling – and indeed, most alarming – was the profusion of small earth mounds, overgrown with a sparse layer of grass and invisible from any substantial distance. Tig ran among these mounds, the highest of which was no more than four or five inches from the ground and vaguely cross-shaped, and eventually found a resting position on one of the least carved boulders. His stiffly crouched figure seemed overwhelmed by fear and regret, his hair sticking out from his head like some bizarre thorn growth, his thin limbs smeared with dirt and crusted with his own faeces. He stared at me with an expression of total confusion and I tried to put him at his ease but he turned half away from me and began to vocalize an imitation of the lark song that echoed around us from the vast early spring population.

I asked him about Burton and he merely clapped his hands together and shrilled all the louder.

You will have the picture – I appeared to be standing in a wide and irregularly laid-out cemetery. Crouching over the nearest mound I excavated a little of the earth away. A few inches below the surface my fingernails raked flesh and came away bloody!

I can't explain it but I panicked completely. Some terrible dread crept into my whole body, some inexplicable fear of what I was witnessing. I left Tig sitting there singing with the larks and starlings and ran back to the crog. I shook for hours and failed to sleep that night. The blood beneath my nails clotted and blackened and when I tried to wash it away it wouldn't come. In my frantic efforts to clean the stain I tore one of my nails right back to the quick and that sudden, appalling pain brought me back to my senses. I can't explain it. My reaction was panic. Something external possessed me for an instant and I was psychologically unready for the power of it. There is something in the ground of that hill, and I don't just mean a body.

I shall return tomorrow and report again.

Farrel left the crog at dawn. The grass was wet underfoot, and across the valley a heavy mist hung silent and sombre. The birds seemed quieter today and what song he heard was often drowned by the murmur of the trees and the disturbing crying of the wind.

Strange, he thought, how mist seems to tangle itself in the forest, hanging in the branches like cotton.

He made his way back towards the strange cemetery on the hill, stopping occasionally to listen to the stillness, hoping to hear Tig crashing towards him, or calling him. When he emerged onto the hillside the mist had lifted and he could see, from the top of the knoll, the river Boyne and the scattered tumuli of the Tuthanach. He could see the hills where, in the next few years, work would begin on the massive sheer-fronted mounds of Newgrange. Who or what, he wondered, would be honoured by that vast structure? And who or what would be honoured by the second and third giant tumuli, built to the east and west of Newgrange at almost the same time (and not centuries earlier as the dating techniques of Farrel's time had suggested).

Of Tig there was no sign. The larks began to sing quite suddenly and sunlight pierced the early morning clouds, setting the forest alive with light and colour. As if – reflected Farrel – some force of night and cold had suddenly gone. Normal service being resumed . . .

Where he had dug in the soil of one of the human burial places yesterday, there was now no sign of interference. The earth was smooth and quite firmly packed. Tig, probably, had repaired the damage.

Farrel wasted no time in excavating down to the flesh again. He felt a cold unease as he cleared the soil from the naked back of the Tuthanach male, that same surge of panic, but today he controlled it. He scooped the earth out of the narrow trench until the man's body lay exposed from head to buttocks. Face down in the mud the man looked dead; his skin was cold and pale grey, the pallor of death. His arms were outstretched on either side and Farrel, on impulse, dug the soil away from one limb to discover the fingers, clenched firm into the earth as if gripping.

Turning the man's head over Farrel felt a jolt of disgust, a fleeting nausea. Open mouthed, open eyed, the earth was everywhere. It fell from the pale lips, a huge bolus of soil, dry, wormy. It fell from his nostrils and from his ears – it packed across his eyeballs, under the lids, like some obscene blindness.

Surely the man was dead; but the flesh was firm – cold, yet not in that rigidity associated with recent death, nor the moving liquefaction associated with decay. Easing the body down again Farrel put his ear to the naked back, listened for the heart.

For a long time he heard nothing. Minutes passed and he felt sure the heart was dead. Then . . .

A single powerful beat. Unmistakable!

Over the course of half an hour Farrel ascertained that the buried man's heart was beating once every four minutes, a powerful, unnaturally sustained contraction, as if the organ were forcing round some viscous fluid and not the easy liquid blood it was used to . . .

An unnerving thought occurred to Farrel and for a second he was ready to cut a vein in the man's hand – but, quite irrationally, fear of what he would find dripping from the body held him back until he recollected the blood under his fingernails and felt a strange relief.

He stood above the body, staring down at the un-dead corpse, then let his gaze wander across the countryside. The spring breeze irritated his scalp by catching the clay-stiffened strands of his hair and bending them at its will. As he stood on the knoll he grew irritated with his make-up and wished he could be clothed in denim shorts and a loose cotton shirt instead of being wrapped in skin that smelled of its previous owner and attracted flies.

Everything, bar this cemetery, was so normal.

The tumuli, the crog, the weapons and pottery, the hunting, the language – it was all just what he had expected, a new stone age colony, conscious of religion, of its ancestry, its future and its agriculture, a colony just a few generations into its life in this green and bountiful land. Further north and south were other communities. Farrel had seen the signs of them, and had read reports about them from previous expeditions to this time. Some were larger than the Tuthanach, some already showing different cultural styles. They all seemed to mix and mingle together (so Tig said) to exchange ideas, to form joint hunting trips during the winter, to compare art forms and techniques of etching them into the rock. They were basically agricultural and peaceful. They feared the Moaning Ones from the earth, and the rock stealers from across the sea, some miles to the east. But for the most part they lived without fear, growing and maturing, becoming ready to accept the new Age of Bronze, still some eight hundred years in their future, at a time when the peacefulness of this country would be shattered by the new sounds of metal clashing with metal.

All those settlements had mixed together and had welcomed Burton – so he had reported – during his first four days in the valley. He had not told them from where he came (his arrival site, like Farrel's) for if the Ceinarc and the Tagda were passively afraid of the Moaning Ones and the Breton raiders, they held a healthy and active hostility for one other thing – crog-Tutha, and the insane settlers from beyond the forest. They would not float their coracles through the wide bend of the Boyne that took them round the foot of the Tuthanach hills, with their scattered mounds and shrieking women. It was a fearsome area, and one where no man could go and return unpossessed.

Reading the reports five thousand years away, Farrel had at first thought this to be a typical piece of forest-fearing, with the settlement on the wrong side of that forest being linked to those same dark forces. He had dismissed them aloud.

Now he realized he shouldn't have dismissed them at all.

There was something wholly unnatural about the people of crog-Tutha. He had travelled more than five thousand years through time and expected surprises – but he had not anticipated being so totally mystified. This was not the simple life of a primitive people – it was something out of the dark corners of the supernatural!

No one up-time would believe him, he was sure of that.

FIFTH TRANSMISSION – SEVENTH DAY (EXTRACT)

. . . and as I filled the grave back in, Tig appeared at the edge of the wood. He ran up the hill and crouched over the mound, watching fascinated as I covered the body of the Tuthanach. I get the feeling that Tig, when he vanishes, is never far away. I always have an acutely uncomfortable feeling of being watched, and I suspect that wherever I go Tig is never far behind. What do I represent to him, I wonder? He is afraid of me still, and still refuses to show me where Burton is buried (if indeed he *is* buried). There are too many mounds on the knoll to excavate them all on an off-chance, so I really do need the boy to open up a little more.

I sat for an hour or so, on a boulder, looking across the forest to where the great crog on Tara was in evidence as a winding spiral of black smoke. The encampment there, Tig tells me, is surrounded by a wooden post-fence and seems to be more hostile than the other crogs. He says they are raising earthworks behind the wooden walls; does that suggest the first dun is being raised on the site? Fascinating. I have no idea how Tig knows this. Tara lies four days to the south. Would he wander that far?

While I watched Tara Tig sat quietly, chewing moodily on the remnants of one of those hares. I didn't ask him about Burton, or about anything. I hoped he would tell me of his own accord. His eyes suddenly grew wide and the bone dropped from his fingers. He was looking up at the knoll and I turned to see what had scared him. It gave me quite a turn too, and I don't blame Tig for scampering off.

One of the graves was moving, as if the body it contained was trying to force its way out. As if . . . ? First the man's hands poked through the ground, the fingers bloody and dirty. Then the earth fell away from where his head was raising up and his whole body followed. He stood upright, black with dirt, and earth fell from his ears and mouth. He spat violently and shook more vigorously, brushing soil from his chest and arms. I hid behind the boulder and watched as the strange apparition turned slowly round, looking upwards into the sky through eyes still caked with dirt. He was sexually aroused and the skin of his penis was lacerated and dripping blood profusely. I have the uncomfortable feeling that he had been copulating with the earth.

Several minutes of brushing and shaking exposed his skin again, cleared his eyes and nostrils and he seemed to get his bearings. He swept back his hair, which showed yellow through the mud, and ran off down the knoll, leaping the mounds and entering the woodlands with loud shrieks and painful crashes.

I followed him to a small stream, a tributary of the

Boyne, and watched him crouching in the flow, washing and splashing, and emptying his bowels of a phenomenal amount of soil. He warbled bird song and laughed in abrupt, almost humourless bursts. He seemed to wash himself for hours, but finally crawled up onto the bank and sat quietly for a while, obviously sensing and enjoying the scenery around him. Then he rose to his feet, waded the stream, and vanished towards the crog.

That all occurred a few minutes ago and it means I shall not return there myself. I'm too puzzled and too frightened if you must know. I have my transmission equipment with me, but medication and field-link pack are still in the crog, which means I'm trapped here for a while, and must be careful not to injure myself.

When Farrel arrived back at the knoll Tig was crouched over one of the mounds, the only one to show a good grassy overlay, and poking at it. He saw Farrel approaching and ran away, leapt onto a boulder and slapped his hands together.

Farrel stared at him for a moment, then at the grave, and an icy unease crept into his mind. Oh no, he thought. Oh God, this is the moment.

The boy gibbered something incoherent.

Farrel asked, 'Ee-eikBurton 'n cruig pad-cruig?' *Is Burton buried here?* . . . (Touching earth, feet on earth?)

'Don't know.'

Farrel sensed the lie. He dropped to his knees and scrabbled at the soil and after a moment he found himself staring at black hair, the back of Burton's head. 'Thank God,' cried Farrel, and grinned at the boy.

What should he do though? It might be dangerous to move the man – the best thing would be to leave Burton alone until the strange process had finished and he resurrected himself in the 'natural' way.

But Farrel found he could not resist examining his colleague in the same way as he had examined the Tuthanach earlier. He scraped back the earth from Burton's head and shoulders.

A funny smell.

For a moment his hands hesitated; he stared silently and motionlessly at the body beneath him. The skin was grey, cold – that was, by all accounts, normal. But there was something wrong, something indefinable, something not quite right.

He reached down and turned Burton's head sideways. Earth poured from empty sockets, worms fell from the gaping, toothy mouth. Where skin remained it was taut and shrunken. Putrefaction rose from the rotting brains through the holes in the skull, driving Farrel to his feet with a terrible cry.

Sweeping back the earth from the torso he found the thigh bone fragment that had been driven into Burton's heart as he lay there, thrusting through the rib cage from behind, ripping skin and flesh and cracking bone. The clenched fists of his colleague took on a new significance. He had died in agony.

For a moment Farrel screamed abuse at Tig for what he had done, then his anger drained away. There was something in the boy's eyes, something in his expression . . . Farrel felt instantly terrified. He reached out towards Tig and shook his head.

'I'm sorry, Tig. Burton called you a beast . . . I understand . . .'

'Not once. Many times,' said Tig. 'I hated Burton. I gave Burton everything he had earned.'

Tentatively Farrel touched the boy's shoulder and when

243

Tig did not flinch he secured the grip and smiled. 'Burton was not my friend . . . but he was known to me and he was important to me. I was upset to see him dead. Forgive me, Tig. I didn't mean what I said.'

'I didn't understand what you said.'

Farrel, guiltily, realized he had shouted in English. He laughed quietly, almost thankfully. He wouldn't have wanted the boy to hear what he had called him. He needed sleep too much and the boy was potentially very lethal.

He walked back to Burton's body and covered it over. A few feet away another mound began to move and Farrel and Tig ran out of sight and watched.

SIXTH TRANSMISSION – EIGHTH DAY

Burton is dead. Tig killed him, perhaps some months ago. I am terrified of Tig now and don't dare question him further about Burton. If only I knew where Burton's equipment was hidden. Tig knows, I'm sure of it. He has hidden it. I pray that in the same way that he indicated Burton's grave to me (uncompromisingly) he will lead me to Burton's records. Burton understood what I have been watching, he must have done – he participated.

Meanwhile I am back in the cave and Tig, now, is in full control. I sleep fitfully and in snatches – terrified of him striking when my defences are down. I woke, last night, to find him crouching over me, peering at my sleeping face. I dare not ask him to refrain from startling me like this. My head hurts and my heart is in pain, as if in anticipation of a long-bone shaft being driven through it.

I can't get my field-link equipment. The crog is active again. Over the last day many Tuthanach have risen

244

from the earth and returned to their homes – men, women, children, they return with bountiful energy and begin to lead a life no different from the Ceinarc or the Tagda – what *were* they doing in the earth? What have they gained? What was the purpose of it all?

SEVENTH TRANSMISSION – TENTH DAY

The trickle of Tuthanach returning to their crog has ceased. They are all home. I remain in the cave, uncertain, insecure. Tig hunts on my behalf, but no longer eats with me. He has become very affectionate, but behind the kindness is a repressed anger that I truly fear. Sometimes he stands in the cave entrance and shrieks with laughter. The garble of words he yells refers to Burton and to me, and I hear 'stone legs' and 'twisting head', two favourite Tuthanach insults. He invariably ends his tirade of abuse by defecating in the cave mouth and elaborately holding his nose and backing away. And a few hours later he brings me a hare or a brace of fat doves, some gift, some appeasement for his show of fury. A bizarre boy and not – I now realize – backward at all, but in some way insane. Listen to me! Do I understand the meaning of my own words any more? What do I mean – *insane*? Is my behaviour sane? Tig is more than just a boy. I suspect he was chosen for his role – Tig-never-touch-woman-never-touch-earth; the only Tuthanach not to touch earth in the strange way I have described . . . why? Why Tig? Or should I ask, why *one Tuthanach*? What was he watching for? What are they asking of him now? What role does he fill?

Tig seems aware of some finality in his role. On his most recent visit he came with a large chunk of meat –

deer, I think. Tears filled his eyes as he passed the joint to me and accepted a small portion back. We ate in silence. As he chewed he watched me, and tears flooded down his cheeks. 'Farrel, my friend, my dear friend,' he said, over and over. The warmth was immense. The Tuthanach have no way of expressing magnificent friendship and he struggled to voice his feelings and I eventually had to stop him. I had understood. 'Farrel and Tig are the only ones not to touch earth,' he said. 'Tig can't, but Farrel . . .'

Time and time again he began that sentence, staring at me. Each time he said it I was filled with his intensity, and with my own anxiety. The thought is terrifying, truly terrifying.

Then the anger from the boy, the shrieking. He raced out into the dusk and vanished swiftly. I face another night alone, more than half afraid to close my eyes . . . not just Tig, though that is certainly a part of it, but the past . . . my past. I am haunted by memories and faces; they fill my dreams, and I can sense my own time in everything I smell or see here. It is insecurity that makes me rue the warmth of civilization, and I shall not bend to any great desire to return; but it hurts, sometimes. Sometimes it really hurts.

Three days after the seventh transmission two Tuthanach males came to the cave and crouched in its entrance watching Farrel. They were both middle-aged, dark-haired, and their skin was decorated with green and blue dye: circles around their eyes, lines across their cheeks, elaborate patterns on their breasts and bellies. They looked angry. Farrel remained quite still, trying to hide his fear.

Then Tig came slipping into the cave, boisterous and

noisy as ever. Farrel tried to piece together something from the boy's excited gabble, but all he could make out were words for 'woman' and the insult 'stone legs'.

A tension grew in the pit of Farrel's stomach and wild thoughts filled his mind. What was Tig up to?

The next thing he knew he was being chased from the cave by the two men. Tig grinned at him, and winked elaborately. 'Soul curers,' he said, pointing to them. 'Make soul good for this Farrel. Make this Farrel's soul ready for earth.' And he patted his loins.

Farrel felt terrified.

They took him to the crog and led him inside the skin wall, past the fire pit and to a smaller circle of skins around which were grouped several women and children. He was led to a small tent and pushed to the ground. Making no attempt to speak to him, nor demonstrating any puzzlement over him, the men left. After a while one of the younger women got up and walked across to him.

By that time, realizing that his sexual need was far more intense than he had admitted to himself for the last few days, Farrel was lost in thoughts of his past.

He saw the Tuthanach woman through a blur of remembered faces, saturated bodies and irritatingly noisy beds. He smelled her through an imagined veil of perfumes, cigarette smoke and the salty and erotic smell of sweat. He felt pain as he remembered these things, a real pain, unlocalized. The woman had crouched before him, her wool skirt drawn up above her knees so that she displayed her white and grossly fat thighs to Farrel's casual gaze. He tried not to think too hard about what he saw.

Then she extended her hand and cocked her head to one side, smiling broadly, letting him see that only two of her teeth were missing.

Farrel took her hand, pressed the cool, firm fingers and

noticed how the woman's palm was sweating like his. The past surged into his mind; agony:

A girl he had known for years as a friend. He had been taking his leave of her small, two-roomed apartment, conscious that his wife would start to worry soon. With his usual calculated shyness he had reached out and shaken her hand again, playing at being nervous. 'I don't like all this hand shaking,' she had said, in a way that made him realize that she had wanted to say it on previous occasions. 'I'd much rather have a cuddle.' So he'd cuddled her, and she hadn't let him draw away. She was tall and lean and felt awkward against his stocky, muscular body. But it had been a long moment, and a good one.

He realized he was excited and the Tuthanach woman was pleased. Her breath was sour as she leaned across him, her left hand gripping him gently between the legs; she kissed each cheek and then the tip of his nose. Then she rose and tugged him to his feet, pulled him into the tent and slipped off her clothes.

She picked up a stone chip, artificially smoothed by all appearances, and made marks on it with a piece of flint. Farrel watched her as he undressed. Her breasts were full and plump at the ends, flat and sac-like where they grew from her body. He hated that. She smelled of animal grease and smoke (as did he) and of something else, something pungent and sexual and offensive. Spitting on the stone she grinned at Farrel and passed it to him, indicating that he should do the same. As he spat he saw the crude phallus she'd drawn on the rock. With her thumb she rubbed the spittle into the sandstone, and laughed as she lay back on the skin-covered floor. She patted her belly with the fragment. She still said nothing.

As Farrel climbed onto her recumbent body and tried to

find her he noticed that she popped the stone into her mouth and swallowed it.

They made love for about ten minutes. At the end of it she was obviously disappointed, and Farrel for no reason that he could identify felt like crying.

EIGHTH TRANSMISSION — FIFTEENTH DAY

It has begun. Newgrange, I mean — the building has begun. Yesterday I crept around the crog and went to the hills overlooking the Boyne, where the cemetery is located. There was much activity down by the river, men and women gathering water-rolled granite boulders for the facing of the mound; they carry these, one per person, in a great chain up the hillside and the piles grow large. Earth is being excavated from several sites ready for the tumulus. Several small tombs on the site have been demolished for the earth and rock they can offer. The past no longer matters. Only the great tumulus seems to concern them now. The first massive orthostats have been dragged to the site, and an artist is working on what can only be the small lintel that will lie above the passage entrance. The work, especially the art, will take many months. The air is filled with the sharp sounds of repeated picking blows as symbols and designs are carved on the dressed rocks, ready for incorporation into the tomb. The speed with which they work is fantastic, but the job they face is enormous. Who will be buried here? Who will be honoured?

I walked closer to the activity, managing to remain undetected behind some trees, and watched the artists at work. Imagine my surprise when I discovered Tig directing the symbol-carving operations! Some thirty men, all old, all frail, were crouched beside or above their slabs and each worked on specifications laid down by the darting, probing, shouting form of the boy.

I watched fascinated for a while, until the sun, beating bright and hot upon my naked back, drove me away to a shadier place. Tig must have caught sight of me because, as I crept down the hill towards the slopes rising to the unbuilt mound of Knowth, he came racing after me, calling my name.

'It will be a huge mound,' he said, breathing heavily. 'A great temple.'

'A temple to who, Tig?'

But he just laughed and slapped his hands together. 'They have all forgotten the symbols of the earth, and the wind, and fire and water,' he babbled happily. 'This is why I was left behind, to remember, to teach them . . .' He was obviously delighted about it. 'Soon this Tig shall no longer be Tig-never-touch-woman.'

'Will this Tig touch earth?' I asked him.

He fell moody, but brightened suddenly and grinned. 'This Tig never touch earth always . . . but this Farrel . . . this Farrel will touch earth soon . . . this Farrel will understand and learn the symbols.'

'This Tig might kill me,' I said carefully. 'Like he killed that Burton.'

He slapped his genitals repeatedly, not hard, but apparently quite painfully for he winced visibly. 'If this Tig kills this Farrel may legs turn to stone.'

And at that moment . . . I felt the compulsion, the fascination to discover, the intrigue, filling me like some uncontrollable ecstasy, like a psychological magnet pulling me down towards the earth. Tig danced happily about . . . had he seen my possession? He ran off, then, shouting back over his shoulder, 'This Farrel knows where to go.'

I am torn between desire to know, and fear of knowing. I keep seeing Burton's rotted corpse, lying there, denied that same knowledge by a thin shaft of bone and a vengeful child. But I also remember the pull of the earth, the feel of magic and glory, the glimpse (for glimpse is what it was) of some great power lying beneath the grass . . .

I will have to make my choice soon.

Farrel knew where to go all right. He thought about the knoll and its now empty burden of graves, and as the night wore on and a heavy rain began to drum across the countryside, sending icy rivulets across the uneven rock floor of his cave, so the knoll, dark and invisible in the night, seemed to beckon to him. Tig writhed before him, a boy at the mercy, the whim, of forces dying, but still far greater than any that man had ever conceived of, either now or in Farrel's own time, far in the future. And yet, perhaps that was wrong – perhaps the people of this time *had* conceived of the sons and daughters of the earth who somehow, inexplicably, were directing the destiny of the Tuthanach. Perhaps it was only with time and greater self awareness that man came to forget the spirits and guardians of all that he surveyed, the rock and stones, the trees and winds, the earth, the vast earth; mother . . .

She called to him and Farrel responded with fear. They had been with him for some time, directing his thoughts, but their touch was tenuous, uneasy. Farrel drew back into his cave and covered his head, blocked his ears and eyes and tried not to see or hear or feel what was coming to him: he tried not to think of it, but he could not empty his mind of their presence.

He screamed, confused and terrified by the strangeness of the contact. Dark-eyed, shivering with cold and terror, he cowered in his cave until morning, and dawnlight, and peace again.

He ran across the storm-threatened land, pacing heavily on the saturated turf, waiting for the next cloudburst. Tig scampered towards him and he felt a great sense of relief.

The boy saw his fear and laughed, jumped high in the air, then clapped his hands together in glee.

'What does it mean?' cried Farrel.

Tig-never-touch-woman-never-touch-earth dropped to his haunches and plunged his fingers between the tightly knotted grass mat.

'This Farrel is being prepared to touch earth,' he said. 'Don't be afraid.'

'But this Farrel *is* afraid. This Farrel is terrified!'

'There is no need to be,' said Tig, suddenly less childish. He watched Farrel through bright, deep brown eyes. Grease and paint were smeared about his cheeks and chin, a meaningless mosaic of colour and half formed design. The wind blew suddenly strong and Tig shivered. He rose to his feet and glanced up, rapping his thin arms around his naked torso. Farrel too hunched up and followed the boy's gaze into the heavens, where dark clouds and lancing sunlight played confusing chase games across the valley.

'What is going to happen to this Farrel?' asked the man.

Tig smiled, almost patronizingly. 'Wonderful things.'

'What is underneath the grass? What is hidden there?'

'This Farrel will soon know. Fear is unnecessary. This Farrel will lose nothing he has not already lost.'

Farrel stared at him, feeling suddenly old, suddenly alien.

'What has this Farrel lost?'

Tig grinned. 'His past, his people, his dreams, his strange images. This Tig never understood them, never understood the words. This has always been between us. When this Farrel has touched the earth they will be gone. We will build the temple together: we will build our dreams and our people together.'

'It sounds magnificent,' said Farrel. 'But this Farrel is still afraid.'

Tig laughed again. 'Afraid of the earth?' He scuffed the ground with his bare feet. 'Afraid of clouds? Afraid of sun?'

'Afraid of . . .' He stopped, unsure. 'This Farrel doesn't know what of.'

Tig slapped his hands together, shook his head. 'This Farrel should go back to the cave. Wait there. When you are called, go to them. Go to them.'

Unquestioningly, resigned to his bizarre fate, Farrel turned and walked back to the overhang.

By dusk it was raining again.

She called to him and again Farrel responded. He was still afraid, but Tig's words, his reassuring attitude, helped him overwhelm that fear and put it from his mind.

He walked through the driving rain, the clay in his hair running into his eyes and mouth, giving him a foretaste of the great oral consummation to come. He swallowed the clay, tasted its texture, wept as he ran through the rain, through the moaning woods. Behind him, high on a hill, torch light burned beneath a skin shelter where an artist worked on stone late into the night, anxious to express the earth symbols that he had relearned from the one boy who had not forgotten. He was an artist who added his soul to the rock and the rock to the temple . . . a temple to the earth gods, Woman in the Hill, Dying Father Thunder, those who inhabited the boulders and the wind, the clouds, and the running mud, the grassy turf of uncountable acres of virgin earth.

Through the night and the rain Farrel ran, until he found himself, without thinking, on the knoll that rose above the woods, the great source of earth energy that he had tapped so briefly, so frighteningly, several days before. And here he lay down on the ground, in the trench left by one of the Tuthanach, and stretched out his arms –

Gripped the mother's flesh –

Penetrated the mother's fertile womb, ejaculated with the ecstasy of contact –

Ate her breast, drank the cold and grainy milk of her glands, felt it flood into his body, through the apertures of his prostrate corpse, driving the substances of his canals before it, replacing his warmth with its own loving cold. Earth closed over his back, the rain filtering through ran down his skin, drained deep into the tissues of the soil below. His lungs filled with mud – he breathed deeply and after a moment his heart stopped, his breathing stopped . . . suspended, touching the earth.

Almost immediately they were there, rising out of the deep rock, flowing through the earth and the pores of the soil, entering Farrel's body through the tips of finger and penis, down the earth bridge that extended along the convolutions of his gut. He was consumed by them, consumed them for his own part, welcomed them and heard their dying greeting, the words that had flowed through the minds of the Tuthanach during the weeks previous . . .

I am earth, Farrel, I am the earth, I am of earth, the earth is within me and without me, I am soil and rock, diamond and jade, ruby and clay, mica and quartz, I am the litter of the dead who live in crystalline echo in the sediments of sea and lake, I am ground, I am woman who suckles the infant flesh of man and beast, I am womb and anus, mouth and nose and ear of the great world lover, I am cave and tunnel, bridge and haven, I am the sand that sucks, the field that flourishes, I am root and clay, I am life pre-carnate, I am dirt, who has been called Nooma and Shaan, and is Tutha and Cein, and will be Ga-Tum-Dug and Nisaba, I will be Geshtin and Tammuz and my branches will be earth against the sky and all will be one, I will be Faunus and I will be Consus, I will be Pellervoinen and Tapio, I will be Luonnotar who floats on white water and touches the wind, I will be Asia and Asia-Bussu, Lug and Jesus, I will be coal and ore and I have existed since a time of desolation and of thunder and of sterility – you, Farrel, who know all these things should know also that this is the moment of our great dying, the breath of wind passing out of the body of earth and into the memory of man . . .

A second voice: I am wind, who has been called Godsinger by the Kalokki who were the first men, and is called Tag and Feng-po, and Huaillapenyi, I am breath and life, I am death, the rising odour of decay, I am storm and rage, light and dark, I am thunder and fear, I am the changing seasons of time, I am the urger of seas and the calmer of wings, I will be remembered as Taranis and Wotan, Thor and Zephyrus and Ga-oh and Hino and my thunder shall be heard until the final fire, but you, Farrel, who know all these things should know also that this is the moment of our great sorrow, where we abandon our domain and enter the minds of men, for only in the minds of man can we continue to survive . . .

And others, then, crowding in, jostling to be heard: I am fire who is Tinedia, who will be Svarogich and Sun and Steropes . . . I am water who is Uisceg . . . I am sky . . . I am serpent . . . All these Farrel heard and consumed, and then they fell away, back into the rock, up into the wind, leaving just a fragment of each god, a morsel of each great being, settling in his crowded mind.

He rose from the earth, shaking his body and feeling the dirt and clay fall from his limbs and his mouth and his eyes. The day was cold; he was conscious of rain, of heavy cloud, of a dullness about the saturated countryside: he loved this. Some greater or lesser part of him was aware that a full two seasons must have passed while he lay in his intimate embrace with the earth. From this same greater or lesser part of him came an alien thought, a last tearful cry from his dead future: *truly a great and noble glory will have gone by my time of glass and steel*.

The new born child turned to regard the virgin land. Rain beat against him, washed him. He opened his mouth to drink it and his laughter joined the gentle sounds of the natural world.

I've found life, at last, at last . . .

The great gods were still there, he thought, as he blinked rain away and stared at the greenness all around him. They were dying, now, committing their great suicide, surviving only in the Tuthanach and their children, and their grandchildren, and so on until they were spread everywhere . . . this they were doing as a gesture of acquiescence to man, but just by staring through the rain, through the unspoiled distance, the man called Farrel could see those gods, could feel them and smell them and hear them.

As he ran down the knoll he could sense them, too, in the brightness of his mind. They were with him by inheritance when he came here, and now they had come direct and he was ecstatic at the greater awareness they had brought him of so many things . . . over the centuries their presence would dilute and become weak and perhaps they had not reckoned on that.

There was plenty of time for them to explore him and understand how things would be. As far as Farrel was concerned there were more important things to do than worry over a day and an age when he would be dust and ashes.

He was a part of the earth, now, a man of the earth, a Tuthanach. His people were building a temple to the earth, and he knew how magnificent that temple would be, for he had seen it. He would mark the rocks of the temple with his soul, raise the walls of the temple with his sweat, and fill the temple with his ecstasy. He ran faster across the rain-soaked land until he could hear the sounds of the stone being carved.

The earth went with him.

The Silvering

It was nine o'clock and the croft was in darkness. Selka was late and Peterson was impatient for her, his anticipation subliming into frustration. He rose from his chair and peered moodily through the small window. The image of the moon was distorted by the coarse glass. The waves, breaking on the shore, were flashes of restless white. He could hear the murmuring rush of the sea, an unbroken sound.

Nothing, yet, was struggling ashore.

He went out into the night, glad of the clear air, the salt-sharp wind. He prowled the sea's edge, kicking through driftwood and weed, staring through the band of silver light on the dark water, below the waning moon. She would follow that light, he knew, swimming from the deep towards the rolling skin of her world.

Back in the croft he cut the cheese and chewed quietly, standing by the window, shivering. Selka liked the croft to be cold. She was uncomfortable in the warmth of a fire.

Peterson was hungry, and he served himself a plate of the cold fish stew that he had prepared for the woman, a concoction of conger eel, crab and codling heads, razor shells, mussels, cockles and periwinkles. There was weed in there too, the softened strands of bladderwrack, and the hearts of anemones, their stings drawn. To help his own taste there was garlic and wine, and a pinch of sea herbs which grew wild on the high ground of the island. He drank some of the wine and became heady. He started to jump nervously at movement and moonshadow in the croft, and took to flashing his torch at the low ceiling, at the rusting metal panels and the dark rugs, nets and harnessings that hung on the cold stone walls.

The sea surged. The monotonous crash and hiss of the breakers was interrupted by the unmistakable sound of a beaching. He heard the driftwood disturbed and the eerie cry of Selka as she rolled on to the land. He smiled, relaxed, and poured two glasses of the chilled Macon. Five minutes later Selka screamed, three short, intense cries of pain, and Peterson blocked his ears. But the shedding of her seal-skin was successful, for a few minutes later she was darkly framed in the low doorway, wet with blood and sea, naked and trembling. She was carrying nothing, no fragment of the wrecked plane, and Peterson was disappointed.

The selkie hesitated, looking quickly round the small room. She seemed disorientated, the same as the first time she had come to the croft. Puzzled by this, Peterson invited her in, reaching his hand for her. She approached cautiously, the merest trace of light in her wide, soft eyes. The smell of the sea was strong on her and water suddenly gushed on to the floor, surprising them both. Reassuringly, Peterson stroked her arm.

'I have a bath ready for you.'

The feel of her was both unpleasant and sensuous. She was slick with the ooze from below the discarded skin, but also firm, muscled. When the slime was washed away she would be slightly scaly, a tickling shagreen, and salt would crystallize in her creases. But with regular baths she could maintain herself in comfort on the land.

Selka knew the routine of washing, but tonight she was behaving strangely, as if unaware of the bath, or the toilet bowl. Instead, she dropped to a crouch and voided her stomach on the floor, alarming the man. The stench of fish and weed was overpowering. Selka wailed and whined as she incontinenced the remnants of her sea life. Peterson filled a bucket with water and mopped up the mess. At last, the woman found the bath and crawled in head first, twisting in the narrow tub and laughing.

Standing watching her, Peterson felt his despair grow into anguish. This was not Selka, of course, despite the similarity of looks. He stared apprehensively at the calm sea, the moon now set and no light available to attract the selkie who had become his lover. This 'new-one' did not appeal. He needed the familiarity of his shared life with Selka, the communication that had so painstakingly evolved throughout the long summer and the bitter autumn nights of the last years, the memories in common.

As the new-one bathed, wallowing and watching with vision that could easily penetrate the Orcadian dark, Peterson walked to the sea's edge and followed the scent trail of the selkie until he found the carefully folded and hidden skin. She had wedged it below an outcrop of granite, high on the shore, and filled the entrance with pebbles and wood. The marine stench would attract flies in the morning, and already tiny hopping creatures were fussing at the part of the skin that she had left exposed.

Peterson carefully withdrew the soft pelt and carried it back to the house. The new-one thrashed in the bath and leapt out, standing shivering in the dark, watching anxiously as Peterson unfurled her marine protection.

'It's all right,' he whispered soothingly. 'If the strand fauna get to this they'll destroy it and weaken you. I'll keep it safe.'

He held the skin towards her, then showed her the cupboard where he placed it, immersed in the deep bowl of sea water he had prepared for Selka.

The new-one relaxed. She was smaller than Selka,

Peterson realized now. His eyes were wide as he stared at the slim, angular shape of the creature. He felt the first signs of desire, not as powerful as when Selka had bathed, undressed him and hugged him to the floor, but strong enough for him to discard his clothes. The new-one watched curiously, then grinned.

'Where is Selka?' Peterson asked. 'Where is the one from before?'

The new-one cocked her head. Weed fragments fell from her hair, which was spidery and greyish. Selka's woman-hair had been silver and very tightly curled, covering half of her face and growing, too, from across her upper lip, an odd moustache that had tickled Peterson when they'd kissed. Selka, as human, had been very hairy, and her scales small, almost unnoticeable. This one was different, but when he touched her it was only at her creases that the skin grated in that fish-scale way. Her breasts were tiny, flattened to her prominent rib cage. The nipples, unlike Selka's, were blanched white and didn't react to his touch.

Peterson couldn't decide whether the new-one was young or old.

'Do you have a name?'

As if she understood the selkie grinned and murmured a series of vowels.

'I thought so,' Peterson responded, referring both to the anticipated incomprehensibility of the name and the fact that the new-one understood him. It had been the same with Selka and the previous ones; all had shed the marine skin and at once seemed to intuit his language. Would it be the same in other countries, he had wondered?

'I can't pronounce your Neptunian sibilants, so I'll opt for Seela. That's clever, you see? Almost a human name, and refers to your primary morphological form. Except that you're not seals, really. Are you?'

He had seen selkies come ashore many times, watching them roll and scream as they had split themselves open to shed the marine skin. They were far uglier than seals, and the human shapes encased within the thin blubber had flexed and forced against the flesh, a bizarre and revolting prey struggling in the grey-blue stomach of the selkie itself. For that was what a selkie looked like: a stomach with an oddly, ugly human face, and matted hair that ran in streaks along the distended carcass.

He knew they were good swimmers, though. He had seen Selka water-dancing in the moon-channel once, and she could leap higher than any dolphin he had ever seen. The dance was old, he knew, but he had never understood the meaning behind the cavorting on tail flippers and the elaborate leaps and dives.

'Seela,' he repeated and the selkie said the name, followed by the word 'Peterson.'

'Ah. You know me then.'

Seela laughed.

'Selka told you. Where is Selka? Why hasn't she come?'

The new-one — Seela — ran to the door of the croft and ducked out into the cold Scottish night. Peterson chased after her and grazed his head on the lintel, swearing loudly. The slim figure of the selkie was standing a few yards away, hunched. Seela had her back to the man, and seemed to be shaking.

Peterson approached her but when he touched the dry, cool skin, the woman darted back into the croft. The wind was increasing and the shore was awash with the noise of the surf. The darkness deepened, but he knew that to use a light would distress the creature this soon after its shedding.

Seela was crouched in a corner, eyes wider now, mouth tightly pinched. Her arms were around her frame and the wet marine skin was unfurled before her. But she had not gone ahead and returned to her marine form. She seemed unsettled, indecisive.

'Are you afraid?' Peterson asked. Seela's teeth chattered.

'I miss Selka,' he went on. 'Please tell me why she hasn't come.'

The selkie drew the skin to her and found the thinner fat of the face. She unfurled the skin and covered her head, crying out as the marine skin began to penetrate her flesh, to renew itself. Peterson was shocked, watching the anguish on the ugly face as the jaw opened and closed and the strange eyes stared steadily into the gloom.

'I won't ask about Selka any more. Come to bed. Come to bed? You'll be cool. You'll be touched. Selka liked my touch. She liked to feel me inside her. She always said that. Come to bed.'

The selkie stopped its mourning sound, peeled off the mask. When Peterson had lain quietly in his rough bed for half an hour, the woman came to him, buried herself into his shape, curled up against him, her hand straying to his pubic hair and gripping the wiry tangle, finding an oddly and painfully secure grip. If she had wanted to love him he would have been prepared for it, but she spent the night half awake and shaking, and at dawn she slept, her mouth open, the smell of shellfish effusing from between the silvery, sharp teeth. She sang in her sleep, the faint sea-songs of her race, just as Selka had done. She sang of the island . . .

Selka had told him that her kin had first come to the island when a sailing ship had foundered, a *long* time before. From her brief description – all that her selkie folklore could summon – he thought it might have been a Viking war galley, blown against the rocks after its long, North Atlantic journey. With that sinking the selkies had come. But they had declined over the centuries, although the skins of two of them had remained on the grave-ledge, cold but still living.

Then the bomber, a Lancaster, had plunged into the deep. Attracted as they were to wrecks, the selkies had returned to the island. They had been present in profusion soon after the crash. Peterson remembered watching them sea-dance as he had converted the ruined croft, incorporating bits of metal and canvas that the sea had washed ashore for those first few months after the drowning. The croft was a shrine to the dead airmen, and Selka always brought him a gift from the deep, some piece of instrumentation, or leather, or harnessing. From other expeditions to the mainland he had collected the rugs, chairs and supplies that made the croft comfortable, and life tolerable on this remote patch of sea rock.

A hard rain freshened the shore just after dawn, stippling the heaving ocean and running from the dark granite above the littoral zone. Wearing only goggles and a thin layer of animal fat, Peterson walked to the sea and plunged in. His senses screamed with shock as the cold assaulted him, but he shivered warm again as he struck out strongly, away from the island and towards the deep pool where Selka used to swim before beaching. The sea was grey and heavy when he peered into its body, but he could see fish there, and the shadows of bigger, darker creatures. They moved close to the falling face of the cliff that widened to deep water where the selkies lived, near to the skeleton of the warplane.

When he was above the pool he drew a deep breath and

plunged, long white hair streaming, beard flowing around him, swimming down vigorously through the hard current and into the warmer stillness. Here he somersaulted to stop himself rising and called for Selka with half the breath he held. In pain, and with his ears threatening to burst, he shot to the surface again and crawled energetically back towards the shore against the drag of the tide. In this way he returned to the pool.

Twice more he plunged to call. The fat was slowly stripped from his skin and the chill began to build in his tissues. He was too old. His seventy years had seen him shrivel and become hard, like an abandoned skin. Cold penetrated fast. He did not like the cold inside him.

It was time to go back.

As he swam for the shore he saw Seela standing at the water's edge, watching him curiously. Before he reached the land she had turned and run beyond the croft, over the grim, stony earth and towards the scrubby trees that grew over the high hill in the centre of the island.

When the rain stopped she returned, screaming. The light hurt her, the day brighter now that the clouds had cleared. She wanted her skin, but Peterson locked the cupboard. The selkie walked backwards around the cluttered room, eyes on his, mouth working silently. She became entangled in nets, and thrashed helplessly and frantically until he released her.

'What happened to Selka?' he asked. Seela covered her face. 'Please tell me.'

She walked out into the day, shining and silver, arms wrapped around her. Her bones were prominent and through her flesh he could see the crushed shape of another creature. Peterson suddenly realized that this selkie was *old*. And with that particular understanding came an awareness of what she wanted from the island. She was not here to be with him, but for her own strange purpose, something that Selka had told him about.

Suddenly she came back into the room, pushing past Peterson with a quick glance that showed him moist eyes. She struggled at the cupboard where her marine skin was being stored, but the lock held fast. She watched him angrily.

'Not ready,' she said. 'Return to sea. Skin please.'

'You want your skin? Then you must tell me where Selka is. Why didn't she come?'

'Please?' Seela ran her hands down the cupboard. Her nails were soft and made no sound, but the flesh whitened with the pressure. Through her skin Peterson could see the wood-form writhing, urgent for release. Its arms in hers were gnarled, its body hard-edged and unpleasant, pushing knobbily through the thinning fat of the woman. Its head, at the top of her chest, seemed to turn and open its mouth, like a child in the womb, flexing and kicking to develop its muscles.

It became quiescent and Seela accepted that Peterson had trapped her.

'Please . . .' she said, the word long and drawn out. 'Luck . . . bad . . . no . . . skin . . .'

'I know about the legend. I know the superstition. I haven't *stolen* your skin, I'm just . . . protecting it. You can have it back when I have the answer to my question. Where is Selka? What has happened to her?'

'Selka went deep,' the new-one whispered. 'Silvering.' She shrank slightly and backed away into the corner. Peterson stepped forward his heart racing. He had heard this expression, but he couldn't remember when or why. One of them, one of the selkies who had attended upon him over the years, one of them had mentioned this. There was a place, over the shelf, over the edge, where the selkies went when they were dying, following the moon down.

'No!' he said. 'Selka was young. She was healthy. She wouldn't have gone deep.'

'Big Tooth,' Seela said. 'Silvering.' Moisture smelling of the sea trickled from her eyes.

Peterson felt his head spin and his legs shake. He leaned against the table, displacing the plates and glasses. 'What do you mean? What do you mean?'

'Went deep,' Seela said. 'Big Tooth. We remember her skin on the ledge.'

'I don't believe you. She was too fast. She could easily outswim a killer whale. I don't believe you. She can't be dead.'

Seela cocked her head. 'Big Tooth,' she insisted. 'Selka went deep.'

Peterson cried out, sitting down hard. He could see his lover so clearly, so svelte, so lovely compared to this scrawny creature. He could feel her hair, the cool skin, the pressure of her teeth in his flesh, her grip, her tenderness. He could hear her laughter. He could hear the clink of glasses, drinking white Burgundy wines, her favourite drink with the cold fish and seaweed stew that was all she could eat.

'Not eaten. No. Not eaten. She can't have been.'

'Not eaten,' Seela said. 'We remember her skin.'

'You have her skin?'

Seela nodded. 'Some. A piece.'

Peterson stared at the selkie through blurring eyes. Did they keep the skin as a memorial? Did they rebirth the selkie? He struggled to remember the conversations with Selka, the night-long murmurings after love in which he had begun to piece together the beliefs and life cycle of the ubiquitous marine creature.

Life is in the skin. Each skin remembers the marine life which is why it is so precious. New-ones come from old skins. They are the same life, although part of the memory is gone. There is a shelf, in the deep water, near to the wreck of the bombing plane. At that shelf the skins are kept. Some of them are very old, waiting for the new-one to emerge and occupy it. This is our island. There has always been a beach here, and the calling of the Beautiful Voice. We cannot resist that voice. We must all go to it at some time in our lives. The Beautiful Voice still calls to me. But I am not ready yet.

The new-one would grow inside the old skin. If Selka was dead she could be brought back, the creature that he loved, the look of her, the feel of her, and part of the memory of her. They could rebuild their occasional life. He could have her back.

'Will you bring me her skin?' Peterson asked. The selkie before him seemed shocked, shaking her head.

'I must have that skin. I need Selka. She has been coming to me for three years. She's a part of me. I love her. Her life is in *my* skin. Please try to understand. Without her . . .'

Seela shivered. The wood-form inside her flexed and stretched and caused her pain. The time of the shedding was close. She would either have to return to the sea or proceed with the cycle. She looked anxiously at the locked cupboard. Peterson, grimly, walked away from her and went out to the beach.

They called it the Island of the Gone Away Ones. It was a magic place to the selkies. There was a call from the island, a Beautiful Voice, and occasionally the call was irresistible. Some who went to the island returned. Some didn't. No selkie knew the fate of those who had Gone Away, but it was assumed they had called down bad luck upon themselves. Selkie superstitions were legion, and told Peterson much about their fear of humankind, which over the centuries had trapped the woman-form after the shedding, or taken the male-form into slavery. *Never shed skin by day. Always swim to the shore along the silver channel of the moon. Selkie blood shed in anger raises the storm from the deep . . .*

And most important of all: *Never let other hands touch the living skin on the shore.*

Peterson had done that to Selka, and now Seela. And Selka was lost . . .

There was a harsh cry from the croft, then the sound of glass breaking. Peterson ran towards the shack, listening to the frantic banging of metal against wood. Seela was shrieking like a seal, a mammalian cry of terror and rage. He knew the reason at once.

She swung round and hurled the hammer at him as he stepped through the door. The cupboard was dented but intact. Where she had dragged the rugs from the wall, the old selkie skins shone in the half-light, the stretched shapes translucently grey where he had pinned them out. She had found all five, and perhaps recognized the distorted faces of some or all of her kin.

'Gone Away Ones!' she howled. 'You!' And then, almost crying, puzzled, 'The Beautiful Voice.'

She knew who he was, now, and her terror was ripe in the air, a salt stink emanating from her.

'My skin,' she hissed. 'Give back my skin.'

'No. Not until I have your promise of Selka's skin. Fetch me Selka's skin.'

'Need skin for fetch.'

She was right, of course. He thought about it, then hardened his heart. 'I'll cut one hand from your skin. You can swim easily enough without it. Do you agree?'

The selkie shuddered at the thought of such mutilation. 'No. Selka gone deep. *Mustn't* touch skin.'

'I want her back. You must help me.'

'Cannot.'

'No skin, then. No skin for you. I'll keep it. I'll keep it safe.'

He already had another idea. It made his witnessing of the selkie's desperation easier to handle. He was not a cold man, he believed, nor heartless, but now he was ruthless in a way he could not have imagined. This was what heartbreak could do to him.

Seela dissolved into despair before him, and he let her run from the croft, compassionately watching her, heart beating hard as he knew what had to be done for his own satisfaction, for the love of Selka.

She tried to get back to the croft but Peterson barred the door against her. He stood in the half-light, leaning against the cupboard where her skin soaked in brine. He thought of Selka's laughter as the new-one hammered and cried beyond the wood.

At dusk she was crouched by the sea, and as the moon rose she swam out along the silver channel and barked and called in the hard tide until moonset brought her back. She was a miserable shape, huddled and dying, curled behind the croft during the long night, and in the morning the wood-form began to split her open.

Peterson followed the trail of pale blood over the rocky ground and into the heart of the island. Seela was limping. She was translucent, but the flexing green and brown of the wood-form gave her an oddly dynamic shape, as if green fire swirled within her. Every so often a grinning face bulged from between her shoulders and Seela's arms flapped as elongated fingers tried to prod and point towards the pursuer. The thing was watching Peterson, which was of no real consequence.

She had come from deep water to the shore, and there she had shed her marine skin to become the woman. Now she had travelled to the tree line and here the human was shed to become the wood-form. It squeezed from her, an insect struggling from its pupa. It chattered and shrieked. It used long nails to shred and tear at the throat and thighs of the skin, parting the fatty fabric, letting its twisted limbs find release. It was human in form and Peterson, watching from the rocks as the shedding occurred in a hollow among the thorns, was revolted by the distended, glistening crotch of the thing. He was reminded at once of the grotesque carvings in stone of the female entity from an earlier, pagan time, the grinning, womb-gaping horror that some called the nagig, or nagigtha, others kali. The consuming, spewing form of woman as nature, or nature as woman. A goblin, a dwarf, a female aspect of the violent reproduction of the world.

She rose from the discarded flesh of the selkie-woman, chattered through tiny teeth and yellow lips, shivered, shuddered, then defecated where she stood, a stenchpile that voided her of the fish of her previous incarnation.

She saw Peterson. The squat form straightened, the eyes were piercing, dark below folds of flesh. She laughed as she hurled three stones at the watching human. All three projectiles struck him glancing but painful blows. When he emerged from hiding, a piece of granite the size of an egg bounced off his shoulder. She was aware of him, accurate, deadly, and no nonsense. Peterson withdrew to a more discreet position.

The nagigtha sighed and stretched. Her lank hair was troublesome and she wound it into braids, then folded the braids into a tall, odd top-knot. More comfortable, she picked up the skin of the marine-form, Seela, and scurried towards the shore, stopping at a rock pool at the head of a deep inlet. The water here was clean from the late tide. She crouched and scrubbed with her fingers at the skin, looking around her defensively, a witch washing the clothes of the dead. Finally, she beat the living fabric against a rock before rolling it tightly, squeezing it out and carrying it up to the trees.

With long fingers she hollowed out a hiding place among the roots of a thorn, wedged Seela into the hole and covered it with stones. Aware of Peterson she flung a stone and drew blood from his chin, but caught in the pattern of ritual events the nagigtha was helpless; she ran among the trees and curled up in shade, melding with the colours of the scrub wood.

Protected against the cold of the sea, he swam out to the pool, then struck back against the tide until his chest ached and his arms threatened to break. He crawled to the shore and collapsed among the driftwood and hard stones, his hand clutching at the beach-dried weed as if it could help drag him to safety. But he was aware of the small shape on the skyline. He watched, from his prone position, and saw the nagigtha slink away from her point of observation.

Each day for a week he swam at dusk. Each time he entered the water the nagigtha watched him, but she could not gain access to the croft, and had disappeared by the time he crawled ashore. She was weakening, he knew that. The cycle, at this phase of a selkie's life, was occurring fast. The nagigtha wanted to take back its marine skin, but there was no breaking the turmoil of hormonal and physical changes that was drawing the creature towards the deep part of the land.

On the eighth day the creature did not appear on the skyline and Peterson ran quickly over the island, crouching on the rise and staring into the thin woods. A pale autumn sun made watching difficult because of the shadowplay of trunks and branches in the gentle wind, but soon he saw the nagigtha. She was sluggish. She looked sick and sad. She crawled to a place in the wood where she burrowed and scooped, perhaps refreshing herself with soil. She leaned back and howled, then moved like an ape lumbering slowly through an oppressive enclosure, walking on hands and knees back to the shade.

In the morning she was shedding. Peterson approached cautiously, wet with dew from his night's vigil. The creature moaned as she saw him coming, but she was already rooted, and the wood-skin was peeling. Her legs were spread and covered with bark, the toes stretching to dig into the hard earth. Her arms were still supple, despite the sprouting of branches, and as Peterson crouched, smiling in triumph, she flicked a stone at him and cracked the enamel on one of his teeth.

He fell back on to his haunches, cursing. 'Damn! Why do you have to be so accurate?'

He massaged his mouth and the pain ebbed. The nagigtha chattered, a last laughter, a defiant gesture now that she knew she was lost. The crusty skin split up to her forehead, dividing the face, but the eyes in the skin – and there was life in the skin, even after it was shed – seemed to watch him. The thorn that was emerging glistened with a resinous material and already flies were arriving to sample the temporary sap. They were caught and died, but the fragrance of the material was strong and pleasant.

'As soon as I have Selka I'll return your skins,' Peterson said. He reached forward to help tug her wood-form away from the new tree. 'I've kept your friends. I don't know why. Impulse, I suppose. I've been here a long time. I like this wood. It gives me shade, it gives me pleasure. It reminds me of home. I love thorns. The mayflower is lovely. It comes late here. I hope you'll blossom for me beautifully . . .' He playfully prodded the trunk and the tree seemed to quiver, but it was beyond movement now. The selkie had rooted and was now at the mercy of nature. If the skin of the wood-form remained among the roots, one day it would grow back over the tree and the nagigtha shape would be regained. But Peterson would perform the role of the occasional animal, stealing the skin, taking it away so that this phase of the creature's life would become permanent, and it would grow and die and shed berries, and spread in a more natural way.

What *did* come of the berries of a nagigtha tree? It was something, an aspect of the selkie lore, that he had never asked Selka. He ought to do so as soon as she was reborn.

He had brought a large can of water to the wood and he poured this around the roots of the new thorn, helping the creature. But he tugged the wood-form skin out of its protecting hole and folded it.

'I don't need this, but I'll look after it for you. When I have Selka back again I'll bring it back to you. This is a promise. But you see, I can't have you running about the island while I'm away. You're too dangerous. So I have to root you for the moment. I need the other skins, the woman, the selkie, but I'll be careful with them. This is my promise. Enjoy the weather. The forecast is good for the next two weeks.'

He hid the nagigtha skin in dry, wormless earth, wrapped around with muslin to keep it safe and cool. It would remain usable for a long time. There was not enough light from the moon to make the right channel, so for two days and nights he drank wine and ate cold fish, sitting in the darkness of the croft, the door open, watching the dark sea, listening to the waves, smelling the salt air. When the moon waxed, when the channel of silver drew his passion again to the task ahead of him, he unfurled the woman-skin and spread it out upon the cold rocks.

When he lay upon it, nude and shivering, the life began to kindle. He clenched his fists and teeth as the pain began, but soon relaxed into a howl of pain, flexing and writhing as his body was invaded. The skin furled around him, probing deeply through his pores, working into his organs, drawing blood into the cold dermis, padding up the fat in an attempt to shape itself to the hard and unfamiliar shape below. It had been expecting the wood-form, something small, something angular; it struggled long and hard to accommodate Peterson.

For a while he felt strangled as the female head stretched and agonized around his chest. His hands were white and puffy as the arms tried to encapsulate them. The skin shuddered and shivered, its own life frustrated by the attempt to enclose him, to find its form, and he felt the breath being squeezed from his lungs, then his anus was probed and stretched, making him arch and kick.

By relaxing, the pain diminished, but for hours he had to cry against the growth and stretching of the woman-form. It crept to his extremities, agonizingly tight against his genitals. The vagina could not open into him, but he felt bruised by the attempt.

By the evening, below a dull sun and warm breeze, he felt at peace. He was enclosed by Seela's skin and the pain had reduced to the feeling of thorns scraping over his body. He stood unsteadily, feeling weak and propping himself against the house. He stared down at the body he had become and saw his corpse, like a pupa, vaguely outlined below the fatty curves.

Worst of all was his mouth. The sharp teeth of the woman had pushed his own teeth out of their sockets. He had swallowed them all. They rested in his stomach. He was still swallowing blood. His jaws ached, and the new teeth pricked the flesh of his mouth.

He slept for a long time, drank water and scooped cold fish from the stewpot using hands that shook violently. His male face was twisted behind the stretched and hideous mask of the female; he was not orientated correctly, so that his mouth could be seen slightly to the right of the thin yet shapely mouth of the woman. His eyes made shadow-eyes behind the slanted sockets of the creature.

He slept for a long time, four days, perhaps, it was hard to tell. In that time his body was digested. Now, when he looked in the mirror, he could see only Seela. Peterson was dormant, down below, hidden; he would hatch out later, when his mission was accomplished.

Again, the skin rolled over him, consuming him. This skin was large, though, and encompassed him instantly, suffocating him in fat, swamping him in images of the deep.

And of men ... the sound of screaming ... the look of fear in eyes ... the cold wind and the long fall to the land ...

There was salt in his lungs, and the flux of cold and warm currents on his flanks. He rolled on the beach, barking and crying, feeling stones and driftwood snag at his back, letting dry weed tangle with his face. The croft door was open. The trees on the hill were silent, stark against the dusk sky. The sea rushed at him, water sucked and tugged at him, then withdrew quietly before surging back. He twisted round and the surge covered his face, cold and welcoming, calling to him. The moon-silver channel was wide.

He eased himself into the water and swam to the pool. There he circled once, then plunged, and having dived deep he kept on going, down along the underwater cliff, towards the ledge where the selkie skins were tied to weeds, their place of remembrance of the dead.

The spars of the bomber's metal hull were weed-racked and corroded. The old plane reached out across the very deep, angled down. It would one day slip from the ledge, broken apart by the weight of water acting upon the corruption of its joints. For the moment, the stub of its starboard wing was wedged in the rock, the port wing long-since vanished below. It was a monstrous and terrifying shape, reaching obscenely from the living cliff. Peterson's mind cleared, a clear-sight leading back forty years to his time in the plane, to the time when he had been human.

He swam through the bomber's empty windows, over the digested leather of the crew seats, through the wires that waved like threads of sea-life. The bones were long gone, long eaten. His friends were in the selkie skins, nourishing the creatures. Perhaps that was why they came ashore, his friends coming home to Peterson, the one survivor.

He had let them die to save his own life. But now, in this place of his sins, his guilt returned, mixed with cold memories of a deeper sea than he could comprehend, of fish, and a freezing emptiness. And selkie memories, too, of the island where the Beautiful Voice sang, his own voice, attracting the selkies before destroying them, all save Selka who had touched his heart, his actions unconscious, perhaps, guilt assuaged with violence after the siren call to the creatures who had consumed his friends. Although the hulk overshadowed everything, although it dominated the grave-ledge and its covering of the shreds of skin of the selkies who had fed here, it was not the great and terrifying tomb that he had dreamed of all these years. He saw it with selkie vision. It was rotting iron, drifting wire, and the home of conger eels. He snapped and shredded one such homesteader, gulping down the screeching flesh, enjoying the meal not for its taste but for the pleasure in the anger he had taken in the killing.

Memories of men faded as he thought of the creature he loved.

Which skin, on the ledge, was Selka's?

He returned to the surface to take breath. He had been without air for a day or more, he realized, and a sluggishness had begun to inhibit him. Male selkies breathed more frequently than the females, but they also swam more deeply, for purposes as yet unknown to Peterson. The female selkies rested for most of their days in a vertical hover against the cliff, slowly turning. Only when danger threatened did they break this pattern and dart into shadow. Peterson swam down among the slowly turning seal-shapes, nudged and nuzzled one to awaken her, but had no success.

*　　*　　*

One morning the males came swimming frantically from the deep, a fan of creatures fleeing from danger. The females broke from their drifting trance and scurried across the cliff. The sea pulsed with sound. Peterson was drawn by the frenzy and by the current, and found himself surfacing towards the pool and the dawn sun.

A killer whale had appeared. Its vast form shadowed the shore for an hour or so, then drifted away. Normality returned.

He beached for a while, relaxing in the air, tempted to shed his skins and drink wine, but the thought of the pain was too much. Another selkie came ashore and watched him. The woman below the skin was plump and ripe, clearly young. But the creature signalled to Peterson and he followed her, slipping back into the waves and meeting in the deep pool.

'Who are you?' she asked him. 'I know your face, but you are not the One who went Away.'

'What happened to Selka?'

As they swam around each other, he realized that his own name for his lover would mean nothing. He tried to articulate the selkie name for the creature whom he loved, and after a while the sound pulses registered on his companion's consciousness.

'She went deep. Big Tooth.'

'But you have a part of her skin. Isn't that right?'

'The skin must never be touched. There is life in the skin –'

'I know. And I want that life back. I want her on the shore.'

The selkie seemed puzzled. 'Don't touch the skin. You must know this. She can never come back if you touch the skin.'

279

'She is *in* the skin,' Peterson said in the selkie language. 'I know that her life is there. She must come back.'

'I don't understand,' the plump female said. 'You know she has gone deep —'

'Into the Big Tooth. Yes. I know.'

He hated the thought of Selka being eaten by the whale. It was good to feel the human response, the masculine feeling below the seal blubber.

'Then don't touch the skin,' the young one urged him. 'You know what will happen.'

'Just show me the skin. Then leave the decision to me. Please?'

'Who are you? I recognize you. But your deeper beings are unfamiliar. Are you male? But you seem to be like me, female. You frighten me.'

'I'm a friend, a dear friend, of your lost companion.' Again, he articulated Selka's marine name. 'There is nothing to fear from me.'

'I'll show you the skin. But if you love your friend, don't touch it.'

She led him down to the grave-ledge, showed him the dull grey fabric that was all that remained of Selka, then spiralled upwards and away, as if fleeing the scene of a crime. Her last words were '*Are* you a female?'

'I'm a Gone Away One,' Peterson said, aware that he would create confusion, yet feeling satisfaction in the simple truth.

'A ghost, then,' his companion said, and for a long time her keening song was poignant in the half-deep waters.

Peterson reached for the skin. He noticed how clean it was, how straight its edges. He had expected tear marks, tooth marks, the signs of the death struggle. This skin seemed to have been cut carefully, someone preserving it. He bit gently into the flesh, loosened it from its tie around the root of a strand of thick weed, and carried it to the cockpit of the drowned bomber.

Memories overwhelmed him again, drawn out of his closed mind by the living presence of his friends in the selkie skin. Names came back to him.

Jackson. Murray. Mitchell. Stevens. He remembered the names clearly. He could see each man, hear each voice, hear the shouts, hear the calm, hear the moment of death, the moment of prayer. Mitchell had prayed. All the way down, Mitchell had spoken words from the Bible. Stevens had yelled abuse. Murray had sung a funny song. Jackson had cried and shouted out a message of everlasting love for his wife, Mary, and his children. They had hit the water and gone down, struggling for release, all failing to escape, as Peterson had drifted down to the island on his silk, sobbing and screaming as the thought of what he had done to save his skin began to haunt him, even as the lives were being crushed from his friends.

The sea had claimed them, then the ridge, then the ledge. The great bomber had settled, wedged, and the creatures of the dark had moved in to feed. The skin, the flesh, the bone, the sinew, the codes, the life, the minds and memories of the men had been greedily and avidly sucked into the hungry jaws of the feeding lifeforms of this shelf by the island.

The selkie that had absorbed them had become the community, days on, reproducing fast, and they lived here, tied to the bomber and the island by the human life that thrived and burgeoned in their pulpy, blubbered bodies.

In Selka, Peterson had recognized the humour of Murray and the passionate family man that had been Jackson. She had even reminded him of Jackson, in her human looks, as if she had been his sister. He and Jackson had always been close. He had found it so easy to form a close relationship with the woman-form of the selkie that had contained so much of that lost essence of friendship.

What to do with the skin?

As he swam lazily through the skeleton of the bomber, Peterson realized that he could not access enough of the selkie Seela's memories to intuit the process by which Selka might reform from the skin. If the skin was the life, and if skin, kept for centuries below the shallow water, could in time regenerate the life that had once inhabited it, then Selka would return.

But how to do it?

There was a disturbance in the water. The iron bones of the plane shuddered, then slipped. Peterson twisted in the cold water and peered into the deep, and his seal-senses made him dart away as the savage features of the whale struck at him. The huge body glided downwards, then struck up again, dislodging the steel girders of the craft. It began to tumble, slipping away from the grave-ledge, dragging the skins of the selkies with it. Peterson struggled out of the frame, grazing his skin and shedding blood. The pale liquid rose in a stream of droplets, up through the murk to the silver surface above.

Blood in the water . . . a storm coming from the deep . . .

He swam furiously upwards, aware that above him the rest of the selkies were small, slim shapes, even now darting into the shallows, to safety. As he rose, as he struggled against the tide, he felt that turbulence around him, the eddying of something monstrous closing fast. He screamed as he twisted, tried to hide his gaze from the maw of the killer. It clamped around him and swept him dizzyingly out of his path, shaking him and savaging him as it plunged down again, into the great darkness.

And yet the teeth had not penetrated his skin, though blood still seeped in bubbles from his cut.

Inside the whale, something flexed, something called to him. In pain, terrified that at any moment the jaws would saw their way shut and sever him, Peterson stared through the skin of the whale . . .

He saw the selkie below, the serene features, the smile. She had her own eyes open, watching him through the eyes of the killer.

Suddenly her face changed – a harder jawline, a narrow look, and Jackson grinned at him, startling him. Jackson's lean features dissolved again and the thick-set face of Edward Mitchell glowered for a moment, replaced by Murray, pursing his lips in silent admonition. Then Selka again, swallowing back the human lives that had nourished her and formed her, as they would have nourished and formed all the selkies at the Island of the Beautiful Voice.

'Why did you follow me?' she seemed to say.

'Because I love you. I thought you had been killed. I thought going deep meant you had died. I came to find your skin, to bring you back to life.'

'There is no coming back. This is the end of my life. This is the silvering. But you can be with me forever. If you've come this far, you must certainly want that.'

Peterson twitched and flexed in the jaws. He wasn't so sure, now. His doubt must have been as transparent to Selka as the whale's flesh was translucent to the selkie soul beneath. It was angry. It turned and swam further down, into a great mass of silent, silver-grey weed.

The killer basked against the gleaming weed mass, stirring the giant fronds with its tail, using Peterson's struggling carcase to whip the strands and suckers into a frenzy of motion.

The life in the weed was awakened suddenly, and like some great squid its fronds stretched, quivered and rapidly enclosed the whale and Peterson. Slowly, Selka was absorbed into the weed, the fronds enclosing her, fusing with her, becoming her main form. Peterson, trapped outside the transformation, understood with clear terror and uninvited irony what he had missed in the life cycle of the selkie . . . that not only did they come to land and shed to become silent, for many years, in the form of a tree, drawing earth into their bodies, experiencing the sky and the storms of the above-water, but also that they went deep, to take on further outer forms, to become the vastest creatures of the sea. Perhaps then they would return to the seal-like creatures that were so familiar to mythology. Or perhaps, this was their final form, and Peterson would never see his lover again.

Selka, the weed-mass, drifted slowly towards the surface.

The whale was consumed, enclosed, and hard, tight fronds gripped the quiescent selkie that contained the ageing human.

'I enjoyed you, Peterson,' Selka whispered from the frond-mass. 'I'm glad you followed me. I want you inside me again. I always did.'

As Peterson screamed and struggled, as they surfaced towards the silver channel of the moon, the horny parts of the frond mass began to cut down to the Peterson-skin inside the seal, to bring him out, to bring him in.

Author's Note

MERLIN'S WOOD owes much to Tennyson (*IDYLLS OF THE KING*), to Joseph Campbell (*THE MASKS OF GOD*), and to Arnauld Lacan, a ghost, whose story came as a sudden and sad surprise in my previous book (*THE HOLLOWING*). Part of the Vision of Magic would never have occurred to me without the Finnish Midnight Sun, in June 1992, and Otto, Irma, Marco, Johanna and Toni et al, whose old tales told through young mouths reminded me of something I have always known without fully knowing it: that evil and enchantment have always been embedded in the words we speak, and that the legend of Merlin is not a story of forgotten magic, or a reflection of shamanism, but of the beguiling power of language, coming raw into bright minds in the long-long-gone, that fascinating and terrifying time when the world could first be described by *illusion*; sleight of tongue replacing sleight of hand! Virtual reality!

EARTH AND STONE was first published in 1980, in INTERFACES, edited by Ursula Le Guin and Virginia Kidd. The story is set in Ireland's own 'Valley of the Kings and Queens', the curve in the valley of the Boyne river where the massive quartz-faced tombs of New Grange, Knowth and Dowth were erected some six thousand years ago, earthen mounds covering monumental carved stones whose symbols remain utterly enigmatic. Excavations continued on the sites throughout the 1980s, especially at

Knowth (the biggest of the tombs) and I have slightly revised the story to reflect new discoveries.

THE SILVERING was written for Chris Donaldson and Paul Oldroyd, who enthused about 'Selkies' one Burns Night when the Oban and Glenmorangie happened to help rather than hinder the creative process. Slàinte! 'The Silvering' itself is one of the ten masks that mark the passages into the Otherworld (see LAVONDYSS). The story was first published in NARROW HOUSES, 1992, edited by Peter Crowther.